Praise for *Welcome to Last Chance*

"A wonderful debut novel. . . . Readers will enjoy the simplicity of *Welcome to Last Chance* and the complexity of Lainie's character."

—*New York Journal of Books*

"Cathleen Armstrong's debut novel is a warm-hearted look at ordinary people living out genuine faith."

—**Crosswalk.com**

"With equal parts hope, charm, and tender faith, Cathleen Armstrong spins a tale as warm and welcoming as a roadside cafe on a dusty highway. Exit from the fast lane and visit Last Chance. It's a place you won't soon forget."

—**Lisa Wingate**, bestselling and award-winning author of *Firefly Island* and *Blue Moon Bay*

Praise for *One More Last Chance*

"Armstrong continues her A Place to Call Home series with this sweet romance that features vivid descriptions of the Southwestern landscape, colorful supporting characters, and engaging relationships subtly shaped by Christian faith."

—*Booklist*

"A gentle love story with a cozy feel. . . . It boasts well-crafted characters who feel like old friends, and its theme of hope leaves readers with the knowledge that for everyone, there really can be one more last chance. This tale is recommended for all fans of sweet and light romances."

—*Library Journal*

Books by

Cathleen Armstrong

A Place to Call Home Series

Welcome to Last Chance

One More Last Chance

At Home in Last Chance

A Place to Call Home #3

At Home in Last Chance

A Novel

Cathleen Armstrong

Revell
a division of Baker Publishing Group
Grand Rapids, Michigan

Published by Revell
a division of Baker Publishing Group
P.O. Box 6287, Grand Rapids, MI 49516-6287
www.revellbooks.com

Printed in the United States of America

Library of Congress Cataloging-in-Publication Data
Armstrong, Cathleen.
At home in last chance : a novel / Cathleen Armstrong.
pages ; cm. — (A place to call home ; book 3)
ISBN 978-0-8007-2248-7 (pbk.)
I. Title.
PS3601.R5747A95 2014
813′.6—dc23 2014029690

This is a work of fiction. Names, characters, incidents, and dialogues are products of the author's imagination and are not to be construed as real. Any resemblance to actual events or persons, living or dead, is entirely coincidental.

15 16 17 18 19 20 21 7 6 5 4 3 2 1

For Bill, Lisa, and Kate
You filled my life with love and purpose

1

Pure and simple, Kaitlyn Reed hated her job. She hated getting up in the early hours of a cold, dark January morning to get there. She hated the curious to outright hostile looks of the diners she served. She hated that she didn't really have a choice about whether to work at the Dip 'n' Dine. But most of all, she hated taking orders from Juanita Sheppard.

Truth be told, she wasn't very good at taking orders from anyone. Her reputation back in Scottsdale as a creative, avant-garde hairstylist had gained her positions in some of Scottsdale's toniest salons, but those jobs never lasted long. Neither did the jobs she held after she left Scottsdale. Kaitlyn simply could not stand being told what to do, and employers always seemed to think they had to give directions. Nine times out of ten, if they had just given her five seconds, she'd have completed the task before they even mentioned it. But they'd go and bark their orders, this white-hot flare would shoot through her, and before she even realized she had said anything, she was out the door, purse and final paycheck in hand.

"Here, refill this and make the rounds." Juanita Sheppard shoved a nearly empty coffeepot into her hands. "And tables four and six need busing, too. Let's keep our eyes open, Kaitlyn, and try to stay on top of things."

Kaitlyn's eyes narrowed. True, her brother had asked Juanita to show her the ropes, but Kaitlyn was about ready to grab that rope and strangle her with it. Holding the pot in both hands, she started after Juanita, who hadn't even paused as she breezed by.

No telling what pyrotechnics the early breakfast diners at the Dip 'n' Dine might have been treated to if her brother Chris, the diner's owner, hadn't intercepted her.

"Why don't I take care of the coffee?" He took the coffeepot from her and gave her a wink. "You go ahead and clean those tables. And Kaitlyn? Try not to throw the dishes in the bin so hard you break them, okay?"

His grin lightened his words but not her temper, and after shooting one last murderous glare at Juanita, who was chatting with a customer and clearly clueless about the apocalypse she so nearly brought down upon herself, Kaitlyn ducked into the kitchen to find Carlos, her one friend and ally in this awful place.

"I just cannot deal with her one more day." Kaitlyn could almost feel steam coming from her ears. She squeezed her eyes shut as Juanita's voice reached them.

"Who? Juanita?" Carlos Montoya pulled a pan of biscuits out of the oven and straightened to look at her. "She's okay. Get's a little bossy sometimes, but you don't need to let it bother you. I don't."

"Well, you don't have to. You're in here. I'm the one she's treating like her own personal servant."

On cue, Juanita appeared at the window to the dining room. "Kaitlyn? Those tables still need busing and we have people waiting for a table. Let's save the chatting for our break, okay?"

Kaitlyn's mouth popped open on its own accord, but before she could say anything, Carlos spoke for her. "She'll be right with you, Juanita. I needed her in here for a minute. The bins are there on the counter, though, if you want to go ahead and get started."

Juanita was silenced, but only for a second. "She wasn't hired to help you, Carlos. She was hired to help me, and I need her out here."

She pursed her lips and raised her eyebrows at Kaitlyn before whirling away, leaving Kaitlyn fighting yet another flash of rage. Carlos shook his head and turned back to his biscuits.

"Take a second and cool off. Here. Eat a biscuit. Then go on out there and bus some tables. Just do your job and let Juanita roll off your back. I mean that." His voice took on a serious tone Kaitlyn had not heard before, and she paused in midbite. "This place doesn't belong to Juanita. It belongs to your brother. He's a good man, and if you think you owe him anything, keep the catfights out of his restaurant."

His dark eyes held hers for a long moment before she dropped her glance and took a thoughtful pull off her biscuit. She hated it that Carlos wasn't just taking her side against the insufferable Juanita, but she had to admit he was right. She did owe Chris. Big time. If there was one person in her life who had always been there for her, it was Chris. When they were growing up, it was he who tried so hard to take the place of their always-busy parents. When she got pregnant at sixteen, it was he who stood by her decision to have the baby when everybody else told her what a bad idea that was. Seven years later, when she decided she was tired of motherhood and had dropped her daughter off like a puppy at a pound, he had taken Olivia in and given her a home. Several months after that, when Kaitlyn found herself alone and penniless and beginning to understand what a world-class idiot she had been, Chris, without a word of recrimination, brought her home and took her in too. Yep. One could say she owed her brother.

"Kaitlyn?" Juanita had appeared at the window again with a brittle smile. "Are you coming?"

Kaitlyn took a deep breath and held it before exhaling in a long slow whoosh. She smiled too and squared her shoulders. "Coming."

She stopped just before pushing her way through the door into the dining room and turned to Carlos. "For Chris."

He raised his spatula in salute. "For the boss."

If Juanita noticed her new, cooperative attitude, she certainly gave no sign. In fact, her instructions, always frequent, seemed more curt and brusque than ever. More than once during the day, Juanita had backed Chris into a corner, and from her glances in Kaitlyn's direction and the fact that she had actually lowered her voice to a near whisper, Kaitlyn could only surmise that the discussions were about her.

Chris listened as he always did. He lowered his head to better look into Juanita's face, nodded thoughtfully as she spoke, then smiled, straightened, said a few words, and put his hand on her shoulder before walking away. Whatever he said could not have been what Juanita was looking for, because she looked Kaitlyn's way, sighed, and shook her head before huffing off.

For Chris. Kaitlyn took another deep breath and held it as long as she could before slowly exhaling. *For Chris. For Chris. For Chris . . . and for my sweet, abandoned Livvy.*

Kaitlyn wasn't sure which was more exhausting, serving tables or trying to keep from snapping back at Juanita, but by the time she climbed into the front seat of Chris's Jeep and let her head drop back against the headrest, she felt as if she never wanted to move again.

"You look beat." Chris's smile may have seemed a bit weary as he slid behind the wheel, but at least he looked as if he had a good chance of remaining upright till they got home. Kaitlyn wasn't at all sure she could if it weren't for the help of the seat belt.

"And you don't. How come?"

Chris shrugged and pulled out onto the road. "Used to it, I guess, and the place is mine. That makes a big difference. For some reason, I used to get a lot more tired when I worked in someone else's restaurant."

They rode in silence for a few minutes before Kaitlyn's frustration burst out again.

"But Chris, I really hate it. It's not only being on my feet all day. I'm used to that. I just can't stand working at the Dip 'n' Dine. It's not as if you really need me. You did just fine before I got here."

"Give yourself some time. It's still really new to you." Chris stopped the Jeep in front of the small brown stucco house where Olivia went every day after school. "You have to do something, Sis, and there aren't a lot of choices here in Last Chance. It's not like you can work at the beauty shop. There isn't one."

"It's called a salon. And I know that. But why can't I just stay home and take care of Olivia after school instead of Elizabeth? Wouldn't that be easier on everybody?"

Chris took a deep breath and Kaitlyn had the feeling she wasn't going to like what he had to say, when her door was yanked open and her seven-year-old daughter appeared in the opening.

"Hey! You guys are late. Hurry up and come in. Me and Miss Elizabeth want to show you something."

Kaitlyn sighed. She had hoped to just wait in the car while Chris went in and got Olivia, but it looked like that wasn't going to happen. She unsnapped her seat belt and slowly unfolded her long legs.

Where in the world did this child find energy at this time of day? By the time she stood next to the Jeep, Chris had joined them, and it was with a twinge that Kaitlyn noticed it was his hand Olivia grabbed and tugged up the sidewalk.

Elizabeth Cooley was waiting on the porch. Even she looked fresher than Kaitlyn felt, and she was nearly ninety and had been riding herd on a seven-year-old for the last few hours. Chris dropped Olivia's hand to give her a hug. "Sorry we're late. I guess the time got away."

"Oh, you're not a bit late. Livvy just started watching early." Elizabeth smiled past Chris's shoulder at Kaitlyn. "Come in. How about a hot cup of tea? With the sun going down, it's really starting to get cold."

Tired as she was, Kaitlyn brightened at the suggestion. Elizabeth always seemed genuinely glad to see her, something she didn't experience from everyone she met, and spending even a little while sipping tea in Elizabeth's warm presence sounded like a great way to put her rotten day behind her.

Chris put his hand on Olivia's head and waggled it. "If you're sure you're not worn out from this one, I bet Kaitlyn could use a cup of tea. She's about done in."

"How about you?" Elizabeth was already on her way to the kitchen to put the kettle on.

"Um, I noticed smoke coming out of Sarah's chimney when we pulled up. I think I'll run down real quick and confirm some plans we made to celebrate her birthday this weekend."

"Wait! I want to show you." Olivia came from the kitchen carrying a plate on which rested the most colorful cake Kaitlyn had ever seen.

"Well, that's a cake if I've ever seen one." Chris was visibly impressed. "Don't tell me you did this all by yourself."

"Yes, I did. Well, me and Miss Elizabeth made the cake part, then she helped me put the white frosting on, but I decorated it all by myself. It's for Sarah."

"She will be amazed. I can tell that right now."

"Well, don't tell her when you go see her. It's supposed to be a surprise."

"Your secret is safe." He caressed her cheek with one hand and smiled over her head at Elizabeth. "That is indeed an amazing cake. So, I'll be back in about a half hour. Will that give you enough time for tea?"

"Plenty. But don't think you need to rush. To tell the truth, I could use a good sit-down and cup of tea, myself."

"Bet you could." Chris was already heading for the door. "See you in a few."

Kaitlyn watched the door shut. She had not said one word since Chris's Jeep had pulled up outside, and no one had even noticed. It wasn't that she was trying to give anyone the silent treatment. It just never seemed to occur to anyone that she might have something to say.

"My goodness, Kaitlyn. You must be just dead on your feet. I don't believe you've made a peep since you walked in this house. Of course, it can be hard to get a word in edgewise around here." Elizabeth rescued the cake from Olivia and motioned for Kaitlyn to follow her into the kitchen. "Let's have our tea here at the kitchen table. Tea just tastes better in the kitchen." She put the cake on the counter and turned to the stove.

Kaitlyn seated herself in the chair Elizabeth indicated, and Olivia came and stood beside her. Kaitlyn slipped her arm around her daughter and pulled her close. She smelled so good, even after a long day at school. "I liked your cake, Livvy. You used so many beautiful colors."

"Well, Miss Elizabeth showed me how I could mix some colors to make other colors. Did you know red and yellow make orange and blue and red make purple?"

"I do now. What else?"

"Well, blue and yellow make green. And just a tiny bit of red in the white frosting makes pink. But I knew that already. But if you mix them all together it makes this yucky brownish color. There. That one. We didn't use very much of that."

Kaitlyn laughed and pulled her closer in a hug. How had it escaped her that her daughter was an absolute delight? "I'm sure your teacher will love your cake."

"I didn't make it because she's my teacher. I made it because she's my friend." Olivia scraped a bit of blue icing off the edge of the plate and popped her finger in her mouth. "She was my friend first, even before Uncle Chris. She took me out to the ranch to ride horses and everything."

"I remember. You told me all about it when we talked on the phone." Kaitlyn closed her eyes against the stab of pain she experienced every time she thought of those runaway-mom days. What could she have been thinking?

When she opened her eyes again, Elizabeth was placing a plate of cookies on the table and sitting down in the chair across from her. Kaitlyn searched her face for the familiar signs of disapproval she found in so many people she had met, not that she blamed them. They could not, even if they banded together and pooled their condemnation, think less of her than she thought of herself.

But Elizabeth just smiled and pushed the cookie plate toward her. "This is nice. I've been just dying to get you alone and have a good visit. But Chris, as much as I love that boy, just doesn't seem to want to let you out of his sight."

Kaitlyn felt her stomach sink again. *Here we go. More little digs. More innuendo.* She picked up a cookie and took a nibble. "Well, I guess he has his reasons."

"Hogwash. You're not going anywhere. I know that and he knows it too."

"I know it too. And I'm not going anywhere either, right, Mom?"

Olivia had climbed into her own chair at the table, and as Kaitlyn looked from one indignant face to another, she couldn't help smiling. It didn't appear Elizabeth shied away from saying exactly what she thought. So much for innuendo.

"No. Unless I'm actually run out of town, I'm not going anywhere."

"No one's going to run you out of town." The teakettle whistled, and Elizabeth got up to make the tea. "Yes, leaving Livvy here and taking off who-knows-where was a big mistake. No one knows that better than you do. But look what came of it. Never underestimate what the Lord can do, honey. He can take the biggest mess you ever saw and make something so beautiful it can take your breath away."

Tears stung Kaitlyn's eyes. "I'm afraid I don't see anything very beautiful right now. Except you." She smiled a watery smile as she reached for her daughter's hand and gave it a squeeze.

"Give it some time. There's just a lot of healing that needs to take place. I think that's the real reason why Chris keeps you so close. He's just worried about you."

"I don't know. I've never had an entire town hate me before."

"Now, don't start feeling sorry for yourself. That's not going to help one bit. Most of this everybody-hates-me is you feeling bad about yourself and seeing blame even when it's not intended. Pshaw. If the hide of everyone in Last Chance who ever made mistakes was nailed to the barn door, you wouldn't be able to get the thing open."

"It would be really gross too." Olivia reached for another cookie.

"That it would." Elizabeth poured tea in all the cups and added a large splash of milk to Olivia's.

Kaitlyn watched her daughter stir sugar into her milky tea. Olivia could seem so grown-up sometimes. Most seven-year-olds would have been carefully excluded from conversations about their disgraced mother, but Olivia took it in stride. After all, nothing said was new to her. Kaitlyn wished with all her heart she could scoop her up and hold her tight and somehow make all the things Olivia had seen and heard and dealt with in her short seven years go away. She felt so helpless and so unworthy of such a beautiful gift.

"Hey. Where is everybody?" Kaitlyn heard the front door open and a man's voice drift in.

"Steven." Olivia heaved a sigh and downed her tea in one long drink. "I think I'll go finish my picture. I'm done here."

"Okay, honey." Elizabeth looked up and smiled as her grandson appeared in the doorway. "We're having some tea. Would you like a cup?"

"I'll skip the tea. But if you have any milk, I'll help you with the cookies."

"In the refrigerator. While you're up, put a few more cookies on the plate, would you?"

When Steven slid the plate of cookies onto the table and plopped into a chair holding his glass of milk, his eyes were only for Kaitlyn.

"I haven't seen you since Christmas. How are you settling in?"

Kaitlyn shrugged. "Okay, I guess."

"Planning on staying long?"

She hesitated. Another dig? But his smile was open and warm.

Besides, Elizabeth was right. It was time to start holding her head up.

Taking a cookie from the plate he offered her, she returned his smile. "Looks like I might be here a while. Chris has me working for him at that diner of his, and that's an opportunity that doesn't come along all that often."

He laughed. "No, I can see how you wouldn't want to pass that up. How is it working out with Juanita? She has a way of keeping everybody hopping. Even Chris, and he's the boss."

"Juanita would like me gone, no question about that. But I'm afraid she's just going to have to deal with the fact that I'm there. Like it or not."

"Oh, don't worry about Juanita. She's one of those people you either take as she is or leave alone." Elizabeth nudged the plate of cookies toward Kaitlyn, who shook her head. "I've known her nearly all her life, and she's been exactly the same. She was in my first class at Last Chance School, you know, and the bossiest little thing you ever saw. She was always trying to organize clubs and name herself president."

It felt good to laugh, and for the first time in months Kaitlyn felt the heaviness she carried in her heart lighten a bit.

"Sounds like you're having a good time in here." Chris walked into the kitchen, smiling and hand in hand with Sarah. "I hate to break it up, but are you ready to go? Sarah invited me to stay for dinner, so I thought I'd run you two home real quick and come back."

"Sure. If Livvy eats any more of these cookies, she's not going to eat dinner anyway." Kaitlyn stood up and gave Elizabeth a hug. "Thanks so much for the tea . . . and everything."

"My pleasure, darlin'. Come back soon."

"Why don't I take them home?" Steven got to his feet too. "Save you a trip. Although I've got to say, bro, if you are voluntarily eating Sarah's cooking, you are hooked really bad."

Sarah took a swipe at her cousin, but Chris grinned. "Thanks. I'd appreciate that. You don't mind, do you, Kaitlyn?"

"No. Why should I mind?" Kaitlyn was careful to keep her voice casual. But truth be told, she was getting pretty tired of having her opinion asked *after* the decision had already been made.

"Then, m'lady, your chariot awaits." Steven bowed and offered his arm.

Oh, brother, just give me a break. Kaitlyn ignored the proffered arm and headed for the front door, calling Olivia as she went.

Steven had to admit he was intrigued. He had heard about Kaitlyn, of course, long before he met her. The whole town knew she had dropped her daughter off at her brother's and taken off for parts unknown on a motorcycle with some guy named Jase. And if any detail of the story had been left out, Juanita was more than happy to fill in the gaps as she refilled coffee cups at the Dip 'n' Dine—always keeping a careful eye to make sure that Chris was indeed out of earshot.

As he watched Kaitlyn walk down the sidewalk to his SUV parked at the curb, he noted that as thorough as Juanita had been, she had left out some vital information—like legs that seemed to go on forever and a shape that could make a grown man cry. Of course, she had a little girl, but that shouldn't be a problem. Kids liked him. As if she could read his mind, Olivia, bouncing alongside her mom, turned around and gave him a glare that would raise blisters on a rock.

Wounded, Steven fell back a step. Where had that come from? Everybody liked him, at least at first. What was there not to like? He was tall, blond, handsome, and built like a Greek god, and if that didn't do the trick, all he had to do was smile and flash that dimple. He decided that Kaitlyn, kid or no kid, deserved the full treatment.

"Here, let me get that for you." He reached past Kaitlyn for the door handle, trapping her between himself and the door just long enough to make her look up so he could give her the dimple treatment. She glanced up, stepped aside so he could open the door, and got in without saying a word.

"Hey, the back door's locked." The kid was tugging at the handle, and as Steven clicked his key chain to unlock it for her, he heard Kaitlyn's seat belt catch and the door slam.

That went well. He turned his attention to the little girl climbing into the backseat. "Need some help, sweetheart?"

She gave him the same withering glare she had tossed over her shoulder and reached for her seat belt. "I can do it myself. And don't call me sweetheart. My name's Olivia."

What's with these people? He walked around the truck and got in. He was taking them home, not to prison.

He turned the key in the ignition and gave the smile another try. "I'll bet you're beat. Why don't I take you and Olivia to San Ramon for pizza or a burger or something? Let someone wait on you for a change."

Kaitlyn shook her head without looking at him. "No, thanks. We need to get home. Olivia's got homework."

"I don't have that much homework. We could get pizza." Olivia still wasn't talking to him, but she didn't sound as angry as she had. He pressed his advantage.

"I'll have you home in an hour and a half, maybe less. You have to eat anyway. Why not with me?" He slid Kaitlyn his aw-shucks grin, which she did not see since she was staring ahead.

"Yeah, Mom, we have to eat anyway."

Steven slowed as he reached the town's main intersection and looked to Kaitlyn for her final word—right to San Ramon, left to the little neighborhood of mobile homes where Kaitlyn lived with her daughter and brother.

"Not tonight. Thanks anyway."

Steven flipped on his left turn signal and looked at Olivia in his rearview mirror. "Sorry, sweetheart, I mean Olivia. I owe you a pizza, though. Don't let me forget."

She glared at him like it was his fault she wasn't getting her pizza, and Steven gave up. It didn't happen often, but sometimes even someone as amazing-looking as Kaitlyn was just more trouble than he cared to deal with. They rode in silence until he turned into the circle drive that led to the yellow-and-white singlewide.

"Thanks for the ride." The words were rote and offered not a hint of appreciation as Kaitlyn got out and opened the back door for Olivia.

"Yeah. Sure. No problem. Glad to do it. Any time." Kaitlyn had already closed her door and Olivia had slammed hers, and Steven sat behind the wheel watching them walk to their front door. What he really wanted to do was spin out on the gravel driveway as he left and raise a cloud of dust that wouldn't settle for a week. What he did do was just as his grandmother had always told him he should do. He sat in the drive and waited until Kaitlyn had fitted her key in the lock. He lifted his hand in a wave as she opened the door and Olivia ran inside. But did Kaitlyn turn and wave back as if to say, "I'm in. Thanks for waiting," like anyone else in Last Chance would have done? She did not.

Steven shifted into first and gunned his engine. The dust cloud was a small one and settled in moments, but it was satisfying nonetheless.

—

"How come we couldn't go out for pizza? We never get to go anywhere." Olivia dropped her pink backpack in the middle of the floor and slumped on the sofa.

"Because it's a school night." Kaitlyn picked up the backpack and handed it to her. "This goes in your room, and you need to take a bath while I fix dinner. Then it is homework and bed time."

"You never *used* to care if it was a school night. We used to have fun." Olivia dragged the pack behind her as she went down the hall to her room.

Kaitlyn sighed. *Yeah, and that worked out really well, didn't it?* She followed Olivia and found her lying facedown on her bed. Sitting next to her, Kaitlyn rubbed light circles on her back. "We'll still have fun. We'll just do it on a weekend. How about Saturday evening? Do you want to go for pizza then?"

"We probably can't even go to the movies, though." Olivia's voice, though muffled, was tragic. Milking a moment was one of her gifts.

Kaitlyn smiled and dug her fingertips lightly into her daughter's ribs. Olivia squealed and flipped faceup, and Kaitlyn bent to kiss her daughter's forehead. "You are something else, you know that?"

"So can we go to the movies too?"

"We'll see what's playing. Now you go hop in the tub and I'll see what I can find for dinner."

"I'll bet Uncle Chris will want to bring Sarah." Olivia headed back up the hall toward the bathroom. "She goes with us almost everywhere now."

Kaitlyn, following close behind, stopped at the door and raised an eyebrow at Olivia. "I thought it would just be the two of us this time. We could have a girls' night out."

"How about Sarah? She's a girl."

"Don't you remember? She and Uncle Chris are going out to celebrate her birthday. Besides, I'd love to have a night with just you. We haven't done that in a long time."

Olivia's expression dimmed just a bit, and she shrugged before pulling her shirt over her head. "Okay, if you think you know the way."

"I'll find it. Don't worry." Kaitlyn's own smile faded after she turned away from the bathroom door and headed to the kitchen. If Olivia wasn't all that excited about spending an evening in her company alone, she really had no one to blame but herself, and she knew that. There was a time, when the two of them lived together in Scottsdale, when Olivia had begged her to spend time alone with her. Kaitlyn had been full of promises then—promises that somehow were always put off for another day. Now, it seemed, the shoe was on the other foot. Olivia was the one with a social schedule that would not quit, and it was Kaitlyn who was adrift and alone.

She was putting dinner on the table when Olivia came in wearing her princess pajamas. "Maybe Steven would come with us for pizza Saturday. He knows where it is too."

"Steven? Why in the world would we take Steven?"

Olivia shrugged and avoided looking at her mother as she climbed onto her chair.

"Livvy, look at me." Kaitlyn put her hands on the table and leaned across until Olivia looked up at her. "I want to have pizza and go to a movie with *you*. Not with Uncle Chris, not with Sarah, and certainly not with Steven. Just with you. Is that okay with you?"

She was bewildered when Olivia's eyes filled with tears. "But what if, when we're having pizza, you make some new friends and want to go with them? How would I find my way back home again?"

The anguish that landed like a blow in the middle of Kaitlyn's chest nearly took her breath away. "Do you think for one minute that I would ever, *ever* do that? I just told you that you're the only one I want to be with, but even if we did meet new friends, I would never in a million years just go off and leave you behind. Don't you know that?"

Olivia stared at her lap and swiped at her nose with the back of her hand.

"Livvy. Olivia, look at me."

Olivia still would not meet her eyes, and Kaitlyn reached across the table and tipped her chin with forefinger and thumb.

"Look at me. Do you really think I would leave you like that?"

Olivia pulled away from her mother's touch and dropped her gaze again. She was blinking hard to keep the tears back, and her mouth worked with the effort. She had not said another word, but she didn't have to. The unspoken accusation filled the room until it crushed the very breath from Kaitlyn's lungs. *But you did. You went away and left me behind, and I couldn't get back home.*

Kaitlyn felt as if she had been turned to ice. She knew she had been walking around under a cloud of disapproval since she came back to Last Chance. But she had been facing down disapproval with complete indifference since she entered her teens. She had taken Chris's forgiveness for granted, and truth be told, she really didn't give a rip what the rest of this tiny little town thought of her. But Livvy! Her own daughter really thought she might be abandoned in a pizza shop. When Kaitlyn could move again, she walked around the table and knelt by Olivia's chair.

"Honey, listen to me." She placed her hands on Olivia's arms, and her heart broke as she felt her daughter shrink under her touch. "I want you to understand two things, so listen as carefully as you can. When I left you here with Uncle Chris, I knew I was leaving you in a good place, a safe place. I wasn't wrong about that, either. You have friends here, you get to ride horses, and you've never done better in school. I think you're happier than you've ever been, and that makes me happy too. But here's the second thing, and it's the most important thing I have to say, so listen very carefully. Leaving you anywhere, even a good place like Uncle Chris's, was a very bad thing to do. I should never, never, never have left you anywhere. Do you hear me? You are my own Olivia, and we belong together, no matter what. I love you and I'm so, so sorry. I wish I could take everything back."

Olivia's tenuous control held almost to the end but gave way in a torrent under her mom's apology. Still on her knees in front of Olivia's chair, Kaitlyn gathered her into her arms and held her, murmuring promises and declarations and more apologies into her hair.

Finally she leaned back and smiled as she brushed damp strands of hair from her daughter's face. "So, are we good?"

Olivia nodded and wiped her nose with the back of her hand again.

"And we can go for pizza Saturday, just you and me?"

Olivia hesitated before nodding again, and Kaitlyn's heart wrenched at the doubt still lingering in her daughter's eyes. She had done more damage than she'd ever allowed herself to imagine. This was going to take a lot of time.

"I'll tell you what. When we go, you can carry my phone, and if ever you feel the tiniest bit scared, you can call Uncle Chris to come get you. How would that be?"

"I won't feel scared."

"I know you won't, because we are going to have a terrific time. But would you like to be in charge of the phone anyway? Just in case?"

Olivia searched her mother's face. Kaitlyn willed the pain and grief from her expression and tried to present one of love and acceptance. Finally, Olivia nodded. "Okay."

"It's settled then." Kaitlyn rose from her aching knees. "Pizza Saturday, and if there is a good movie on, we'll do that too. And you are in charge of the phone. Now go blow your nose and wash your face and hands. Dinner is getting cold."

As Olivia skipped off, Kaitlyn hugged herself to keep the pain from spilling out all over the kitchen. Leaving Olivia with Chris had been Jase's idea. He was the one who convinced her it would be easier on everybody if they just slipped away quietly at sunup. But even as she tried to blame him for all the heartache she had caused, the attempt fell flat. She was the one who listened. In fact, now that she thought about it, most of the trouble she had ever been in had begun because she listened to some guy with a good idea.

The splashing in the bathroom had stopped, and Olivia's light, running footsteps headed her way. Kaitlyn straightened her shoulders and pasted what she hoped was a cheerful smile on her face. Well, her days of listening to good-looking guys with bad ideas were over. Everyone in town, including Chris, had good reason to think she didn't deserve someone as wonderful as Olivia. Truth be told, she agreed with them. But the past was past. Olivia was the most important person in the world to her, and if there wasn't room for anyone else, well, that was just the way it was going to be.

—∞—

"You're back." Elizabeth stuck her head in from the kitchen when the front door opened. "I thought you were heading back to the ranch after you dropped Kaitlyn off."

"I thought I'd swing back by. I didn't get much of a chance to talk to you earlier." No need to mention Kaitlyn and how thoroughly he had been shut down. He had a reputation to uphold, even if he was just talking to his grandmother.

"Have you eaten? I'm just fixing to have supper." Elizabeth had returned to the kitchen.

Steven wandered in after her and turned a kitchen chair around to straddle. "Yeah, I could eat something." He folded his hands on the chair back and rested his chin on them.

Elizabeth gave him a look. "Well then, please let me fix you dinner."

"Sorry, Gran. I didn't mean to be rude. I was just thinking. Here, I'll set the table." He got up and gave her a one-armed hug before getting plates out of the cupboard.

Gran was really good at setting you sharply back on the straight and narrow and then moving on as if nothing had happened, and while she chatted on, Steven went over his short trip to take Kaitlyn home. Was she mad that Chris was having dinner with Sarah? She didn't seem like a possessive sister. In fact, the few times he had seen them together, Sarah and Kaitlyn really seemed to get along. Maybe she'd had a bad day at work? That was a distinct possibility, now that he thought about it. Working at that pokey diner had to be a real bore for someone who had been around as much as Kaitlyn Reed. A brief consideration that it might have been him personally that repelled her came and went without even stopping. Nah, couldn't be that.

He realized that his grandmother had stopped talking and was looking at him with expectation. Clearly, some response was required, and he hadn't the slightest idea what she had been talking about.

"You caught me, Gran. My mind was wandering. Care to run that by me again?"

But Gran was much more interested in his wandering mind than she was in repeating herself. "What's going on with you, Steven? All this thinking isn't like you. Is something wrong?"

He flashed his dimple and ignored the comment about thinking being foreign to him. "Nope, not a thing's wrong. Just daydreaming." He dropped into his chair, waited for Gran to say grace, and passed the green beans before casually bringing Kaitlyn into the conversation.

"Chris's sister sure doesn't seem very happy here. Think she'll be around long?"

"I hope so. I like Kaitlyn. She hasn't had an easy time of it, and I think Last Chance might be just the place for her to rest awhile and find out who she really is."

"From what I hear, what you call a hard time, she calls a fun time. I give her six months tops." Steven plopped a scoop of potato salad onto his plate and offered the bowl to his grandmother.

"Really. Is that what you hear?" Gran's blue eyes had gone stormy. "That's disgraceful. I'm surprised you'd even listen to such trash, and even more disappointed that you'd pass it on."

"Sorry, Gran." Steven stabbed at the slice of cold ham on his plate. The evening was not going well. He fancied himself—with good reason, he had to admit—pretty darn irresistible when it came to the ladies. But so far, every female he had come in contact with today, from a seven-year-old girl to his own grandmother, had treated him like he had something on his boots. Gran *always* took his side. At least she used to.

Dinner was pretty quiet. Steven kept glancing up at his grandmother, who seemed lost in her own thoughts. From the time he was a kid, Steven could count on Gran trying to set things right after she had barked at him. She never backed down on what she had said in the first place, but it had always been important to her that the waters had been calmed before they went on. But he really must have messed up this time, because she did not have a lot to say.

Finally, he broke the silence. "Gran, I know I was out of line with the comment about Kaitlyn. You're right. She hasn't had it easy."

Elizabeth looked up with a frown. "What? Oh, that." Her face relaxed into a smile. "I'm not upset with you, honey, but I guess I *was* thinking about Kaitlyn. It just breaks my heart that someone as young as she is seems to go around acting as if her life is over. I'm sorry. Here, have some more ham."

"No, thanks. I'll just grab a few cookies and head on out to the ranch. Uncle Joe Jr. runs a pretty tight ship, and morning comes awful early up there."

Elizabeth got to her feet and reached for her apron. "I'm sure he appreciates the help. When do you go to the academy?"

"Not till spring." He grinned. "So I'll be leaving about the time they could really use the help."

"Well, you'll make a fine law officer. I'm proud of you." She held up her cheek for a kiss. "You take care."

"Can't I help with these dishes before I go?" Steven started to clear his plate, half expecting his grandmother to wave him away as she always did.

"You know, if you'd just stack them in the sink, I'd really appreciate that. I may just leave them till morning this time."

"You're not letting that little girl of Kaitlyn's wear you out, are you?" He took an armload of dishes to the counter. "I never did think her coming here after school was the best idea, you know."

This time Elizabeth did flap a hand at him. "Oh, pshaw. Livvy's no trouble at all. She's a sweet little thing and I love having her. I'm just a little tired tonight, that's all."

"Then you go sit down and watch your shows, and I'll be done here in a minute."

"I'll do that. Thank you, darlin'."

Steven watched her rest her hand briefly on the doorjamb for support when she passed through to the living room. Gran was slowing down. Okay, she was eighty-seven and maybe she was entitled, but that didn't mean Steven liked seeing it.

3

Kaitlyn was curled up on the sofa watching an old movie when she heard Chris's Jeep pull up outside and the door slam.

"Hey, how's it going?" He almost had to duck when he came through the front door a few minutes later. "You got home okay, I see."

She hit the Mute button on the remote and looked up him. "You've got lipstick all over your face."

When Chris immediately rubbed his hand over his jaw and examined his fingers, she grinned. "Gotcha. Have a good time?"

He just glared and ignored the question. "Olivia in bed?"

"Yep, hours ago." Kaitlyn got up and followed him into the kitchen. She leaned against the counter and watched her brother rummage through the refrigerator. "That Steven Braden who you pawned us off on—and thanks so much, by the way—sure is impressed with himself. Who is he, anyway?"

Chris emerged holding a piece of cheesecake that looked slightly dry on the sides and cracked on the top. "I didn't mean to pawn you off on anybody. All you had to do was say no. I'd have been happy to drive you home. Why? Did he try to pull anything?"

"No, not really. He just seemed to think I should be so impressed that he even looked my way. Then when I didn't fall all over him, he acted like a spoiled kid."

Chris sniffed at the cheesecake and took a tentative bite. It must have tasted okay because he finished it off and opened the cupboard to see what else he could find. "Yep, that would be Steven. He's sort of the family black sheep. Sarah says he's been getting by on charm and good looks all his life. Seems to work too, from what I hear."

"This is the guy you sent your sister and niece home with? Nice."

Chris found a bag of chips. "Honey, I'd back you in a bear fight."

If that was supposed to make Kaitlyn feel better, it didn't. Okay, it was true that if Steven had tried to get physical, he probably would have wound up with something broken, but still . . . She watched Chris grab a handful of chips from the bag and stuff them in his mouth. "Why are you eating? Didn't you ever get around to dinner?"

Chris threw her a warning look. "Yes, we had dinner. But cooking isn't exactly one of Sarah's strengths, so I'm still a little hungry, okay?"

"Sheesh. Sorry. Well, cooking's not one of my strengths either, so if you're looking for leftovers from tonight's dinner, knock yourself out. I'm going back to my movie."

She had curled back onto the sofa when Chris joined her with his bag of chips. "What are you watching?"

"It's an old Hitchcock movie. I can't believe this guy. He's supposed to be the good guy and he's nothing but a creepy stalker."

Chris finished his chips and wadded up the bag. "Well, I hope it's almost over. We're out of here awful early in the morning. I'm going to bed." He took careful aim with his chip bag and made the three-point shot to the wastebasket in the kitchen. "And the crowd goes wild . . ."

"Chris, wait a minute." He had already started down the hall but turned when she called.

"Yeah?"

"I'd like to take Livvy to San Ramon Saturday after work, all right?"

A tired frown crossed his face. "Saturday? I can't, Kaitlyn. You know it's Sarah's birthday. We're going out."

"I'm talking about just Livvy and me, so all I'm asking is that you take Sarah's car. We haven't had much chance to just reconnect, and I'd really like some time alone with her." She was about to tell Chris of the wrenching remorse she felt at leaving Olivia as she did, but when his frown deepened to one of real concern, she changed her mind. She just couldn't go there with him yet. "So I'd like to take your car. We wouldn't be out too late."

She lifted her chin to meet his troubled gaze, and after a moment, almost as if he willed it, his face relaxed into a smile. "Sure. Why not? You two need some time together. Have fun."

He started down the hall to his room, and Kaitlyn slumped against the sofa. She clicked off the television and closed her eyes. Everyone made mistakes, but it seemed hers were the kind that just kept on giving.

"Kaitlyn?"

Kaitlyn jumped and her eyes popped open. She hadn't heard Chris come back in the room. He sat down on the sofa next to her.

"I have to ask." He draped his arm across the back of the sofa and looked into her eyes for a long moment before speaking. "Saturday. You're just going up to San Ramon for the evening, right? You're coming back?"

"Seriously, Chris?" Her voice rose to the breaking point, and her brother glanced down the hall at Olivia's door. "I'm going to kidnap my own daughter and steal your car? You really think I would do that?"

"Look, Kaitlyn, don't get mad. I'm sorry if I got this all wrong. But you did take off once, and I know you're not all that crazy about Last Chance."

"No, I'm not all that crazy about Last Chance." Kaitlyn jumped up and stood over Chris, swiping a shaking hand across her eyes. "But Olivia is here, and I'm not leaving her again. Ever. I guess I don't need to remind you why I can't just take her."

"Kaitlyn . . ." Chris got to his feet and reached for his sister.

She backed away. "I knew what a rotten mother I was when I signed those papers. I knew Olivia deserved so much more than she was getting from me. She's changed so much since she's been with you. I can see that too. But she's not the only one who's changed, Chris, in case you haven't noticed."

"I've noticed. And maybe it's because you've changed that I worry sometimes. I know you're going to want Olivia back one of these days, and when that happens, nothing will stop you from just taking her away. I don't think I could stand losing both of you again."

Kaitlyn felt her rage turn to something else. Tender frustration? Frustrated tenderness? Her brother, looking at her with such sadness in his eyes, loomed larger than life, both in physical size and in the role he had always played in her life. He'd been her hero and champion, always ready to take on anything or anyone who threatened her. But that couldn't continue forever. She was grown now and needed to fight her own battles, and Chris, if his moon-eyed devotion to Sarah Cooley was any indication of things to come, needed to be able to get on with his own life too.

She stepped over to him and stood on tiptoe to kiss his cheek.

"You're not losing either of us, ever, no matter where we all wind up. Now, good night. I'll see you in the morning."

He gave her a hug. "I stopped in your trailer and turned the heat on for you when I got home. Should be toasty warm now. G'night."

"Thank you, Chris. Sleep tight." Kaitlyn took her coat off the rack by the door and wrapped herself up in it before letting herself out into the icy stillness of the winter night. She stopped on the porch a moment to gaze at the heavens. More stars than she ever dreamed existed had exploded against the black sky, and the cold made them glisten like a million shards of ice. Pulling her coat more tightly around her, she jumped off the porch and ran around the singlewide to the tiny travel trailer parked in back.

Chris was right; it was warm and welcoming. He had been almost apologetic about the little trailer when he brought her back to Last Chance, explaining that his house was just too small for another person, but she had loved it from the first moment. It was hers, one room though it was, and in it she could feel safe and protected and almost ready to begin the process of learning to forgive herself.

Leaving the single room in darkness, she sat at the little dinette and gazed out the window at the sky again. Across the short expanse of desert, she saw first the kitchen light, then the bathroom light, and finally Chris's bedroom light go out. The yellow-and-white singlewide became a gray shadow. And over everything—the singlewide, her little trailer, and even the sleeping town of Last Chance—arched a sky so immense and so bright with stars that it should have made Kaitlyn feel small and insignificant but for some reason made her feel protected and looked after.

Without turning on a light, she got ready for bed and climbed beneath the down comforter. Even from her bed she could see the stars through the window. Nothing about her past actions had changed, and she knew she'd still be facing hard expressions of disapproval when she got to work in the morning, but something about that sky made her realize that there was more. She was still gazing at the spangled heavens when her eyes drifted shut and she slept.

—ꟷ—

The worst thing about the alarm going off in winter was that it went off in the dark. The second worst thing was the phone call that always came about five minutes later.

"Rise and shine, baby sister. Time to get going."

"I'm up." Kaitlyn's voice came as a croak, and she cleared her throat to sound a little more convincing. "I'm up."

"Then turn on your light." Through her own window, she could see Chris, dressed and ready for the day, standing at the window of his brightly lit kitchen.

"Aren't there Peeping Tom laws in this place?"

"All I can see is the shape of your trailer, so shut your blinds and turn on your light. We're out of here in half an hour."

Mentally going over her catalog of torments that should be administered to those who woke other people from sound sleep, Kaitlyn shut her shades and groped for her lamp, squinting against the harsh light that forced the gentle night from her room. She briefly considered just going back to bed with the light on, but it was too late. She was awake now.

She was standing before her mirror buttoning her uniform and wondering who in the world could design such an ugly garment when she heard running footsteps outside and Olivia burst through her door.

"Hey, Mom, could you do my hair?"

"Well, good morning to you too, sweet cakes." Kaitlyn smiled at her daughter and reached to give her a hug.

Olivia danced out of reach and shrugged out of both coat and backpack. "Mo-o-o-m, Uncle Chris said I have exactly two and one half minutes, and I want you to do those two braids on the side that go into that sort of inside-out braid in the back."

"That's going to take more than two and a half minutes, babe." Kaitlyn took the brush from Olivia's hand and began to gently tug the nighttime snarls from her daughter's hair. "How about wearing your hair down today? I'll just pull the sides up high on your head. See? You've got this waterfall of blonde down the back. Beautiful."

She gave Olivia a hand mirror, and her daughter turned from side to side trying to see the back. Finally, she nodded her approval and reached for her coat as two quick honks from the driveway reminded them that the two and a half minutes were up.

"Mom?" Olivia reached for her mother's hand as the two walked around to the front where Chris waited in the Jeep. "Do you think you could do Emma A.'s hair sometime? She always tells me she likes my hair now. She likes the braids best, but I bet she'll like the waterfall, too."

"If she'd like me to." Ignoring Chris's pointed glare, Kaitlyn got in the front seat and fastened her seat belt. Truthfully, she couldn't see Emma's mother allowing her precious daughter anywhere near Kaitlyn, but maybe Olivia wouldn't press it and it would all go away.

One of the things that hurt her most when she came to Last Chance was the bedraggled, off-center ponytail that Olivia wore so defiantly. It took several weeks before she allowed her mother to even touch her hair, and even longer before she let her trim the ragged ends. During those long weeks, Kaitlyn ached to draw her daughter onto her lap and never let her go, filling every one of her senses—touch, smell, sight, even taste—with the daughter she had so carelessly let out of her life, but Olivia had not forgotten and was not ready to forgive. Not for a long time. If Olivia had shouted her anger and pain, Kaitlyn would have welcomed it. They would have had a place to start the healing. But from the moment Kaitlyn stepped off the bus in San Ramon to find Chris and Olivia waiting for her last November, Olivia had treated her with the same casual indifference she treated any stranger. In those first days back in Last Chance, Kaitlyn had tried to talk to Olivia, to explain, or try to explain, why she did what she did, even to ask forgiveness. But Olivia would just shrug, look away, and mutter, "S'okay."

So Kaitlyn waited, treasuring every tiny step toward her that her daughter allowed her to take. The pedicure came first, then the manicure—if you could call dabbing polish on those bitten scraps of nail a manicure—and finally the good-night kiss. But Olivia had still worn that scraggly ponytail like a badge of honor. Whether it was to prove to her mother that she did not need either her or her skills, or whether it was to show the world that in her own eyes at least, Olivia was still motherless, Kaitlyn could not guess, but it broke her heart. The day Olivia had had an angry fight with the rubber band entangled in her hair and Kaitlyn had deftly removed the offending band, brushed out Olivia's hair, and put the ponytail back—dead center this time—had passed without comment by Olivia, but it had been a day that set Kaitlyn to singing. Now, under Kaitlyn's care, Olivia's hair shimmered like watered silk and fell just past her shoulders in a smooth, even layer.

Kaitlyn looked over the seat and smiled at Olivia. Let the shoemaker's children go barefoot; the hairstylist's child would look like a princess—from the neck up, anyway, and principally from the back.

"Carlos is already here. We're late." Chris pulled up in front of the Dip 'n' Dine, dark except for the light from the kitchen, and shut off the engine. Before Kaitlyn could observe that Carlos always got there first and that she didn't call three minutes "late" when the diner wasn't due to open for another hour anyway, Chris was out of the Jeep and unlocking the front door.

By the time she and Olivia followed him in, he had turned on the lights and was heading for the thermostat. Carlos, already at work in the kitchen, lifted a spatula in salute. "Just in time, *chica*. I've got some pancakes for you. Pull up a stool there at the counter and breakfast is served."

Olivia's coat and backpack hit the floor where she shrugged out of them on the way across the room, and Kaitlyn stooped to pick them up, wondering if Olivia even knew she didn't have them with her anymore. It was as if her little body and her head didn't communicate with each other much. Kaitlyn tucked the coat and pack away and went to take the plate of pancakes and bacon from the window and put it in front of Olivia, now perched on the counter stool.

"Want some milk?" She smiled at her daughter as she set the plate down. "How about some juice?"

"Juice." Olivia, busy with the pancakes, didn't look up.

"Juice, please."

"Please." Olivia still did not look up.

"Juice, please, mother darling."

This time Olivia did glance up from under her bangs, but it was clear from her dark look that Kaitlyn was going to have to be happy with a simple *please*.

Kaitlyn laughed and headed for the kitchen. "I'll get your juice."

Chris, emerging from the storeroom with a carton of paper

napkins, glanced at the clock as Juanita came in. She was running even later than usual this morning, and clearly he wasn't too happy about it. If he had planned to mention it, however, Juanita beat him to it.

"Don't anyone say one word to me, and I mean it." She sent a warning look Chris's way as she took off her coat. "I got here just as quick as I could, all things considered. Besides, you know I can get all my side work done in about fifteen minutes."

Kaitlyn tried to ignore the little flash in her chest as Juanita disappeared into the storeroom. She knew she was the one who needed the extra time, and she knew Juanita was taking another opportunity to remind her of it.

"Morning, Carlos. Those biscuits smell heavenly." Juanita, having gotten in the first dig of the morning, seemed in a better mood. "Don't you look pretty this morning, Miss Olivia."

Neither Carlos nor Olivia responded, but that didn't seem to bother Juanita. She tied her apron on and set about doing her fifteen minutes' worth of tasks, chatting as if everyone was hanging on her every word. It didn't seem to matter to her that no one was paying any attention, and Kaitlyn wondered again how, under these circumstances, Juanita still managed to convey the distinct impression that her conversation included everyone but Chris's wayward sister.

4

Good morning, beautiful." The sun had just spilled down the side of the mountains that rose east of Last Chance when Steven let himself in the front door of his grandmother's house. He hadn't been sure that he'd find his grandmother up yet as she was more a night owl than an early bird, but there she was in her recliner with her Bible open on her lap and her fuzzy pink slippers propped up on the footrest. "How about a little breakfast?"

"Steven! What brings you out so early?" She smiled up at him as he crossed the room to kiss her cheek. Gran always made him feel that just his turning up made her day. Not too many people did that. In fact, now that he thought about it, Gran was the only person in his life who was always glad to see him.

"I have an errand to run for Uncle Joe Jr. in San Ramon. I thought I'd come in a little early so I can take you out to breakfast."

"Why don't I just fix you something here?" Elizabeth closed her Bible and set it on the little table next to her chair. "I've got some sausage in there, and I can make eggs."

"Nope, you're not cooking this morning. I'm taking you out, so finish up what you're doing there, and then go get dressed. I'm not in a hurry." He took a *Yarn Lovers' World* magazine off the coffee table. "This any good? I'll just read this. Take your time."

Elizabeth seemed more exasperated than pleased. "Steven, I am just a mess. I have a hair appointment in San Ramon this afternoon, and I'm not fit to be seen right now. Why don't you just let me fix you some breakfast here? The coffee's already made."

Steven tossed the magazine on the table and stood up. "I want to take you out to breakfast this morning, okay?" He held out a hand to help her out of her recliner. "Your hair looks fine. You always look beautiful, don't you know that?"

This time she didn't return his engaging smile, and she waved away his hand as she struggled out of her recliner.

"All right. Give me about a half hour." She stopped before heading down the hall. "Steven, I do appreciate your coming by to take me to breakfast, but I'd also appreciate a little warning next time."

Steven leaned back against the sofa and watched her go. That was twice in twelve hours that he had turned on the charm and had it fall flat. Three times if you counted Kaitlyn's kid. That sort of thing just didn't happen. Was he losing his touch—getting old or something? The thought made him feel hollow, and he pushed it away. Passing by a small wall mirror as he went for coffee, he smiled, flashing his dimple. Nah. He still had it. Which was good, since, after thinking it over, he had decided to give Kaitlyn Reed another chance at breakfast this morning.

"Well, good morning!" Juanita greeted them at the door. "We don't usually see you this early, Elizabeth. Are you headed up to San Ramon for a doctor's appointment or something?"

"No, Steven's the one going to San Ramon. He was just sweet enough to take me out to breakfast before he went." If Elizabeth was still annoyed at being hustled out of her robe and slippers way too early for her own preference, you couldn't tell it by her voice.

Steven didn't say anything. He guided his grandmother to a booth as he looked around the diner. No sign of Kaitlyn. A wave of annoyance swept over him. Okay, he would have taken Gran out for breakfast, or for lunch, anyway. If not today, then another day. He and Gran got along great. But her presence with him today was supposed to prove to Kaitlyn that she had him all wrong. He was a nice guy, one who looked after his old granny. He knew Kaitlyn had to love Gran. Everybody did. And if she could see how much Gran loved him, well, then, how bad could he be?

While Gran and Juanita talked, Steven gazed out the window. There was no point in even opening the menu. Everyone in town had it memorized, and despite the well-known intention of Chris to get something else on the menu, so far Carlos had won out and nothing had changed. While he watched, Chris's Jeep pulled up out front and he watched first one and then the other of Kaitlyn's long legs appear beneath the open door of the driver's side.

Over his head, he heard Juanita huff. "Well, look who's finally back."

Elizabeth followed their gaze and smiled. "Did she take Olivia to school?"

"Yes, Chris used to run her over and be back in no time. I have no idea what takes Kaitlyn so long."

Kaitlyn pushed through the front door and stopped at the sight of the three of them looking at her. Steven smiled to assure her that no matter what the others said, she had a friend in him, but it was Elizabeth's warm welcome that she responded to.

"Kaitlyn! I was hoping we'd see you in here this morning. How are you, sweet girl?"

It was clear from Juanita's solid stance as she turned to face Kaitlyn that she was trying to dissuade her from coming over, but Kaitlyn came anyway, ignoring Juanita.

"Hi." Kaitlyn took the hand that Elizabeth held out to her and ignored Steven. "I'm glad I didn't miss you."

"I've got this table, Kaitlyn. Get your coat off real quick and then you can go take care of table four." Juanita pulled out her pad and raised an eyebrow at Kaitlyn, who nodded, smiled again at Elizabeth, and turned to go.

"Would you mind if Kaitlyn took care of us?" Elizabeth turned her smile on Juanita.

"Well, if that's what you want, I guess it's all right, but we have a way of doing things around here, you know." Juanita waited for a response, but Elizabeth had already turned her attention to Kaitlyn. After a second, and with another little huff, Juanita went to take care of table four.

"You didn't answer me." Elizabeth still held Kaitlyn's hand. "How are you doing?"

"Okay, I guess. You're out early."

"Well, we have Steven to thank for that. He turned up at the crack of dawn to take me to breakfast."

At the mention of his name, Kaitlyn finally turned her eyes on Steven. He grinned up at her. "You wouldn't believe how hard it is for me to get a good-looking woman to have a meal with me. I have to catch 'em early, before they get their wits about them."

Kaitlyn actually laughed, and Steven loved the way it made her face soften and look young. "Well, good for you. Let me put my coat away and I'll be back to take your order."

Steven was admiring her retreating form when Gran brought his attention back to the table. "What was that all about?"

"Hmm? Oh, I tried to get Kaitlyn and her kid to go out for pizza with me last night after we left your house, but she shot me down."

"I see." Gran raised an eyebrow, and Steven was afraid that she indeed did see. "In the first place, Kaitlyn's little girl is named Olivia, and in the second place, the last thing Kaitlyn needs right now is someone like you in her life."

Steven sat back and stared. If she had hauled off and socked him in the jaw, she couldn't have surprised him more. To tell the truth, he'd had slugs to the jaw that hurt less. "What do you mean, someone like me?"

"I guess that sounded pretty awful, didn't it?" She reached across the table to put her hand on his arm. He just looked at her. "I wouldn't hurt you for the world, my darlin', but even you'd have to admit you're something of a playboy."

"Playboy? Haven't heard that one in a while." Steven pulled his arm out of reach of his grandmother's hand.

"Well, you know what I mean, whatever you call it now. I do wish you'd get that pout off your face. You look like you're about twelve years old."

Steven picked up his menu and read it like he had never seen it before. It gave him something to look at besides Gran's piercing blue eyes, and even then he could almost feel her gaze drilling into his forehead. A conversation with Gran was never over until she said it was, and he had the uneasy feeling that there was more to come on this one.

"Okay, what can I get you?" Kaitlyn appeared with the coffeepot, and as she filled their cups, Steven tossed his menu aside and waited for her to look his way.

"I guess I'll just have a scrambled egg and some of that good sausage." Elizabeth hadn't even opened her menu. "Oh, and I'll need a little green chile with the egg."

"I'm learning. If it doesn't have syrup on it, bring on the green chile. And if it does have syrup, ask anyway." The smile Kaitlyn gave Elizabeth was different from the ones Steven had seen before. It was open, easy, and not so guarded. Steven liked the way it made her face look and decided he'd try to get a smile like that for himself.

"I'll have the huevos rancheros, eggs over easy." *Ditch the man-of-the-world leer, stow the country-boy grin, and just give her a sincere, from-the-heart smile.* He caught her gaze and held it. "I'd appreciate a couple extra tortillas too, if you don't mind."

"Sure." Her smile faded and she looked away. "I'll get this right in."

Steven watched her cross the room to post the order and shook his head. *What was wrong with her?* When he looked back across the table, Gran was looking at him with her mouth all pinched up. *Oh, brother, here we go.*

"Steven, that is exactly what I was talking about." Gran kept her voice low enough not to be heard by anyone else, but Steven got every word. "You were staring at Kaitlyn like you were trying to hypnotize her. I half expected her to stick both arms out in front of her and her eyes to go blank."

"I was just ordering some eggs."

"Oh, pshaw. Steven, who do you think you're talking to? There's not a look that crosses your face that I haven't seen a thousand times." She sighed, but at least she didn't look mad anymore. "Honey, I know you've liked the girls since the minute you noticed everybody God created wasn't a little boy. And you've got every bit of your daddy's charm, and then some. I guess you can't help that, but you can help how you use it. All I'm saying is, just let

Kaitlyn be. She's got a whole lot she's trying to figure out right now, and I just don't think she needs the kind of complications you offer."

Steven clenched his jaw and looked out the window. If he opened his mouth now, he was pretty sure he'd wind up regretting what came out. Instead, he rehearsed it all in his mind, using language Gran wouldn't approve of either. Finally, he looked back at his grandmother, ready for round two.

"So what are you saying? You don't even want me to talk to her? Just act like she's not there?"

Gran's smile was sweet and unperturbed as she took a sip of her coffee. "Oh, for Pete's sake, Steven, of course not. I've said my piece, and you know exactly what I meant, so let's just enjoy our breakfast and talk about something else." There was rarely a round two where Gran was concerned. "What does Uncle Joe Jr. have you going up to San Ramon for?"

Steven took a deep breath and slowly let it go. He didn't want to admit it, even to himself, but Gran probably had a point. Kaitlyn was a good-looking woman, no doubt about that, but part of what intrigued him about her was the stories swirling around Last Chance since she came back. He had thought of her as something of a kindred spirit, not bound by the outdated values of this backwater town. But as he watched her make her way from table to table and the conversation stop as she refilled coffee or brought plates and the looks follow her as she moved away, he saw a spirit not kindred but broken.

When she brought their order and put it on the table in front of them, Steven didn't go through his repertoire of smiles to decide which one to present. He just looked up and smiled at her and said, "Thanks. This looks great."

Kaitlyn smiled back and said, "Well, enjoy."

That was all, and it felt good.

Kaitlyn found her thoughts turning to Steven more often than she would have liked them to as the day wore on. He was a hard one to figure out. There were times—most of the time, in fact—when she thought she had him pegged. He was kind of a self-satisfied jerk. But every now and then, like this morning, she got the distinct impression there was a nice guy in there somewhere, even if he did try to keep that guy suppressed.

In the kitchen, Carlos hung up the phone. "That was Elizabeth. She's still up at the beauty parlor and might be a little late. She said to bring Olivia over here after school, and she'll stop by and get her on her way home." He went back to his stove, muttering something about not being a blamed secretary.

Juanita, sitting at the counter with a cup of coffee, ran her fingers through her hair. "That is the number one thing I miss, now that I've started working. I do not have one minute to myself to do something as simple as go get my hair done. I need a haircut and a perm so bad I scare the dog, but when in the world am I going to find time for that?"

Kaitlyn, on the way to the kitchen with a bin of dirty dishes, glanced at Juanita as she passed. "I could cut your hair and give you a perm, if you want." *Where did that suggestion come from?* Kaitlyn could have bit her tongue the minute the words were out of her mouth—not because she didn't think Juanita could use a bit of an update in her hairstyle, but because she had just set herself up for another one of Juanita's cutting remarks.

But Juanita just held her cup in both hands and cocked her

head. "That's right, you were a beauty operator back in Arizona, weren't you?" She took another sip, and Kaitlyn could almost feel the scrutiny of her own short, asymmetrical style. "Well, it's nice of you to offer, but I'm afraid those fancy new hairdos are just not for me. I just need a nice, normal cut and perm, nothing fancy, just wash and go."

"I know what you're talking about." Kaitlyn paused at the counter where Juanita sat. "I did a ton of them in cosmetology school. Every two weeks some of us would go to a nursing home and do the ladies' hair."

"Well, I don't think I'm quite ready for nursing home hair." Juanita fluffed her own hair again. "Just, you know, something normal and nice."

Actually, the style Juanita had been describing hadn't been the norm for decades, but Kaitlyn decided to keep that information to herself. "Well, I'm going up to San Ramon on Saturday. Let me know if you want me to pick up a perm."

She continued into the kitchen with her bin of dirty dishes. When she came out, Juanita was still fingering her hair. "They were always real happy with what you did? You didn't ever get real cute and dye their hair green or something to surprise them, did you?"

"Of course not. I liked those ladies, and I liked seeing them happy with the way they looked. They were just different people after they got their hair done, you know?" Her smile faded at the worried look on Juanita's face. "But if you're concerned, don't worry about it. It was just a thought. Maybe we can get Chris to give you some time off to go up to San Ramon, and I can cover for you here."

"What kind of perm do you think I'd need?" Somehow, the offer *not* to do Juanita's hair seemed to be the deciding factor.

Kaitlyn reached over and rubbed a strand of hair between thumb and forefinger. "Your hair is pretty damaged from all the processing. We'd have to get something really gentle, and a good conditioning treatment wouldn't hurt either."

"You two do realize that this is a restaurant, not a beauty parlor, right?" Chris had joined the conversation and he did not look happy. "Go wash your hands, both of you. What if we had customers in here right now? They'd be totally grossed out, and I wouldn't blame them."

"Well, if we had customers in here, Chris, we'd be waiting on them, wouldn't we?" Juanita slid off her stool and smoothed her apron. "And in case you're worried about it, I do not have cooties."

Juanita disappeared into the restroom, and Chris turned to Kaitlyn. "Come on, Kait. Give me a break here. Don't make things harder on me than they are already."

He pushed through the door into the kitchen, and through the window Kaitlyn could see him settling at his desk. She wasn't quite sure what he was talking about, but she certainly hadn't intended to make things harder on Chris. She hadn't intended to offer to do Juanita's hair for her either, but it looked like she had managed to do that as well.

She crossed the room and stood looking through the glass door at the highway that briefly turned to Main Street as it passed through Last Chance. A tumbleweed bouncing down the center of the street in a gust of winter wind disappeared under the wheels of a passing eighteen-wheeler. She couldn't see the driver well, but he looked young, and Kaitlyn followed the truck with her eyes as long as she could see it. What if she had run outside and flagged him down? Would he have stopped long enough for her to climb in? And if he had, where would they be off to now? For a moment she let herself imagine leaving everything behind—all of it—Last Chance, the Dip 'n' Dine, Juanita, those judging looks that seemed to follow her everywhere she went. She wouldn't even stop for her coat. But even as the image of flight filled her with exhilaration, another image supplanted it—that of her daughter whom she had promised never to leave again. She turned from the window. She wasn't going anywhere.

5

The wind was still blowing when Elizabeth pulled up outside the Dip 'n' Dine but did little to disturb the helmet of tight white curls that now adorned her head when she got out of her car and came inside. Olivia, who had been sitting in a back booth doing her homework since Kaitlyn had picked her up from school, ran to meet her at the door.

"Here's my girl." Elizabeth smiled over Olivia's head as she enveloped her in a hug. "I'm sorry I'm so late, but Linda was running behind. She can talk or she can do hair, but she doesn't seem to be able to do both at the same time. It doesn't take long before things start to just back up."

"Well, guess who my new hairdresser is?" Juanita started to pat her hair but caught Chris's eye and dropped her hand. "Miss Kaitlyn over there is going to cut my hair and give me a perm next Sunday afternoon. Sunday's okay, isn't it, Kaitlyn?"

"Um, I guess." Kaitlyn hadn't been sure until that moment that Juanita even wanted her to do her hair.

"You don't mean it. Well, aren't you smart? I wish I'd thought of that." Elizabeth watched Olivia run to the booth where she'd been sitting and start stuffing her papers in her backpack. She smiled back at Juanita and Kaitlyn. "Remember when you had energy like that this late in the day? I don't."

"Are you okay? Can I get you a cup of coffee or something?" Kaitlyn had come to think of Elizabeth as eternal as the hills around Last Chance, but today she looked frail as she rested her hand on the back of the booth nearest the door for support.

"Oh, I'm fine." Elizabeth waved Kaitlyn's concern away and stood a little straighter. "Just a little weary, that's all. That trip to San Ramon takes more out of me than it used to. Linda's a sweet girl and all, but listening to her go on and on about absolutely nothing just wears me out. I'll just grab my girl here, and we'll go home and both of us have a cup of tea."

"Are you sure?" Olivia, pink backpack thumping along behind her, had skidded to a stop next to Elizabeth. Kaitlyn smoothed a wayward strand of her hair. "If you need to get some rest, Livvy can stay here with us this afternoon."

Olivia gave her mother a look of mild outrage, and Elizabeth slipped an arm around her shoulders. "No, we'll be just fine, won't we, Olivia? She's the highlight of my day."

"Okay, let's go." Olivia tried to edge Elizabeth toward the door as if she was afraid that further delay might result in someone deciding she should stay after all.

Elizabeth squared her shoulders and settled her handbag on her arm. She looked as eternal as ever, leaving Kaitlyn wondering if she had imagined the frailty. Olivia raced past her, as far as her oversized backpack allowed her to race, but Elizabeth stopped at the door. "You know, I don't know what you're charging Juanita, but if your prices are at all competitive, I'll bet you could get yourself a nice little business right here in Last Chance. I know I'd come to you in a heartbeat."

From the expression on Juanita's face, it was clear that she hadn't given actually paying Kaitlyn much thought, but Kaitlyn just smiled and shook her head. "I'm not charging anything. My license is in Arizona."

"I don't know how hard it would be to get a license in New Mexico, but you might think about looking into it. It sure would be handy to have a shop right here in town."

Through the window they could see that Olivia had climbed into the passenger side of Elizabeth's pickup truck and from her stare was willing Elizabeth to stop talking and come drive her home.

"That's an awful big truck, Elizabeth. Don't you think you'd be happier with something easier to handle?"

Elizabeth shook her head as she started to push her way through the door. "I just waited too long, I'm afraid, and now I'm between a rock and a hard place. I'm not about to go get me a new car at this stage of the game, so I'll just drive that thing until it's too much for me, and then I'll hang up my keys, I guess. I'm sure not looking forward to that."

She opened the door and waved as the wind made another unsuccessful assault on her white curls. Kaitlyn watched her pause at the open door of her pickup for a moment as if to gather her strength. But when she did hoist herself inside, it was with one smooth and practiced move. Elizabeth looked up as she fastened her seat belt and smiled and waved again when she saw Kaitlyn watching her.

"Chris, are you sure Elizabeth is up to keeping Livvy every afternoon?" Kaitlyn turned to Chris, who had just come up behind her. "She can be such a handful, and I'm not sure Elizabeth is as strong as she'd like us to think she is."

"Hmm? I think she's okay. Elizabeth's one tough lady. She pretty well knows what she can and can't do. She'd tell us if Livvy was too much for her, and if she wouldn't, Sarah would. She's real protective of her grandma." Chris was taking advantage of the afternoon lull to check his phone messages, and he scowled at the screen. "Mom called. I wonder what she wants."

He wandered back to his desk in the kitchen with his phone pressed against his ear, and Kaitlyn poured herself a cup of coffee and slid into a booth by the window. There would probably be a few more diners before they closed, but the day was for the most part over. Afternoon shadows faded into early winter twilight, making the boarded up High Lonesome Saloon across the road look even more abandoned. It had been Steven's once, so Kaitlyn had been told, or it would have been if he had wanted it. But when it came right down to staying in one place and going to work every day, even at the bar he and his dad had dreamed of running together, he had taken off. So boards had been nailed across windows, and weeds pushed through and then took over the gravel parking lot in front. His cousin Sarah said he claimed it was because his dad died and he didn't have the heart for it anymore. But Kaitlyn guessed the reality was that anything that threatened to hold Steven in one place just put him on the road again.

"Looks like we're getting some company." Chris broke her reverie by sliding into the booth across from her. "Mom and Dad are coming down next week for a couple days."

"Why? Don't tell me they miss us."

"Actually, I think they do. Especially Olivia. But they say they're coming to bring you your stuff. Remember? You left an apartment when you took off with Jase. I guess mom finally got it cleaned out."

"Oh, this is going to be a fun visit, I can just tell."

Chris stood up as the flash of headlights cutting through the gathering dusk announced the arrival of customers. "Well, you've got to face the music sometime, baby sister. Might as well get it over with."

Kaitlyn watched a tumbleweed the size of a bushel basket bounce across the deserted parking lot of the High Lonesome Saloon before it lodged in the fence that bordered the property. That was the trouble with thinking yourself rootless and fancy-free. Just when you think nothing can stop you, you hit that barbed wire fence.

—m—

It was nearly dark when Steven pulled the ranch pickup truck up behind the ranch house. Through the window, he could see his aunt Nancy Jo putting food on the table in the brightly lit kitchen.

"Looks like we made it just in time. Come on, Speed Bump." He scooped a small, dirty white dog from the seat beside him and headed for the back door.

"You must have smelled dinner cooking." Nancy Jo turned from the stove with a smile that faded when she saw what he was carrying. "What in the world do you have?"

Steven looked down at the scraggly bundle under his arm. "It's a dog, I think."

"I can see that. What I want to know is whose dog is it, and why is it in my kitchen?"

"I found her on the side of the road on my way back from San Ramon. She was running back and forth looking at every car that passed like she was waiting for whoever dropped her off to come back for her. The jerk." He put the dog on the floor and got a cereal bowl from the cupboard and filled it with water. "I knew it wasn't going to be long before she was roadkill or some coyote's dinner, so I stopped and put her in the truck."

Nancy Jo took the cereal bowl from him, dumped the water

into the sink, and reached under the counter for a couple plastic margarine tubs. "Here. Use these, not my good dishes. You can put her there in the service room while we eat. Get a can of dog food from the cupboard over the washing machine. Poor little thing. Who would do something like that?"

Steven headed for the service room with the little dog at his heels. "Beats me. I'd sure like to have about five minutes to tell them what I think about it, though."

As Steven opened the can of dog food and scooped it into the butter tub, his little companion fixed a stare on his hands and swallowed convulsively, barely able to keep all four feet on the ground at the same time. She had her nose buried in the dish almost before Steven set it on the floor.

"You were hungry, weren't you, Speed Bump? Did they starve you before they dumped you?" He watched the little dog gulp down her food a moment before returning to the kitchen. "You know, some people need a whippin' more than they need a dog."

Nancy Jo looked at him and sighed. "Steven, we can't have that dog in the kitchen while we're eating. She's filthy. Just put her back in the service room."

Steven glanced over his shoulder. The service room was empty and Speed Bump, no bigger than Steven's boot, sat right next to it. "Hey, I thought you were hungry. Come on, you."

He led the way back to the service room with the dog at his heel, but this time the food held no interest. Speed Bump was going where Steven went. He bent down to scratch her ears. "Look, you need to stay in here, so eat your dinner and I'll see you after I eat mine."

She stayed right with him as he walked to the door and flipped on the light. After gently pushing her back and closing the door,

Steven waited a minute, listening for scratching or whining, but there was only silence. He shrugged. "I guess she'll be okay."

"Of course she will. Now scrub your hands and we'll eat." Nancy Jo looked up and smiled as Joe Jr. came in carrying bags of groceries in each arm.

"Were you planning on leaving these in the back of the truck all night?" He set the bags on the counter.

"Oh, man, I forgot. I'll go bring them in right now." Steven headed for the door.

"That boy would lose his head if his hat didn't hold it down." His uncle was already at the sink scrubbing up for dinner.

"Oh, I think he just got distracted by the dog." Nancy Jo intercepted his reach for the dishtowel by handing him a hand towel.

Steven made it out the back door before the puzzled look on Uncle Joe Jr.'s face found expression. When he came back with his first armload of groceries, Joe Jr. was standing with the service room door open looking down at the scruffy bundle of dirty white fur sitting in the doorway looking up at him.

He turned to Steven. "What in the world?"

"Just found her on the highway. I couldn't leave her there for the coyotes." He added his bags to the ones Joe Jr. had just put down.

"Well, what are you going to do with her? I don't see how she can hold her own around here. This is a lap dog, not a ranch dog."

The little dog, on seeing Steven come back in, made a wide circle around Joe Jr.'s boots and trotted up to Steven, who scooped her up. "Come on, Speed Bump, back in the service room."

"Oh, for Pete's sake, Steven, you just washed your hands. Wash them again, and hurry. This food is going to be stone cold by the time we get to it." Nancy Jo slipped off her apron and seated herself at the table.

After Joe Jr. asked the blessing, Nancy Jo passed Steven a bowl of potatoes. "Did I hear you call that poor creature Speed Bump? That's an awful thing to do, even if you only keep her long enough to find out who she belongs to."

"The folks she belonged to dumped her out on the side of the road like an empty soda can. I don't think they're getting her back." Steven helped himself to the platter of pork chops.

"You don't know what happened. She might have jumped out of the car when her owners stopped to change a tire or something. Or she might have been taken from someone's yard by somebody who decided they didn't want her after all. You have to at least make an effort. She was someone's pet, you can tell that."

Steven turned his attention to his meal without answering. He could feel Aunt Nancy Jo's gaze. Finally she spoke.

"Don't you ignore me when I'm speaking to you, Steven. That is just not going to fly. Now promise me you'll put an ad in the San Ramon newspaper."

Silence while Steven chewed his pork chop. When he heard Uncle Joe Jr. clear his throat and push his chair back, he looked up. Not much riled his uncle, but lack of respect for his wife headed the list.

"Okay. I'll put an ad in the paper tomorrow. First thing." He smiled, but from the look on Joe Jr.'s face, he hadn't done enough. "I'm sorry. I didn't mean any disrespect."

Uncle Joe Jr. nodded, and everyone went back to eating and discussing the day's events. Steven stifled his irritation at having his behavior called out like he was a kid. Though if he thought about it, he had to admit to himself that age really didn't have anything to do with being set straight. He'd heard Gran, with a sharp word or two, call Uncle Joe Jr. back into line. It was just family. The younger generation had to answer to the older, and that was all there was to it. It lasted until there was no generation older than you to answer to.

After dinner, Aunt Nancy Jo looked at her counters and sighed. "I'm going to have to put all those groceries away before I do dishes. There's no space."

"Need my help?" Steven was ready to get back into her good graces.

"No. I'd never find anything if you helped. Why don't you see to your dog? She probably needs to go out."

Speed Bump was sitting just inside the service room door when Steven opened it. Her food was untouched beyond what she had eaten when Steven first put it down.

"Hey, I thought you were hungry." Steven scooped up the dog and set her in front of the food bowl. But though she swallowed a few times and her little tongue swept across her nose, her eyes were only on Steven, not the food in front of her. He sat cross-legged on the floor and leaned against the washing machine. "Eat up. I'm not going anywhere."

The dog took a tentative bite, eyes still on Steven, and then another. Finally, as she became convinced that he might not disappear again, she buried her nose in the bowl and in seconds was licking the last specks of dog food from the empty bowl.

"There you go. You've got to feel better now." Steven, still on the floor, scratched behind her ears, and she crawled into his lap. She was awful dirty and had more than a few stickers caught in her coat. He absently pulled them from her fur as he stroked her. "You need a bath, kiddo."

He stuck his head in the kitchen where Nancy Jo was cleaning up. "Hey, is it okay if I bathe the dog in the laundry sink?"

"That wouldn't be a bad idea. She can sure use a bath." His

aunt set an armload of dishes on the counter and cast a baleful glance at the dog. "Use that flea shampoo on the shelf next to the dog food. I'll go find you some old towels to use. Oh, and don't forget to rinse out the sink with bleach water when you're done. No telling what she brought in."

If the little dog looked scrawny when dry, she looked downright rat-like when wet. And miserable. Everything about her, from ears, to eyes, to tail, drooped. Even her back legs began to buckle as if she had nothing left within her to hold her upright. She trembled from the moment Steven lifted her into the sink until he was rubbing her dry with the towels Aunt Nancy Jo brought him.

"You've got to feel better now, Speed Bump." Steven tossed a wet towel aside and reached for a dry one. "Although, I've got to say, you looked a little tougher before you cleaned up. I hope you don't get your feelings hurt when the rest of the ranch dogs bust out laughing."

A double sudsing of the flea shampoo had left the little dog's coat pure white, and the more Steven rubbed it with towels, the fluffier and curlier it became. Finally, he set her on the floor, a fleecy white cloud disrupted only by two black eyes, one black nose, and bottom teeth exposed by a slightly underslung jaw.

Uncle Joe Jr., sitting at the kitchen table reading, lowered his newspaper and just shook his head when Steven and the dog emerged from the service room. "I don't know what you found out there on the highway, Steven, but that ain't no dog."

"Oh, she's precious." Aunt Nancy Jo bent down and reached out her hand, but the dog just looked at her and edged closer to Steven. "She knows how her bread is buttered, that's for sure. What are you going to do with her now?"

"I thought I'd keep her with me tonight. It's a little late to introduce her to the other dogs."

"I'll say." Uncle Joe Jr. folded his newspaper and got to his feet. "They'd laugh themselves sick and then have her for a midnight snack. I'm going to go see what's on TV."

He looked down at the dog, who met his gaze with one of her own, and shook his head as he left the room. "That's a cat, that's what that is. A cat or a rabbit, one, but I'm telling you, that ain't no dog."

While Aunt Nancy Jo tried to make friends with Speed Bump with a few bits of pork chop she scraped off a bone, Steven found a scrap of paper and a pen in the junk drawer and sat down to compose the ad he had promised his aunt he'd place in the paper.

To the yahoo who dumped a little white dog on the Last Chance Highway: You may be glad to know I found her before a car or the coyotes got her. If you think you want her back, call me. We'll talk.

6

Brooke and David Reed had said they'd probably get to Last Chance sometime in the late afternoon Monday, and Kaitlyn spent most of the day watching the clock and trying to quell the feelings of impending doom. She felt exactly as she felt in high school after she had been suspended again, waiting for her parents to get home to deal with it.

Grow up, Kaitlyn. You know by now they're not going to kill you. It's not even like they can take privileges away. You don't have any privileges.

"You know, that's the fifth compliment I've had today on my hair." Juanita brought Kaitlyn's attention back where it belonged as Lurlene left. "And more than one person asked if you were going to set up shop here in Last Chance. I'd give it some thought, if I were you."

"Maybe." Kaitlyn shrugged. She'd never looked more than a few weeks ahead, but then she'd never really considered how her actions would affect anyone but herself before either. Now there was Olivia to think about.

Funny. Olivia had been hers to think about for seven years and she had taken that gift for granted. In fact, having a daughter had seemed more a burden than a blessing in those days when she was a single mom back in Scottsdale. Letting Chris assume guardianship had seemed like a win-win for everybody. But now, not so much.

It wasn't that Chris rubbed her nose in it or anything. They both loved Olivia and cared for her, corrected her when she got a little sassy, and reminded her to do homework and take baths, but if Kaitlyn decided tomorrow to pick up and leave Last Chance, she'd have to go alone. That, she knew, was never going to happen, but it still didn't mean she wanted to open a salon in Last Chance and live here for the rest of her life. She shuddered at the thought.

"Have you given any thought to what you might call it?"

"Call what?" Kaitlyn gradually became aware of the fact that Juanita was still talking to her, although Juanita didn't seem to notice that Kaitlyn hadn't been listening.

"Your little beauty shop. What do you think of Curl Up and Dye? I saw that someplace and I just thought it was the cutest thing ever."

"Yeah, I've seen that too. I don't know, Juanita, there are so many things to think about. Opening a business is huge. Ask Chris. And it takes a whole lot more money than I've got. I think you're stuck with me here at the Dip 'n' Dine for a while." Kaitlyn tried to smile, but truthfully, the thought depressed her so much she wanted to cry.

"I bet you that's your folks. They're not from around here, I know that much." Juanita stood, hands on hips, looking out the front window as a steel gray Lexus eased into the parking spot closest to the front door.

"Yep, that's them, all right." Kaitlyn watched her mother, slim, blonde, and wearing a faux fur bomber jacket and knee-high boots, and her dad, nearly as tall as Chris, but considerably trimmer, emerge from the car. They didn't have time for much that wasn't work related, but workouts with their personal trainers were never neglected, and it showed.

Kaitlyn could only imagine what her dad was thinking as he stood by the car and looked down the road that ran through Last Chance. Her mom was leaning into the open back door and emerged holding a cat carrier. Oh, great.

"Chris, they're here." Kaitlyn didn't even try to put any enthusiasm in her voice.

Her brother came out of the kitchen and headed for the front door with a big smile on his face. Sure. They liked him. She watched as he shook their dad's hand and walked around the car to greet their mom. He came close for a hug but stepped back when he saw the carrier. They were still talking when the three of them came through the door.

"Mom, we can't have a cat in here. Can't you keep him with you just till we close? It won't be long now."

"No, I cannot. You can just put him in your own car until you're ready to go home. He has meowed, without stopping, at least once every two seconds since the minute we pulled out of the driveway at home, and I am not getting back in the car with that cat. That's all there is to it. Hello, Kaitlyn, dear. I brought you your cat, and a few other things as well."

"Hi, Mom." Kaitlyn pasted a smile on her face and kissed her mother's cheek. Dad was always easier to get along with, and Kaitlyn went to him for the hug she knew she'd find.

"Where's Olivia? I thought she'd be here." Brooke looked around the diner, her eyes resting only briefly on Juanita.

Chris lifted the cat carrier off the table where Brooke had put it and peered inside before placing it on the floor. "She goes to a lady's house after school, Mom. We'll pick her up after we close, unless you want to go get her. I know she's been looking forward to seeing you."

Brooke looked at her watch. "Didn't you say you were about ready to close up anyway? We'll just go check into our motel in San Ramon and meet you somewhere for dinner. How would that be? I can't wait to see that sweet girl. I've brought her some presents."

"You know, Mom, we have a nice motel right here in Last Chance. I told you about it."

"Yes, you did." Brooke didn't elaborate. "See you soon, dear."

David Reed prepared to follow her out. He looked around the room and smiled. "Nice place you've got here, son. Not quite where I thought you'd end up, but you're young yet."

Juanita, apparently tired of being overlooked, stepped forward with outstretched hand. "I'm Juanita Sheppard. Welcome to Last Chance. It's so nice to finally meet you. I can't say enough nice things about your son."

Brooke touched Juanita's hand with her fingers and nodded. "Hello. Yes, we've always been proud of him." Her voice was as cool as her smile. She turned to Kaitlyn. "Come with me to the car, dear. I have all of your cat's paraphernalia in the backseat. You'll need that."

Nodding again to Juanita and lifting a cheek for Chris to kiss, she led her husband and Kaitlyn back outside. Kaitlyn braced herself for the worst, but after handing her all the cat's stuff, her mom leaned against the car and actually smiled at her. It wasn't the warmest smile Kaitlyn had ever seen, but it wasn't the tongue-lashing she had been fearing since she found out her parents were on the way.

"Well, dear, I hope what we did was all right with you. We never heard anything from you, so we weren't sure what you wanted us to do with the apartment you left." She waited a moment as if to give her daughter a chance to explain herself.

Kaitlyn didn't say anything. What was there to say?

Brooke raised an eyebrow and continued. "At any rate, we liquidated everything but your clothes and a few knickknacks that we thought you might want. They're in the trunk."

"Liquidated?"

"We sold everything, dear. The furniture was ours anyway, but we considered it yours for liquidation purposes. The rest went to a woman who puts on yard sales, and what didn't sell went to charity."

"All my stuff's gone?"

"Well, dear, we didn't think it meant anything to you since you just walked off and left it."

Kaitlyn just looked at her mom. She had no words.

"Since you and Olivia are here with Chris, this will probably serve you better anyway." Brooke fished in her purse and pulled out a check. "This is everything we made. Dad and I paid the expenses, so it's all profit for you."

Kaitlyn took the check and looked at it. It was certainly larger than any check she had seen her name on in a long time. But still, everything she had considered hers was gone.

"You're free as a bird, my sweet Kaitlyn." Brooke's smile had broadened, and she patted Kaitlyn's cheek. "No ties left in Scottsdale. Except us, of course, and we want you and Livvy to come visit us as often as you can."

Kaitlyn watched her parents wave as they pulled out of the parking lot. She put the cat's stuff in the back of the Jeep and walked back into the diner, still holding her check.

Chris had picked up the cat carrier again and was poking his finger through the grate. "Well, you survived. They didn't even look all that mad from here."

"No, it was weird. Dad didn't say anything, and Mom was

using her real estate voice—all cheerful and businesslike. They gave me this."

Chris looked at the check and raised his eyebrows. "Wow. That's sure not what you were expecting. Feel better?"

"They sold all my stuff. This is what they got for it."

"You're kidding. Without even asking you what you wanted?"

Kaitlyn shrugged. "Mom said it couldn't matter much to me since I walked off and left everything. But it just felt like they were saying they were done with me. Like they were paying me off and cutting me loose."

"Well, just between you and me, I think it's time." Chris's smile softened his words. "I don't think Mom and Dad were doing you any favors by bailing you out of any mess you got into all the time. And you know what? I'm betting you're going to do just fine."

"It's just not what I thought was going to happen. I thought Mom would yell and Dad would look all stern and they'd tell me to get in the car because I was going back to Scottsdale, and I'd say no, and we'd have this big fight."

"And you'd say you weren't a child anymore? Looks like they beat you to the punch." Chris laughed and put the cat carrier back on the floor so he could pull her into a hug. Kaitlyn closed her eyes. She wanted to just stay where she was and feel safe, but after a minute Chris pulled back and looked down at the carrier where the cat was still yowling his dissatisfaction with his confinement. "Look, would you take this cat home? You and Olivia can come back for me and we'll go on up to San Ramon and get Mom and Dad for dinner."

Kaitlyn sighed as she picked up the carrier and peeked inside. "Hey, cat. Long time no see."

Steven's SUV was parked outside Elizabeth's when Kaitlyn pulled up and got out of the Jeep. Olivia met her at the door holding a little white dog.

"Hey, Mom, look! Can we keep her? Steven says if it's okay with you I can have her. Her name is Speed Bump."

Kaitlyn shot a look at Steven, who shrugged and gave her a guilty grin before she turned back to Olivia. "Well, I don't think Meeko would like it very much if we brought a dog home, do you?"

Olivia froze. "Meeko?"

"Yep, your grandparents brought Meeko. He's out in the car right now waiting for us to take him home."

Kaitlyn found herself holding Speed Bump as Olivia raced to the curb and jerked open the back door of the Jeep. "Do not open that carrier until we get home, do you hear me?" She turned to Steven and handed him the dog. "You promised her a dog before you even spoke to me about it? What were you thinking?"

"It wasn't exactly like that." Steven still sounded guilty. "She asked whose dog it was. I said I'd found it. She asked if she could have it and I said we'd have to talk to you. That's all that happened."

"That's true, Kaitlyn." Elizabeth came from the kitchen. "It was all pretty much Livvy's idea. Although you didn't do a whole lot to discourage her, Steven." A low, warning wail came from the back of the sofa, where a large gray tabby crouched, ears back and tail lashing. "Oh, for Pete's sake, Sam. Hush up. That dog's not about to bother you. You're twice his size, anyway."

Kaitlyn reached over and scratched Speed Bump's ears. "He is cute. Where'd you find him?"

"It's a she, and I found her on the highway." Steven told the story of the abandoned dog, winding up with, "So unless I can find the owner, I guess I'll keep her."

Kaitlyn smiled. "It doesn't sound like you want to find the owner that bad."

"Well, not to give the dog back, anyway." Steven held the dog up to look in her face, and on the back of the sofa, Sam arched, hissed, and spat.

"Steven, honey, I'm going to have to ask you to take that little thing outside. She's worrying Sam to death, and he's about to drive me to distraction. I bet she'd be happy in your truck for a little while. Kaitlyn, how about some tea?"

"I'd love to, but I've got to get that cat home and settled and then go get Chris. Our parents are in town and we're meeting them for dinner in San Ramon."

"Oh, that's lovely. Will they be here long? I'd love to meet them."

Kaitlyn looked around Elizabeth's fussy little living room, with its crocheted afghan and framed pictures of family on every surface. She had no doubt what her mother's reaction would be, and she had no intention of allowing Elizabeth to feel her mother's cool, dismissive gaze. "Um, I'm not sure how long they're going to be here, and they're sort of making San Ramon their base."

As if she could read Kaitlyn's mind, Elizabeth put a warm, comforting hand on her arm. "Well, I'd love to meet them just the same. I want to tell them how much I've come to care for you and Olivia and Chris. And unless I'm entirely mistaken, I think they might want to meet Sarah and her family."

Sarah. Of course. Kaitlyn closed her eyes for a moment. Chris was bound to want their parents to meet Sarah. He was so besotted with her, it wouldn't even occur to him that his mother might find Sarah a bit beneath them. But even if Chris didn't see it, Kaitlyn was pretty sure nothing would get past Sarah. She did not see this as the beginning of a beautiful friendship.

"Mom! Hurry! Meeko really wants out." Olivia was back and tugging at Kaitlyn's hand.

Kaitlyn smiled at Elizabeth and gave her a hug. "You're right. You probably will meet them sooner or later, maybe sooner. But be prepared. They're sort of . . ." She broke off. How do you tell someone your parents are complete snobs?

"Honey, don't you worry one bit. If they're your parents, I know we'll get along just fine."

Olivia was already back at the car, and Kaitlyn followed her down the walk. Having people think they knew what kind of parents she had because they knew her was nothing new. But having that be a positive thing was.

"Mom? Do you think Meeko and Sam could be friends? Both of them don't like dogs." Olivia buckled herself in the backseat and pulled the cat carrier next to her, then wiggled her fingers through the grate.

"I don't think so, honey." Kaitlyn watched Steven, his dog still under his arm, saying good-bye to his grandmother on the porch. She couldn't help smiling at how ludicrous a picture he presented standing there in boots with his cowboy hat pulled low over his eyes and holding that little ball of white fluff under his arm.

"Mom? What's a speed bump?"

Kaitlyn pulled away from the curb. "It's a little bump they put in the road so cars will slow down when they run over it."

There was a moment of silence, broken only by another protesting howl from Meeko.

"Steven named his dog *that*?" Olivia could not have sounded more horrified.

"I'm sure he just thought he was being funny. He did save the dog from maybe being run over, you know."

"Well, it's *not* funny. I'm going to tell him that the next time I see him too. That's just mean."

"Okay." Kaitlyn was barely aware of Olivia's running conversation, sometimes directed toward her, sometimes toward her cat as she drove the few miles home. She pulled to a stop in the carport. "Do you think you can manage the cat carrier? I'll get the rest of Meeko's stuff. Don't open it yet, though. We'll fix him a nice little home in the bathroom, and then we have to get Uncle Chris and go have dinner with BeBe and Pops."

"But Meeko doesn't want to stay in the bathroom." The carrier was almost too big for Olivia to carry, but she pulled away when her mother tried to help her. "I can do it."

"It's only till we get back from dinner. He'll feel safer in a small place since everything is so unfamiliar."

"Then he can live in my room?"

"That will be up to Uncle Chris." Yep, all decisions were to be deferred to Chris, even simple ones like where the cat would sleep. Kaitlyn felt another pang of regret that she had allowed things to get this far, but she pasted a smile on her face. "Now, let's get everything into the bathroom and you can finally let poor Meeko out while I get him all set up."

The neon sign in the big window that fronted the Dip 'n' Dine was out and the parking lot was deserted when Kaitlyn and Olivia pulled up to the front door a half hour later. Kaitlyn smiled at Olivia when she got out to go around to the passenger side. Olivia had protested a bit, but she had cleaned up really well. She was wearing new jeans—not a scuff or a hole anywhere—and a pale blue sweater the color of her eyes. Kaitlyn had even got her to put the cat down long enough to give her hair a good brushing, and it fell to her shoulders like silk, the sides pulled up and held with a blue grosgrain bow. If Olivia had ever looked like a motherless waif, those days were gone. Kaitlyn wondered if her own mother would even notice.

"You ladies look sharp." Chris got in behind the wheel. "Get your cat all settled?"

"He's in the bathroom so he'll feel safe, but we're going to let him out when we get home, right, Mom?"

Kaitlyn shrugged when Chris glared at her. "Well, we can't keep him in the bathroom forever. He doesn't much like being cooped up, you may have noticed."

"How 'bout if he lived out in your trailer with you?"

"No!" Olivia's outrage was clear. "He's my cat. He has to live with me."

They rode in silence for a while. Finally Chris heaved a sigh. "You know, I don't remember signing up for a cat."

Kaitlyn smiled. "You didn't sign up for a lot of things. But you have an awful lot on your plate right now, don't you?"

He glanced at Kaitlyn with what he probably thought was a glower, but she saw a smile trying to keep from showing through. "You got that right."

7

Brooke and David Reed were already sitting at a table by the window when Chris brought the Jeep to a stop. Neither looked particularly happy.

"You're kidding me." Kaitlyn sat a moment to gather strength before reaching for her seat belt. "I've never known Mom to order from a menu in lights over the counter in my life."

"Well, they found the pickings kind of slim. It was here, the all-you-can-eat buffet, or Mexican food. Mom said at least there was a salad bar here."

"I love this place!" Olivia scrambled from the backseat. "You can get all the chicken nuggets and ice cream you want for free."

Kaitlyn couldn't help it. As she watched her elegant mother surrounded by noisy families and servers delivering plastic platters with thin steaks and loaded baked potatoes, she started to giggle. As all the tension and worry she had been carrying since she found out her parents were coming took over, she found herself laughing until she had tears rolling down her face.

Chris looked at her in concern that seemed to border on alarm. "Are you all right? What is so all-fired funny?"

Kaitlyn just shook her head and sniffed. Her laughter was turning into real tears. She waved him away. "I'm fine. Go on in. I just need a minute."

"Mom?" Even Olivia sounded troubled, and Kaitlyn made an effort to smile. She never wanted Olivia to worry about her again. Ever. "I'm just being silly. You go give BeBe and Pops a big hug and tell them I'll be right in."

She watched Chris, with Olivia running in front of him, greet their parents. Olivia threw her arms around each grandparent in turn and was welcomed with hugs and kisses, and when her mother held Olivia at arm's length, Kaitlyn knew she was telling her how pretty she looked. Finally, someone must have asked where she was, because Chris gestured through the window and everyone turned to look at her. She waved and tried to smile, and they waved back with a little "come on in" gesture before turning back to each other. Olivia slid in the booth next to her grandmother, and Chris pulled a chair to the end of the table, leaving a space next to their dad for Kaitlyn. The family picture looked complete, and even as Kaitlyn told herself to grow up and stop being such a crybaby, she wondered if they even knew, really knew, or cared, that she wasn't there. She leaned her head against the seat and watched them for a while. Chris and their dad were deep in animated conversation while their mom, with Olivia tucked under her arm, looked on with mild but proprietary interest, as serene as any queen. It was the family she never felt part of or approved by. Olivia kept leaning past her grandmother to peer out the window at her. Kaitlyn waved, but she still wasn't ready to go in. Finally, Olivia jumped down and headed for the door, ignoring obvious calls for her to return to the table.

"Mom, what's wrong? Are you coming in?" Olivia looked worried as she yanked open the door.

"I'll be there in a second." Kaitlyn tried to make her smile reassuring.

"But what's wrong? Why are you crying?" She hoisted herself up so she was standing in the doorway.

Kaitlyn pulled Olivia onto her lap. What could she say that her daughter could understand and not be too worried by?

"Do you remember when we left our home in Scottsdale with Jase?"

Olivia's brow wrinkled in a scowl as she nodded. She hadn't liked the motorcycle ride, and she had liked Jase even less.

"Well, BeBe and Pops had to take care of everything that we left behind, and you can see how that wouldn't make them very happy."

"Is BeBe going to get you in trouble?"

Kaitlyn smiled and hugged her daughter to her. "No, she's not, but that wasn't a very nice thing for me to do, and I feel kind of bad about it."

Olivia leaned back to look up into her mother's face. She still looked worried. "But they got to play with Meeko all that time, so they should be happy about that."

Kaitlyn kissed the top of her daughter's head. Even this benign explanation wasn't working. If Kaitlyn was sad, Olivia was making it her responsibility to make things better, and Kaitlyn hated that this residual of their former existence still colored Olivia's life. She took Olivia's face in both hands and smiled into the worried blue eyes.

"You know what? I had forgotten about that. They *did* get to play with Meeko all that time. That should make anybody happy. Let's go inside."

All three sitting at the table looked up and smiled. Kaitlyn couldn't help thinking how different each smile was, and how easy to read. Chris's said, "Still don't know what's wrong, but I hope everything's okay now." Dad's said, "Here's my girl." He always found the role of detached observer the easiest one to take. But Mom just looked at her and her eyes and frozen smile said, "I'm going to try to just overlook this outburst. Again."

"I want to sit by my mom." Olivia folded her arms and stood by the table.

"But, honey, there'll be more room if we sit this way. Don't you want to sit by me? I haven't seen you in such a long time." Brooke reached out a hand to Olivia, who stepped away and slipped an arm around Kaitlyn's waist.

"It's okay." Kaitlyn leaned down to give Olivia a squeeze. "You sit by BeBe, and I'll sit over here."

After another second or two's hesitation, Olivia slid into the booth next to her grandmother, and Kaitlyn gave her a wink as she sat across the table with David.

"I see Olivia is still taking good care of her mommy. And she looks so grown-up." Brooke was still smiling, but she almost always smiled, even when she intended her words to cut. She turned to Chris. "I've never seen her happier or look more cared for. You are doing such a good job with her."

Kaitlyn felt the old anger flare, and she had opened her mouth to retort when a server interrupted. "Um, you guys know you have to order at the counter, right?"

"Yes, dear, we *guys* do know that. We were just waiting for the rest of our party to arrive. Thank you." Brooke gave Olivia a little push to get her moving. "Oh, by the way, I'd like a glass of wine. Is there a list?"

"Not a list, but I can tell you what kinds we have."

Brooke raised an eyebrow and waited.

"Red, white, and pink."

"Never mind." Brooke closed her eyes for a long moment, sighed, and shook her head. "I'll just have water. You do have bottled water?"

The server nodded.

"Well, that's something." She slid out of the booth and headed for the line snaking toward the counter.

Chris came alongside and draped an arm over her shoulder. "You know, Ma, servers work really hard trying to keep folks happy. I know for a fact that's not always easy, so if you could cut her a little slack, I know she'd appreciate it. I'd appreciate it too, for that matter."

Walking behind them, Kaitlyn waited for the explosion. Mom did not do well with any criticism, because she simply never erred.

But Brooke just sighed and rested her head for a moment against Chris's shoulder. "You're right, dear. I'm just exhausted from the trip and I suppose a little annoyed by all the usual drama, but I should not take it out on our poor waitress. We'll leave a nice tip to make up for it."

Chris gestured for Kaitlyn to fall in line behind their mother, but she shook her head and stepped back. He shrugged and got in line, and as Kaitlyn stared at his broad back she felt her frustration mounting again. If anyone, *anyone*, but Chris had said those things to Brooke, she would have quickly and neatly severed head from shoulders. But Chris could do no wrong.

"Mom, can I go get some chicken nuggets now?" Olivia clearly saw no need to stand in a line when the real attraction lay at the appetizer bar.

"Sure. I'll order for you. What do you want?" Kaitlyn took a deep breath and let it out slowly before turning a smile on her daughter. Whatever her pain was, it had nothing to do with Olivia.

"I don't care." Olivia was already gone.

Waiting behind Chris, comfortably walled off from the rest of the family, Kaitlyn took a few minutes to regroup so that by the time the family reassembled at the table, she was able to join the conversation with a smile.

"So, Mom and Dad, when are you going to meet Sarah? She's adorable, and I know you'll just love her."

"Oh. Sarah." Brooke looked as if she had bitten into something she did not want to swallow. She looked at Chris and sighed. "I suppose this is still serious?"

"Yes, Mom, it's serious." Chris sounded incredulous. "We told you that when we called."

"But nothing official, I gather?"

"No, nothing official."

"Well then, I think we have plenty of time." Brooke smiled and turned to Olivia to change the subject. "How are the riding lessons coming, Olivia? I'll bet you're turning into quite the horsewoman."

Before Olivia could answer, Chris spoke again. "Mom, Dad. I want you to meet Sarah. It's time. We want to take you two out to dinner tomorrow night."

Brooke gave a little puff of exasperation and started to speak, but her husband interrupted. "I think that'd be great." He clapped Chris on the shoulder. "We had planned to head on home tomorrow since we all are so busy, but we can put it off a day."

"But I have that breakfast meeting—" Brooke began. She clamped her mouth shut and sent her husband a "we shall discuss this later" look when he interrupted again.

"You can make a phone call or two." He answered her look with one of his own. "I think this is important."

Brooke stabbed her salad, forked in a bite, and stared out the window.

Chris put both hands on the table and pushed back a bit. Kaitlyn could almost see the steam coming out of his ears. "You know what? I'm beginning to think this might not be such a good idea, after all. I'm not sure I want to put Sarah through this."

Brooke turned to Chris and leveled a stare at him that made Kaitlyn shrivel inside. The Look. The cold, expressionless expression that warned against taking the next step, saying the next word. "Put Sarah through what, dear?"

"This." He waved a hand over the table. "This need to impress, to intimidate. She's better than all this. And, truthfully, if you ever said one word to hurt her, I'm not sure what I'd do. But I can almost bet you wouldn't like it."

"Who has the Big Roundup, medium rare?" The server snapped open the stand she held in one hand and carefully set the huge tray she had balanced on her shoulder upon it.

Chris pulled his gaze away from his mother and looked up. "That's me."

"The Cattleman, medium?"

By the time each plate had been delivered to the proper diner, the iced tea glasses refilled, and the server assured that there was nothing else anyone needed, the tension at the table had eased a bit.

"I suppose I *could* postpone the breakfast meeting so we could stay an extra day, if it's that important to you." Brooke dipped the tip of her fork into the dressing by her plate before taking up another bite of salad.

"No, the more I think about it, the more I think this is probably not the best time for you to meet Sarah. Maybe we can drive up to Scottsdale one weekend. I'll see what she says." Chris barely glanced up from his steak.

His mother took another tiny bite of her salad. "Suit yourself. But keep in mind that we're busiest on the weekends."

Finally the check came, and David picked it up, scrutinized it, and handed the server his card. Kaitlyn saw Chris glance over while his dad added in the tip, and she also saw him slip a bill from his wallet and leave it on the table after the others headed for the door.

"Kaitlyn, dear, let's be sure to get your boxes out of the trunk. That's why we came, after all." Brooke's smile was cool and poised again as she reached the car and leaned in to kiss her daughter's cheek. "I'm so glad to see you settled so nicely here. There doesn't seem to be much here to get you in trouble."

She may have meant her laugh to be light and teasing, but it just fell on the pavement of the parking lot with a thump. Kaitlyn took a deep breath and tried to smile. "Nope. Things are pretty quiet."

"Chris, I am looking forward to meeting Sarah sometime. Maybe you're right that now's not the best time, though. This is such a rushed trip." She lifted her face so Chris could give her a kiss too. "It was so good to see you, dear. Thanks for taking such good care of my girls, both of them." She slid gracefully into the front seat.

"Sure." Chris nodded, but Kaitlyn could see he was seething.

David returned from transferring Kaitlyn's boxes and clapped Chris's shoulder with his left hand while extending his right. "Son, it's always good to see you. Say, do you think you can get that girl of yours to the diner early tomorrow? I'd love to take her to breakfast."

"I don't know, Dad. She has to be at school pretty early in the morning."

"I don't care. If she can be there, I'll be there too. Just give her a call and let me know."

"Yeah, I'll do that." Chris's face relaxed into the first real smile Kaitlyn had seen all evening as her dad reached for her and drew her into a hug.

"You're looking great, sweet cakes." How many years had it been since he had called her that? "I wouldn't have dreamed it, but I think this place suits you."

He opened his door and paused for a wave just before he got inside. "I hope I see you both tomorrow morning."

Chris slid an arm around Kaitlyn's shoulders as they stood in the parking lot and watched the Lexus pull away. "Well, that four hours zipped by."

Kaitlyn looked at her watch and grinned. They had been at the restaurant for exactly forty-five minutes.

"Hey, come on. Meeko wants out of the bathroom." Olivia was already buckled in and ready to go.

Chris gave Kaitlyn's shoulders a squeeze. "Still sorry you're stuck in Last Chance and not back in Scottsdale?"

Kaitlyn watched the taillights of her parents' car disappear. Was she sorry she was stuck in Last Chance? Good question. When she joined Chris and Olivia in the Jeep, Chris was already on the phone, and from his goofy grin, she had little doubt who he was speaking to.

It was still black as midnight the next morning when the Lexus glided into the empty parking lot and David Reed got out. His black leather jacket didn't look like it afforded much protection against the predawn cold. Kaitlyn met him at the door.

"You're here early." She gave him a hug. "Mom didn't come?"

"I always get up early to get a run in before work; this was sleeping in for me." He grinned. "And no, your mom was still asleep when I left. I'll pick her up after breakfast and we'll hit the road. We'll be back in Scottsdale by noon, maybe a little after."

"'Morning, Dad." Chris came out of the kitchen smiling. Like his dad, he was a morning person, and like her mom, Kaitlyn was not. She went to pour her dad a cup of coffee and take another long drink from the mug she had had going since the first coffeepot finished brewing.

"Hi, Pops." Olivia, sitting at the counter eating breakfast, waved a spoon at him.

"Hi there, sweet cakes." David crossed the room to give his granddaughter a hug before looking around the room with an amused smile. "So this is the Dip 'n' Dine we've heard so much about. Can't say it bears much resemblance to the places you've worked before. I thought you were more of a high-end chef."

"Well, I'm pretty proud of the place, just the same." Chris's smile looked a little fixed. "Come on, let me show you around."

He led his dad into the kitchen where Carlos was already at work.

"Man, something smells out of this world. Whatever it is you're cooking, I want some." David grinned as he extended his hand to Carlos when Chris introduced them.

Carlos, well known for hating small talk as much as he hated being interrupted, stopped what he was doing and returned the smile and the handshake. But that was David. People just liked him on sight. That was why he and Brooke made such successful business partners. He might not remember a person's name or anything about them five minutes after leaving them, but Brooke did. She was the one with the head for business, and she didn't forget anything. In her mind, Kaitlyn referred to her parents as Bait and Switch.

She glanced through the window as she checked the clock and went to unlock the front door. Dad was leaning against Carlos's prep table, arms folded easily across his chest, chatting with Carlos as if he had known him for years while Chris looked on. Poor Chris. Dad always knew just what questions to ask to get someone talking about themselves, and he would nod and ask follow-up questions like he was talking to the most interesting person in the world. But he didn't even try to pretend to Chris that he had an ounce of interest in the Dip 'n' Dine.

8

Look, Mom, it's Speed Bump!"

Steven's truck was in the parking lot of the elementary school when Kaitlyn pulled in to drop Olivia off at school, and his dog was perched on the dashboard staring at the school door as if willing his return. A few of the kids had gathered around, but Speed Bump was oblivious to them.

"Speed Bump, what are you doing?" Olivia jumped out and joined the others, full of importance that she, and she alone, knew the dog and could call her by name.

Kaitlyn sat a moment and watched Olivia revel in her place as center of attention. She had come a long way since she had been suspended for fighting shortly after her arrival in Last Chance. She'd still probably never be voted Miss Congeniality, but she didn't seem to assume that everyone she met was her enemy either.

The little dog on the dashboard seemed to rivet to attention, and Kaitlyn looked up to see Steven ambling across the parking lot, his hat pulled low over his eyes. She got out and leaned against the door of the Jeep, and he looked up and smiled. But before he could say anything to her, the kids took over.

"Your dog is so cute. Can I pet him?"

"It's a 'her,' but sure, why not?" Steven opened the door, and his dog all but jumped into his arms. He leaned against the seat with his boots still in the parking lot and held the little dog in front of him. The kids gathered around.

"He's so little."

"Where'd you get him?"

"Why did you name her Speed Bump?" This was Olivia, and her outrage was unmistakable. "People run over Speed Bumps. Is that what you want?"

"No, of course not. She was on the side of the road when I found her. I was afraid she would get run over; that's why I picked her up in the first place. And that's why I named her Speed Bump."

"That's still an awful name. You should call her something else."

"Yeah." Someone else chimed in. "No one's going to run you over now, are they, puppy?"

"No Speed Bump?" Steven didn't sound convinced as he held his dog up and looked into her face.

"No!" The chorus was loud and unified.

"Well, what should I call her?"

"How about Flat Road?"

"Mmmmm. Any other ideas?"

"What about Fluffy? She's just the fluffiest dog." A little girl reached over and stroked the curly white fur.

"Yeah, Fluffy! Here, Fluffy. See, she likes that name."

"How about something like Spike or Fang? See? Look at those teeth. They're fierce." Steven turned his dog's face so the kids could see the tiny canines exposed by Speed Bump's underbite.

"Noooo." The chorus came as one voice. "Fluffy!"

If the kids were in agreement that his dog should be called Fluffy, Steven did not seem at all convinced. He met Kaitlyn's eyes, and his expression clearly said, "Help me out here." She just smiled.

The bell rang, and each of the kids jostled each other for one last pat of the dog before they headed for the school door.

"Bye, Fluffy."

"Bye, Fluffy."

When Kaitlyn and Steven were left alone in the parking lot, she couldn't help laughing at how dubious he looked as he held his dog up and looked into her face again. "Fluffy?"

"Hey, I think Fluffy's a great name. I had a guinea pig once named Fluffy. It looked a lot like your dog."

"Careful. If you make her mad, I won't be able to control her." Steven looked severe as he tucked his dog under his arm and stood up.

Kaitlyn laughed again. She had forgotten how good it felt to just laugh. "What are you doing here this morning? Still working off the detentions you racked up when you went to school here?"

"Nope. Got those all taken care of. Actually, Mrs. Martinez wanted to talk to me about a coaching job."

"Coaching, really? I thought you were going to the police academy or something."

"I am, but not till spring. This would be volunteer, anyway. We were talking about an after-school basketball program through the winter. We could probably get enough teams together to have some kind of tournament."

"Girls' teams and boys' teams?"

Steven shrugged. "I'll let them get that all sorted out when they start playing high school basketball. We'll just have teams. It's all about fun and learning teamwork, anyway."

Kaitlyn cocked her head. "You know, I'm kind of surprised to hear you talk that way. I'd heard you hold records that still haven't been broken yet at the high school. I thought you'd be all about the competition."

He shrugged again. "As I said, there'll be time for that later. They're just kids. And speaking of kids, I'm telling you right now that I'm planning on getting Olivia involved. As tall as she is, I'll bet she's a natural."

"Well, as someone else who was always the tallest girl in class, I'm telling *you* that's not always the case. But if she wants to play, I'm all for it." She glanced at her watch. "I need to get back. I think Juanita has a stopwatch that she times me by. You and Fluffy have a good day now." She smiled and turned to get back into the Jeep.

"Kaitlyn, wait just a second."

She stopped with one hand on the door.

"Listen, I know we kind of got off on the wrong foot, but do you think we can start over?" He smiled, and Kaitlyn saw none of the cockiness he had exuded every time they met. "Would you like to go to a movie up in San Ramon this weekend?"

He must have seen in her eyes the apprehension she felt, because he hurried on before she could respond. "Everything really low-key. A movie and maybe a cup of coffee afterward. I really would like to get to know you better."

Kaitlyn hesitated. Everyone from Sarah and Chris to Juanita had managed to let her know that Steven could be trouble. But something about him today—maybe the interest in coaching kids, or that silly dog, or maybe even that smile that insinuated nothing and promised a lot—made her decide to take a chance.

"Sure. I'd like that."

When she looked in her rearview mirror as she drove from the parking lot, he was standing watching her go, hat pulled low over his eyes, one hand tucked into his jeans pocket and the other cradling a fluffy white dog.

Only a few of the tables held diners when Kaitlyn got back to the Dip 'n' Dine, but Juanita still glanced pointedly at the neon clock over the pie safe.

"So what did Dad say about Sarah?" Kaitlyn found Chris behind the counter. She tried to keep her voice low, but Juanita joined them anyway.

"I'd say they got along like a house afire." Juanita didn't even try to keep her voice low, but then, she never did.

"What exactly does that mean, Juanita? What does getting along have to do with burning houses? I've always wondered." If Chris was trying to throw Juanita off the subject, it didn't work.

"It means they got along, Chris. Don't overthink it." She barely rolled her eyes before getting back to the subject at hand. "Your dad, on his own, is absolutely delightful, and as you well know, no one can resist Sarah."

Kaitlyn hid a smile. It sounded like Dad had turned the charm on Juanita as well, and since she had come in this morning still bristling from last night's near snubbing by Mom, she was more than ready for a little ego balm.

"This concerns the two of you . . . *how*?" Chris tried to slip past the women standing in front of him, but they held their ground. He sighed and shook his head. "Okay, if you have to know, he said he liked her. Can we get back to work now?"

"That's all? He liked her?" Juanita never did care for the condensed version of anything.

"Pretty much. We have work to do; let's get to it." This time he did push past them and disappeared into the kitchen.

"You know, I'd have thought your dad would have a lot more

to say than just that he liked her." Juanita picked up the coffeepot. "He just hung on every word she said, and I don't think I've ever heard her talk so much. She was giggling like a schoolgirl. She never acts that way with Chris."

"I can hear you, you know." Chris appeared in the window to the kitchen, and he did not look happy. "And so can everyone else, so would you just get to work?"

"Oh, for Pete's sake, Chris, you don't need to be so touchy all the time. Between your mother and your dad, I can sure see who you take after." Juanita huffed an exasperated sigh and went to refill coffee cups.

Chris watched her go and then turned his glare toward his sister, who just smiled at him. "Sounds like everything went great. What's the problem?"

He shook his head, muttered something under his breath, and disappeared back into the kitchen.

Kaitlyn pushed through the door and followed him. "Okay, so what's up?"

Chris had dropped back into his chair and pushed back so he could look up at Kaitlyn. After a second or two he got up and gestured for her to follow him. At the back door, he took Carlos's jacket off a hook and tossed it to Kaitlyn. "You don't mind if we borrow your jacket for a minute, do you?"

"Nope." It was good that Carlos was a man of few words, because Chris didn't even wait for an answer before heading out the back door.

Kaitlyn slipped her arms into the sleeves and sat down beside Chris on the back step. He just stared off toward the distant hills for a while. Finally, Kaitlyn nudged his shoulder with her own. "So? What did Dad really say? He likes her, but . . ."

Chris sighed and leaned back on his elbows. "No, he thinks she's wonderful, and as far as I could tell, she thinks he's great too."

"Then what's the problem?"

"Me. I'm the problem. Dad took me aside before he left and let me know that he was really impressed—even amazed—that I had found someone as special as Sarah. Then he let me know that if I wanted to keep her, I was going to have to set my sights a lot higher than this place."

"What place? Last Chance or the Dip 'n' Dine?"

"Both, I think. He said that a class act like Sarah—that's what he called her, a class act—was meant for better than this, and if I didn't see it, someone else would."

"But Sarah loves Last Chance, and the Dip 'n' Dine too, for that matter. She's already said she'd never live anywhere else."

"That's what I told Dad, but he said that's what they all say, until they leave."

"Oh, come on, Chris." Kaitlyn bumped his shoulder again. "He spent what? Less than an hour with Sarah and he knows everything about her? Sarah loves you. Even more than Last Chance, I think, and that's saying something. Dad doesn't know what he's talking about."

Chris just nodded slowly without turning to look at her. "But you know? Just once in my life I'd like to hear him say, 'Ya done good.' Just once."

"Aww." Kaitlyn leaned her head on his shoulder and held up a hand where her forefinger gently brushed across her thumb. "Know what this is?"

"Yeah, the world's smallest violin." His grin was rueful. "I guess I sound pretty pathetic, huh?"

"Truthfully? I think we're both pretty pathetic to spend so much time worrying about what Mom and Dad think about us when the reality is that they probably don't think about us all that much anyway. The disapproval is on autopilot. I pretty much have it coming, but you have never been anything but perfect your whole life long. That's what makes me mad."

Chris draped his arm over her shoulders. "Not anywhere near perfect, Kait, and you know that. But you're not the same person who came through town on that motorcycle last summer either. I wish they had taken the time to notice."

"You know, I really didn't expect they would."

Kaitlyn was beginning to think she was going to have to use her tiny violin to accompany her own pity party when the back door opened and Juanita stuck her head out.

"Here you are. I asked Carlos where you'd gone and he just said you stole his coat and left. I hate to bother you, but if you can spare the time, I could use some help in here." She was filled with righteous indignation, her favorite kind, and gave every indication that she would stand there with the door open all day if it took that, but she was not going back inside without them.

Chris gave Kaitlyn's shoulder a squeeze and moved to get up. "Come on. We need to get back at it."

He went inside, and after giving her another vexed look, Juanita followed. Alone on the back porch, Kaitlyn let her gaze cross the desert to the mountains beyond. Usually they called her, promising highways to places she'd never been, and people she hadn't met yet, and cities filled with lights. Usually only thoughts of Olivia held her in this tiny town working in her brother's diner, but the call to run didn't seem quite so strong this morning, and Last Chance didn't quite seem the end of the road that it had. She shook her head to clear it and got up to go inside.

Steven checked his list as he got back in his truck at the post office. No one left the ranch without a list of things that needed to be done or picked up while in town, but this one hadn't been especially long. He hadn't even had to go to San Ramon, which was too bad. The more he thought about Mrs. Martinez's basketball idea, the more interesting it sounded, and he would have really liked to have stopped by the sporting goods store to start figuring out what he needed.

"What do you think, Speed Bump? Think we have time to run up there real quick? It probably wouldn't add an hour to my time, if I really booked it."

His dog just looked at him.

"Yeah, you're right. I can get lost in a sporting goods store, and since I want to talk to Uncle Joe Jr. about funding the program, I don't want to start out on his bad side. Better save it for another time."

Speed Bump settled into the passenger seat and rested her chin on her front paws. Since she couldn't see out the window, even with her front paws on the armrest, there was no point in even trying.

"But I think we can spare a couple minutes to run by to see Gran. You need to work things out with Sam, anyway. You're going to have to go somewhere when I leave for the academy, you know, and Gran's would be the perfect place for you."

Gran was right where Steven knew he'd find her—sitting in her recliner with her Bible open in her lap. She looked up when he opened the door, but her welcoming smile faded when she saw his dog under his arm.

"Steven, honey, I've told you that dog just worries Sam to death. You really need to let her wait for you in your car."

"But I want you to get to know her, Gran. Besides, look. Sam's leaving."

Sam, who had gone into an ear-flattened crouch on the back of the sofa at the sight of Steven's dog, leapt down and headed toward the back of the house without ever actually getting out of his crouch.

Elizabeth sighed and set her Bible on the table beside her to make room on her lap. "Well, let me see this little thing then."

Steven put his dog on her lap, and she rested a gnarled hand on its head. "What did you say her name was?"

"Speed Bump."

"Steven Braden, you did not call this unfortunate beast Speed Bump."

"Well, I thought it was pretty clever, but I seem to be a minority of one. The kids at school today made me rename her Fluffy."

"Fluffy. Well, it's better than Speed Bump, I guess." Gran smiled as she continued stroking the little dog. "I keep expecting her to start purring, but dogs don't do that, do they?"

"She'd better not. I spend half my time trying to convince folks she's a real dog as it is."

"With those bottom teeth sticking out, maybe you'd better call her Fang. I think it kind of suits her, don't you?"

"I do, and I tried to get the kids to go for that one, but they got stuck on Fluffy."

"Here, take her, honey." Elizabeth handed the dog up to Steven and struggled to get out of her recliner. "Have you had breakfast? I'm not about to go out this morning, but I'd be happy to fix you something here if you're hungry."

"Sounds great. I think I can manage a few more minutes without getting on Uncle Joe Jr.'s wrong side. Besides, there's something I want to talk to you about." He followed his grandmother into the kitchen and sat at the table while she poured a cup of coffee and set it in front of him.

"Oh?" She put an iron skillet on the stove and pulled a package of sausage from the refrigerator.

"I wanted to tell you before you heard it from Olivia or someone, but I'm taking Kaitlyn to the show on Saturday."

Elizabeth turned to him with a sausage patty still in her hand, and the gaze from her piercing blue eyes pinned him to the wall. "Steven, I asked you to leave that poor girl alone. She has more than enough to deal with right now."

"Gran, I know what you said. And to tell the truth, it kind of ticked me off that you were treating me like I was some kind of predator and she was an unsuspecting lamb or something. I know I've been around a little bit, but so has she, you know. She can take care of herself, and I'm not a bad guy."

Elizabeth's expression softened. She rinsed off her hands and dried them with a dishtowel before coming to sit across from Steven. "Honey, I know you're not a bad guy. You have a huge heart. But sometimes you let your own wants take precedence over the needs of somebody else."

Silence filled the kitchen for a moment, broken only by the gurgle of the coffeepot. Steven didn't have to meet his grandmother's eyes to know she was referring to the way he had let his brother Ray put his life on hold to run their father's bar for him while he was in the military, only to let it go without even a thank-you.

He cleared his throat before he spoke. "Yeah, well, people can change, you know."

Elizabeth reached across the table and took his hand. "People can try to change. Sometimes they can even do a fair job of it. But, honey, real change only comes when God does the changing, and I haven't seen him working in your life since you first figured out how to skip Sunday school."

Steven tried to take his hand back, but Gran held fast. She didn't often try to talk to him about God, and that suited him just fine. It was bad enough knowing she was praying for him all the time. When Gran prayed, things happened.

9

Steven turned the collar of his coat up and jerked the rim of his hat down as he walked around the car after closing Kaitlyn's door. His spirits were considerably lower than they had been all week as he thought about tonight and his plans with Kaitlyn, but that had little to do with the cold wind that had picked up at sundown.

He slid behind the wheel and glanced in the rearview mirror. "All buckled in back there?"

"Wait a second. Okay. Yeah."

"You're sure you don't mind?" Kaitlyn smiled at him across the front seat. "She's been so excited."

"Mind? Are you kidding?" Steven pulled out onto the road and headed for the highway. "Olivia and I are old buds, aren't we?" He glanced in the rearview mirror again.

"It's just that the new Pixar movie is out, and Chris and Sarah already had plans, and—"

"Hey, it's fine. Really." He stopped at Last Chance's only traffic light and looked over at her. Man, she looked amazing. Everyone he had seen all day had been wearing jeans, but no one, *no one* wore jeans like Kaitlyn Reed. And the way her super short hair fell across one eye just did him in. A short beep behind him reminded him that the light had changed, and he dragged his gaze back to the road.

"Where's Fluffy?" The question was accompanied by a light kick to the back of his seat.

"She's home." Steven decided to ignore both the kick and Kaitlyn's muffled snort of laughter. "I asked her if she wanted to come, but she said she already saw it last week."

A moment of silence, then, "She did not!"

"Yeah, she did. She also said she's not real crazy about being called 'Fluffy' either." He sneaked another glance at Kaitlyn, who was trying pretty unsuccessfully to hide a smile. "The other dogs on the ranch are laughing at her."

"Sadie and Beau are nice. They wouldn't laugh at her."

"Well, they're nice to you and they like each other, but you know how dogs are. A new dog comes around and they have to kind of prove who's boss. Fluffy is just not a very tough name."

"Oh, I don't know. I kind of like 'Fluffy.' It suits her." Kaitlyn was laughing now. "Besides, with all her attitude, I'll bet she can get Sadie and Beau to fall in line in no time."

Steven meant for his scowl to be forbidding, but he got distracted by her smile. It changed her face completely, made her look really young and just plain happy. He liked that smile . . . a lot. And if calling his dog Fluffy kept the smile there, well, Speed Bump was just going to have to deal.

"No, Mom. It's not fun being new and having everyone make fun of you. We can't let Sadie and Beau be mean to her."

Kaitlyn's smile faded, and she turned away to look out the side window. Steven sighed and pulled his gaze back to the road. "You know I was kidding about Sadie and Beau, right? Dogs don't really laugh, and they really don't care about what people name them."

"But I don't want them to be mean to Fluffy. It's not her fault someone left her on the side of the road." Olivia's voice was beginning to quaver, and Kaitlyn was still staring out the side window.

Steven blew out a gust of a sigh. This was not going well at all. He tried again. "Well, she's got a good home now, and that's what counts. I'm going to introduce her to Sadie and Beau tomorrow. Do you want to come make sure they are nice to her?"

"Can we, Mom?" Even Steven was touched at the eagerness in Olivia's voice. He glanced at Kaitlyn for confirmation. A smile had returned to her lips, but that's where it stopped. The rest of her beautiful face held that air of sad resignation she had carried since her return to Last Chance.

"It would have to be after church. Uncle Chris likes for all of us to go, you know."

Steven found himself wondering what it would take to get that happy, carefree expression back. "Why don't I meet you there? I'll get Gran and we can all come back to the ranch for lunch."

"You might want to check with your aunt before you start inviting people to Sunday dinner." Kaitlyn still had that sort of wry smile going.

"I will, but she's one of those people who starts trying to feed you before you even get in the house. I'm sure she'll be fine with it."

"Come on, Mom. Can we?" Olivia probably didn't even realize she was kicking the back of his seat.

"I guess it would be all right." Kaitlyn spoke after a few seconds of consideration. "If you're sure it would be okay with your aunt, and if you're sure that there won't be any trouble introducing Fluffy to the others. I don't want Olivia in the middle of a bunch of doggie drama."

"Drama? Nah. Sadie and Beau are pretty mellow. They've already been checking each other out as I've carried, um, *Fluffy* from my car to the house, anyway. I'll tell you what. After we get to San Ramon, I'll call Aunt Nancy Jo and ask her about lunch. How would that be?"

"Okay, thanks. I'd feel better if you did that."

"Yay!" If Kaitlyn's response was a little tepid, Olivia's enthusiasm more than made up for it. Steven hoped he wasn't going to have to ask her to stop kicking his seat.

Steven was waiting in the hall when Kaitlyn ushered Olivia out of the restroom at the theater after the movie. He slipped his phone in his pocket and smiled.

"Aunt Nancy Jo said she'd love to have you for lunch tomorrow. Looks like we're having a party, in fact. She said Sarah had just called and she and Chris are coming too. See? What'd I tell you?"

"Wow." Kaitlyn shook her head. "She can go from, what, two or three for lunch to a full-fledged party just like that? You're sure it's not going to be too much trouble for her?"

"Aunt Nancy Jo could probably feed the county on a day's notice, and since she doesn't get into town that often, she loves the company. She's looking forward to this." Steven fell in beside them as they walked through the lobby of the theater. Olivia, holding her mother's hand, positioned herself between them.

Kaitlyn was beginning to wonder what she had allowed herself to get into. She'd never been the sort of girl that guys took home to meet the family, and though this couldn't be construed by anyone as *that* sort of meeting, she did feel awkward and on the spot. Knowing Chris and Sarah, and even Elizabeth, would be there made her feel safer. Maybe she could just fade into the crowd or something.

"You look so serious." Steven grinned at her over Olivia's head. "You're not still worried, are you?"

"No, not really." Kaitlyn returned his smile as she tried to shake off those old feelings of defectiveness. "I was just thinking that your aunt must be pretty amazing. My mom never had people over for a meal—she had dinner parties, and she obsessed over every last detail from guest list to menu, even to the height of the centerpiece, for days."

"Well, Aunt Nancy Jo's amazing, I'll give you that. But she does take a few shortcuts. The centerpiece is likely to be mashed potatoes, and the guest list is anyone in the house at mealtime. Saves a lot of wear and tear."

"I'm hungry." The voice came from below their line of vision and was accompanied by a tug on Kaitlyn's hand.

"With the popcorn, and the candy, and the slushie? How can you be?" Kaitlyn looked down at her daughter.

"Well, I am."

"You read my mind, Liv." Steven pushed the door of the theater open to a gust of cold wind. "There's a place just around the corner that serves terrific burgers and shakes. How does that sound?"

"Great."

"Olivia." Kaitlyn's voice was little more than an exasperated whisper as she buttoned her daughter's coat to the top and tugged her hat over her ears.

"It's just down this way. We'll be out of this wind in a minute." Steven turned his own collar up and jammed his hat further down on his head as he led them down the street.

Warmth and the sound of the Everly Brothers met them when they entered the burger joint, and the aroma of potatoes sizzling in hot fat made Kaitlyn's mouth water. Since she had foregone the candy and taken only a small handful of Olivia's popcorn, she had to admit that a burger sounded really good.

"I know you can find retro diners all over, but this is the real deal." Steven led them to a booth and slid in on one side while Olivia and Kaitlyn took the other. "This place looked just like this when my folks would bring me here after a movie when I was a kid, and as far as I know, it was the same when my dad brought my mom here on dates. Not even the music has changed."

"What's this?" Olivia had found the booth-side jukebox and was flipping the tabs.

"That lets us choose what music we want to listen to." Steven dug in his pocket for quarters and placed them on the table. "Let's order first, and then I'll show you how it works."

After the waitress left, Kaitlyn watched as Steven helped Olivia read the titles of the songs and punch in the numbers. He tried to steer her toward a romantic ballad or two, but when Olivia's preference clearly leaned toward novelty songs and those with an animal in the title, he gave in with grace. Kaitlyn smiled to herself. Olivia seemed to have taken over both Steven and the date, but that was okay. It took a little of the pressure off.

"Oh my gosh, Steven. Is that you? I haven't seen you in, like, forever." The dark-eyed brunette who stopped at their table was obviously addressing Steven, but her eyes kept flicking to Kaitlyn.

"Jen, how's it going?" Steven slid out of the booth to give her a hug. "Yeah, not since high school, huh? What've you been up to? Thought you got married and moved away after graduation."

"I did, but I'm back. Divorced, no kids, working at the bank. But look at you. Married and with a little girl even. I never would have guessed it." She extended a hand toward Kaitlyn. "Hi, I'm Jennifer. Steven and I go way, way back. Don't we, Steven?"

The knowing smile Jennifer sent Steven's way did not escape Kaitlyn's notice. Nor was it supposed to, she suspected. She returned the smile but said nothing. Let Steven deal with this.

"Nope, not married." Steven took a step back, putting some space between himself and Jennifer. "This is my friend Kaitlyn and her daughter, Olivia."

"Oh? Good friends?" How could a smile look catty one second and predatory the next and really not change all that much? Maybe it was the eyes.

"Mere acquaintances." Kaitlyn tried to make her own smile benign, but Olivia didn't even try.

"Steven, I need you to help me. I still have two more quarters." The look Olivia gave Jennifer was easy to read: *Go away. We don't like you.*

"And here's our dinner." Steven stepped further out of the way as a waitress appeared with their order. "Jen, it was good seeing you. Hope we bump into you again sometime."

"Oh, me too. Wait a second." She fished in her purse for a pen and wrote something on a slip of paper. Tucking it into his hand, she moved in for another hug, which Steven returned with an awkward pat on her back.

She gave Kaitlyn that toothy smile and wiggled her fingers at Olivia before she left. Steven looked at the paper in his hand and wadded it up, but Kaitlyn noticed that he did shove it in his pocket before he sat down.

"Old friend?" Kaitlyn tore the paper off her straw and took a sip of her Diet Cherry Coke.

"I knew her in high school. I haven't seen her since we graduated, though." Steven's voice was casual, but Kaitlyn noticed he seemed a lot more interested in getting mustard on his burger than he was in meeting her eyes.

"I gathered. And what a long and painful fifteen years it must have seemed for her." Kaitlyn couldn't help it. Hassling Steven was becoming a favorite pastime. "Finding you seems to have given her life new meaning."

Steven's brow furrowed, and Kaitlyn bit the inside of her cheeks to keep from grinning. "It hasn't been fifteen years. How old do you think I am, anyway?"

"You know, I really hadn't thought about it. But when I saw Jennifer, I guessed fifteen years. At least." Kaitlyn made her smile sweet and innocent.

Steven sat back and looked at Kaitlyn. He looked so frustrated that Kaitlyn couldn't help laughing. "I'm just teasing you. She is awful pretty, though, and I think running into you just made her day."

The look Steven gave her made her laugh even more, but he did seem to relax as he picked up his burger. "She was cute in high school. And she sure knew it too. She just sort of expected crowds of admirers to form wherever she was."

"And were you in the crowd?"

"Nope." He took a bite and shifted it to his cheek. "I had my own crowds."

Kaitlyn grinned and shook her head as she picked up her own sandwich. "I'll just bet you did."

"Let's pick another song." Olivia claimed Steven's attention again, and as he turned away to help her read the titles on the jukebox, Kaitlyn felt surprisingly at ease, if a bit disappointed.

She had been so nervous since Steven had asked her out, even to the point of finding a reason why Olivia had to come with them. It wasn't that everyone had warned her about Steven. The only guys she had ever been interested in were ones people warned you about.

But she wasn't looking for that anymore. And the Steven who she had seen carrying that silly dog around seemed to have changed too. But he had taken Jennifer's phone number—what else could it have been?—and put it in his pocket. He was a lot of fun to be with, and he seemed to like Olivia, which was a plus, but he was not who she hoped he might be. And since she wasn't completely sure she could trust herself yet, she wouldn't be seeing Steven again—at least not as anything but the most casual of friends.

Steven felt great as he got back in his truck after seeing Kaitlyn and Olivia to their front door. Kaitlyn hadn't asked him in, but that was all right. There'd be time for that later, because he planned to see as much of Kaitlyn Reed as he could. Okay, he'd admit that it was her amazing looks that first caught his attention. She was, to put it plainly, drop-dead gorgeous. She looked almost exotic, like an orchid that had suddenly appeared among the cactus flowers. And that standoffish attitude of hers had presented an interesting challenge too. But she was funny! Who knew? And when she laughed, he found himself wanting to walk a fence or do a pratfall—anything to keep her laughing—just like he was in the fourth grade.

A gust of wind rocked his truck as he turned onto the highway and headed to the ranch. His headlights picked out a coyote loping across the road ahead, and a tumbleweed blew under his wheels. This was a night to be home. He found himself wondering what sitting at home on a night like this with Kaitlyn would be like. Sitting on the sofa watching a movie, maybe, with a bowl of popcorn. He sighed as the picture completed itself: Olivia sitting between them, holding the popcorn bowl.

Well, one thing was sure enough—any picture with Kaitlyn in

it had Olivia squarely in the middle. Everyone in town knew that she had dumped her daughter with her brother and taken off last summer. And deserting your kid was a pretty hard thing to get forgiven for in Last Chance. But Kaitlyn didn't seem to expect it or even look for it. She just came back and became one of the most attentive, loving parents Steven had ever seen. He didn't know a whole lot about kids and parents, but if you could tell how a parent was doing by looking at the kids, Kaitlyn must be doing a pretty good job. The chip Olivia had worn on her shoulder since she came to Last Chance didn't seem to be there anymore. She was pretty mouthy by local standards, but on the whole, she seemed like a normal, happy kid. And Steven, who'd never had much time for kids since he quit being one, liked her. That in itself came as something of a surprise.

He could see Speed Bump, or Fluffy, sitting on the back of the sofa looking out the window when Steven drove up the gravel drive. Her ears perked up when she saw the truck, and she immediately disappeared as she jumped down. In a second, she was back, and then gone, and then back as she tried to monitor the front door and watch his arrival simultaneously.

The wind really howled now, and Steven shrugged deeper into his sheepskin jacket and held his hat on his head as he hurried to the house. He jammed his free hand deep in his pocket as he went, and his fingers found the crumpled piece of paper he had left there in the diner.

"Right. Like that'll ever happen." He pulled the scrap from his pocket and dropped it. A gust of wind snatched it up before it hit the ground and carried it away high over his head and into the dark night.

10

Steven had two choices when he stepped into church after the service had begun the next morning. He could slip unnoticed into the back pew, or he could clomp all the way down to the front where his grandmother sat in the pew she claimed over sixty years ago. He sighed and let his gaze wander down the row. There they all were. Gran on the aisle, her white curls barely visible through the crowd behind her, then Sarah's dark curls; next came Chris, towering over them all, and finally Kaitlyn. And beside Kaitlyn, an empty seat. That made the choice a no-brainer. Holding his hat in his hands, he almost tiptoed down the side aisle and slipped in next to Kaitlyn.

She looked up at him and smiled as Steven took one side of her hymnbook. He gave her a wink and turned his attention to the front of the church where Lurlene, the worship leader, caught his eye and beamed at him. Steven smiled back. When they finished the hymn and everyone sat back down, Rita Sandoval, sitting right behind him, patted his shoulder and whispered, "It's good to see you!" He sent a brief smile over his shoulder, and when he turned back to the front, Gran was leaning forward so she could see him, her face a mask of delighted amazement. Good grief. You'd think he'd never been to church before.

He took the hymnbook from Kaitlyn and slid it into the rack. For a minute or two he almost wished he had stayed in the back after all, but as he sat next to Kaitlyn, feeling the warmth of her nearness and smelling the fragrance of her hair, he decided that he liked being just where he was. A lot. And if he were honest with himself, he'd have to admit that Gran and the others might have reason to show a little wonder. He'd never been a real dedicated churchgoer. In fact, once he got too old for someone to tell him to get in the car, he'd usually found someplace else to be on a Sunday morning. But this was nice. In fact, sitting here in church with his family and Kaitlyn's just seemed right this morning.

After church, and after Brother Parker had slapped his shoulder, pumped his hand, and told him how glad he was to see him, Steven joined the others in the parking lot just as Kaitlyn returned from the Sunday school rooms with Olivia. If left to arrange things himself, Steven would have put Gran and Olivia in Chris's car, but before he could say much, Kaitlyn had taken Olivia's hand and invited Gran to ride with them. Then she insisted that Gran take the front seat while she and Olivia sat in back.

"How was Sunday school, Olivia?" Elizabeth half turned so she could see into the back seat. "What was your lesson about?"

"Jesus."

"I can't think of a better subject. What did you learn?"

While Elizabeth and Olivia talked about Sunday school, Steven glanced at Kaitlyn in the rearview mirror. She gazed off to the side, a sad and resigned look on her face. He looked back at the road and lightly thumped the steering wheel once with his fist. Where did she go when she got that faraway look on her face? And why was she so sad when she was there? He had seen her face light up like Christmas when she laughed. Just the thought of it made him want to follow her around like a puppy in case she laughed again.

Gran and Olivia were still the only ones talking when Steven bumped over the cattle guard onto the dirt road that led to the ranch house. A float of dust over the road told him that Chris's Jeep was not too far ahead. When he stopped in front to let Gran out, Chris and Sarah had just reached the front porch and were being greeted by Aunt Nancy Jo. She waved an arm over her head as Steven drove up.

"Welcome, everyone. You're just in time. Dinner is almost ready. Come in this house."

Steven smiled to himself as he got back in his truck after helping Gran out and up the steps. You'd think from all the hugging and carrying on that everyone had just returned from a trip to the South Pole. He parked in back and came through the kitchen to the living room where everyone was still talking and shedding coats. Actually, Gran and Aunt Nancy Jo seemed to be doing all the talking. Sarah was awfully quiet, an event he had rarely seen, and Chris looked as uneasy as a sixth grader on report card day. Olivia, oblivious to them all, had scooped up Speed Bump and was cuddling with her in a big chair.

Aunt Nancy Jo ushered Gran and Sarah off to the kitchen, and Uncle Joe Jr. ambled back to his chair and the televised football game. Steven went over and knelt by the chair where Olivia and Speed Bump nestled.

"What you got there?"

Olivia looked up. "I was just telling Fluffy that Sadie and Beau were real nice, and she shouldn't worry about whether they were going to like her."

"Oh, she'll be fine. Wait and see." Steven reached over and

scratched his dog's ears. "But I have to tell you, Livvy. I just can't call her Fluffy. I've tried. I really have. But it's just not her name. Do you think maybe Speed Bump could just remind people to drive slowly and carefully? That's all real speed bumps do, you know."

Olivia looked down at Speed Bump, and Speed Bump looked up at her. "I guess. Is it okay if I call her Fluffy sometimes, though?"

"Hey, if it's okay with her, it's fine with me."

Chris cleared his throat, and Steven noticed he was still standing in the middle of the room.

"Um, Mr. Cooley, I was wondering if I could have a few words with you in private before dinner, sir."

Steven had never heard anyone call his uncle Mr. Cooley before, and it sounded just odd. People had called Granddad Mr. Cooley, but that was Granddad. However, Uncle Joe Jr. wasn't a bit confused about who was being addressed. He gazed at Chris a moment over the top of his glasses and then got to his feet.

"Sure, son. We can go in my office." His voice was light and easy, but Steven had been on the wrong side of that expression before, and he was mighty glad it was Chris disappearing behind that closing door and not him.

He looked at Olivia and discarded the idea of asking her what was going on. Whatever it was, it didn't look like it was the kind of thing someone would discuss with a seven-year-old. He settled himself on the sofa to watch the game.

When the door opened a few minutes later, Steven looked up, ready to bring them up to speed on what they had missed of the game, but Uncle Joe Jr. only stuck his head out and hollered.

"Nancy Jo! Sarah!"

Okay, that's enough. Steven got to his feet and headed for the kitchen. On the way, he passed Sarah and his aunt. Nancy Jo's face was crunched in a worried frown and Sarah, just behind her, mouthed, "Pray for me," as she went by. He raised his eyebrows. Something big was going on, and whatever was being discussed in the office, Steven was pretty sure it was going to wind up in a wedding.

"What's going on?"

Gran was just releasing Kaitlyn from a hug when he walked in the kitchen.

She looked at Kaitlyn. "Can we tell?"

Kaitlyn shrugged and lifted her hands shoulder high. "I don't think it's much of a secret anymore."

"Chris asked Sarah to marry him. He's in there asking Joe Jr. for his blessing right now." Elizabeth looked like she could have started dancing.

"Wow, that's fast work. Any particular reason why they're in such a big hurry?" Steven didn't have time to worry about the look of disgust that settled on Kaitlyn's face before Gran waded into him.

"Steven Braden, if you're implying what I think you're implying, you ought to be ashamed of yourself. In the first place, that's just plain none of your business, and in the second, you might try thinking the best about people instead of automatically assuming the worst. This is your family you're talking about."

"Sorry, Gran." How many times had he said those words in his life? "But you didn't see Uncle Joe Jr.'s face. I've seen that look on his face more times than I'd care to admit to, and it's never meant anything good."

"Oh, pshaw." Elizabeth flapped a hand at him. "He's just being a father. If he doesn't have sense enough to see that he won't find a finer son-in-law anywhere than Chris Reed, I'll be happy to remind him of a few things."

"How long have you known about this?" Steven looked at Kaitlyn, who had turned her back on him and was busy making the salad.

"Since last night." The words floated over her shoulder. "When he got home, he told me he had just asked Sarah to marry him, but he swore me to secrecy. Sarah insisted that no one should know anything until she and Chris talked to her parents."

"But he told you."

Kaitlyn turned to face him. "And that was fine with Sarah. I'm Chris's family. And I know how to keep a secret."

There it was again, that reference to family. Despite being surrounded by relatives all his life, Steven was beginning to wonder if he even had a clue as to what that meant.

"She sure does know how to keep a secret." Elizabeth put her arm around Kaitlyn's waist and gave a squeeze. "Butter wouldn't have melted in her mouth until Joe Jr. started hollering and Nancy Jo and Sarah took off."

"Then you spilled the beans." Steven grinned, trying to get a smile, even a tiny one, from Kaitlyn. He had blundered big-time, and he knew it. His attempt didn't work. Kaitlyn just gave him a look before she turned back to her salad.

"Do you think she needed to say a word?" Elizabeth opened the oven and peeked at the biscuits. "My lands, Steven, how many of these announcements do you think I've seen in my day? In fact, the only one I wasn't party to was your parents'." She stood up and gave him a glare as if he was somehow at fault. "They just ran off and got married. And let me tell you, whatever is going on in that office right now is nothing compared to the talking-to your granddad gave your dad when they got back."

"Yeah, I heard about that." The story of his mother and the

rodeo bum was family legend. To tell the truth, Steven didn't see it as the scandal everyone else in the family seemed to. His parents loved each other to the last day of their lives. And he was kind of proud of his dad for daring to face the wrath of his formidable grandfather, even if it was after the fact.

"These biscuits are going to get too brown if I don't get them out of the oven." Elizabeth set the pan of hot bread on the stove and looked around the kitchen with her hands on her hips. "In fact, everything's ready to dish up now. Let's get dinner on the table, and if they're still not finished talking, I'll go get them. Joe Jr. can talk till he's blue in the face, and he's not going to change a thing."

Setting Kaitlyn and Steven to work carrying platters piled high with fried chicken and bowls brimming with mashed potatoes and green beans simmered with bacon to the dining room table, Elizabeth took off her apron and headed down the hall to Joe Jr.'s office. Steven watched her go. Uncle Joe Jr. was a force to be reckoned with, all right, but nobody messed with Gran.

When he turned to go back to the kitchen, he found his way blocked by Kaitlyn.

"I need to talk to you." She glanced through to the living room where Olivia still played with Steven's dog. "In the kitchen."

Puzzled, Steven followed her. Ordinarily, Kaitlyn wanting to talk to him in private would interest him greatly, but from the expression on her face, he wasn't sure he wanted to hear what she had to say.

In the kitchen, she leaned against the counter and brushed back that lock of hair that always fell over one eye. "That comment you made about Sarah and Chris needing to rush their marriage . . ."

Aw, man. Is that what this is about? Steven started to speak, but Kaitlyn held up a hand to stop him.

"Let me finish." She took a deep breath. "Do not judge my

brother by me. Yes, I have a daughter. And no, I've never been married. But my brother is not me. You will not find a finer, a more respectful, a more loving, a more godly man anywhere than Chris. And believe me, present company is not excluded—not by a long shot." Her eyes filled with tears, and she batted her lashes to keep them from falling as her voice threatened to break.

Steven spun so his back was to Kaitlyn and dropped his head back as if looking for help from the ceiling. *How can you be this stupid and still live, Braden?* He turned back to Kaitlyn, who had crossed her arms over her chest. "Kaitlyn, I swear, I wasn't even thinking about you, at least not in that context. In fact, I think it's pretty obvious I wasn't thinking at all. It was just a really dumb comment that I never would have made if I had given it a second's thought. I am so sorry."

He took a step toward her, but she held up a hand to stop him. "Shhh. They're coming."

Voices approached, and Kaitlyn gave her eyes a quick brush with the heel of her hand as she headed down the hall. "Livvy, put the dog down and go wash your hands. We're going to eat now."

Dinner conversation was dominated, not surprisingly, by wedding talk. And also not surprisingly, almost entirely by the women sitting at the table. Chris was occasionally drawn in to answer a question or two, but after asking the blessing, Uncle Joe Jr. said little beyond asking for the gravy or the biscuits to be passed. Olivia matched his indifference, which surprised Steven since she was supposed to be flower girl or something, but mostly he was just thankful to be ignored. He had said enough on the subject for one afternoon.

Finally, as Nancy Jo and Sarah got up to clear the plates in preparation for dessert, Uncle Joe Jr. put both elbows on the table and clasped his hands. "I just don't see what the big fat hurry is. You two barely know each other."

Nancy Jo and Sarah sat back down again.

"Daddy, that's just not true." Sarah was one of the few people, the others being Aunt Nancy Jo and Gran, not intimidated to silence by Uncle Joe Jr. "I may not have known Chris as long as you think I should have, but I know him as well as I've ever known anyone in my life. He's the only man I've ever known who comes anywhere near being as fine a man as you are. And, you know, I had pretty much decided there were none like you left."

She smiled at her dad, and Steven could see his uncle beginning to show signs of giving in, but he clearly wasn't ready to capitulate completely quite yet.

"Okay, be engaged. It looks like you already are, anyway. But take some time. You don't need to get married this spring." He fastened his glare on Chris. "Again, what's the hurry?"

Chris cleared his throat. "Well, sir, with Sarah teaching all winter and the food and music festivals we have scheduled for the summer at the Dip 'n' Dine, it just seemed like Sarah's spring break was the only time available."

"But why *this* spring?"

"Oh, for Pete's sake, Joe Jr., you are just being obstinate." Elizabeth leaned back in her chair. "They're getting married this spring because they love each other and they want to begin their lives together just as soon as they can. Surely you can understand that. I remember what a tear you and Nancy Jo were in to get married, even if you don't. We tried and tried to get you to wait till you finished college, and you know how well that went."

"Well, we'd known each other a lot longer than these two have, that's for sure."

"Honey, you had known each other all your lives. Chris and Sarah would have to have a twenty-year engagement to catch up. Is that what you want?"

"Maybe." Joe Jr. still scowled, but it was clear he had given up, and Sarah jumped up to give him a hug. Her dad patted her arm, and if Steven hadn't known his uncle to be such a tough old bird, he would have sworn there was a mist in Joe Jr.'s eyes.

Nancy Jo got up again and began gathering dishes to carry to the kitchen, and Gran and Kaitlyn joined her. In a moment just Chris, Steven, and Joe Jr. were left sitting in awkward silence. Olivia was also there, but since Kaitlyn had whispered that if she asked to leave the table to take Fluffy outside one more time before dinner was over, she was going to spend the afternoon sitting on a chair, she had slumped down in her seat and wasn't talking to anyone.

Finally, Joe Jr. broke the silence. He leaned back in his chair and gazed at Chris over his glasses. "Well, it looks like this is a done deal. Welcome to the family, son."

"Thank you, sir." Chris sat tall, and Steven was impressed with the confidence in his smile. "You can rest assured that I will devote my life to Sarah's happiness."

"I know you will."

His tone made the words sound more like a warning than an affirmation, but Chris's smile never wavered as he met his future father-in-law's eyes. Steven took a sip of iced tea to hide his own smile. He was going to have to get to know Chris better, maybe learn his secret.

Steven was relieved when dinner was finally over and he and Olivia could head out back with the dogs. As he had predicted, he had no trouble introducing Speed Bump to Sadie and Beau. She was little, of course, but she had big dog attitude. And since she, like Beau, was willing to accept Sadie as alpha, everyone got along just fine.

Olivia was right in the middle of the three dogs, trying to boss them all around, and Steven was sitting on the back steps when Chris joined them.

"Hey, congratulations." Steven grinned and held out his hand as Chris lowered himself to the back step. "Sarah's always been my favorite cousin. Looks like she found a good man."

Chris nodded as he picked up a stick and threw it, sending the dogs, followed by Olivia, racing across the yard. "Yeah, well, Sarah is one amazing woman. I'm the lucky one."

Steven laughed. "You better not let Gran hear you talking like that. She doesn't hold much with luck. She'd say it was God who brought you two together."

If Steven thought Chris would join him in smiling at his grandmother's old-fashioned ways, he was mistaken. Chris couldn't have looked more serious as he nodded.

"Yep, and I thank him every day for it. I have no idea why he decided to bless me like he has, but believe me, I am surely blessed."

Steven didn't have much to say about that, and silence fell between them as they watched Olivia and the dogs. Chris had this funny little smile, and Steven guessed he was thinking about Sarah.

"I escaped! Take me away." Sarah burst through the back door, and Chris's smile broadened into a wide grin as he stood to grab her up in a hug. "I told them what I want. I want Gran to make me a pretty white dress, and I want to get married right here in this yard. I want barbecue and I want music and I want everyone in Last Chance to come help us celebrate. But Gran's saying I have to get married in the church, and Mom's talking about taking her wedding dress out of mothballs, and I just had to get out of there."

Steven stood too and shoved his hand in his front pocket. He grinned at Chris. "You going to try to get your two cents into these plans, or are you just going to bow to the inevitable?"

"Oh, he doesn't care, do you?" Sarah looked up at Chris, who just shook his head.

"Nope. As long as when it's all over I've got you, nothing else matters. You could wear a gunnysack for all I care."

Clearly that wasn't the right answer either. Sarah drew herself up to where she almost reached Chris's shoulder. "Well, I hope you care a little more than that how I look. It will be our wedding day, after all."

Chris tried to backtrack, but Sarah wouldn't let him, and she was still needling him when they headed off together, Chris trying to take Sarah's hand and Sarah refusing to let him. They hadn't gone halfway across the yard before Chris snatched it anyway, and Steven heard Sarah giggle.

He stood on the steps and watched them walk down the road toward the corrals, accompanied by Olivia and the dogs. They seemed good for each other. Sarah was a lot like Speed Bump—tiny but way full of attitude. Chris was big and pretty quiet, but he seemed like a good guy. And if he was half the man his sister thought he was, Sarah had a good life ahead of her.

At the thought of Kaitlyn, Steven turned and looked in the kitchen window behind him. He could see Gran and Aunt Nancy Jo talking a mile a minute, most likely still planning Sarah's wedding. Kaitlyn stood at the sink drying dishes. She was wearing a different smile than he had seen before, neither sad nor teasing. She simply looked content. Her face looked softer, less guarded.

He found himself wanting that for her every day, whether he was around or not.

A sudden gust of wind made him shrug deeper into his jacket and reach for the back door. With the wind came an unexpected sense of loneliness. He'd never much felt the need for family. They were always there, and more often than not trying to get him to do something he didn't want to do, or to stop doing something he did. But for the first time, he found himself wondering just what the difference would be to anybody if he were taken away permanently. And he had to admit, probably not much. The thought chilled him more than the wind. With a last glance through the window at Kaitlyn, he let himself through the back door and headed to the family room to see if Uncle Joe Jr. was still watching the game. He would have stopped in the kitchen to talk, but he didn't think he could bear to see that smile disappear when she saw him.

11

What is this news that I hear?" Juanita was talking as she came through the front door. "You are one fast worker, Mr. Reed, even though I predicted as much the day you two met, remember?"

Chris had glanced at the clock when Juanita came in five minutes late as he always did, but this time Juanita didn't even roll her eyes. She pulled off her coat, tossed it over the back of the booth nearest the door, and headed for Chris with arms open wide. Kaitlyn watched her brother's annoyed employer expression fade into a goofy grin when Juanita drew him into a hug. How did people around here know things as soon as they happened? Sarah said it blew on the wind, but really, that just didn't make sense.

"Now, this is going to be interesting." Juanita picked up her coat and headed for the storeroom. "Ordinarily, Rita and Lurlene would be planning this wedding in a minute, but I have a feeling that Elizabeth and Nancy Jo are going to have plenty to say, and they are certainly forces to be reckoned with."

"Well, Sarah and I thought . . . ," Chris began, but Juanita had already disappeared into the storeroom.

Kaitlyn picked up the tray of silverware she had been rolling into napkins and bent to slide it under the counter. "Doesn't seem to matter a whole lot what you and Sarah thought, does it?" She straightened up and smiled at her brother. "I guess you can count yourself lucky that you got to choose who you were going to marry, because that's about all you get to decide."

"Don't underestimate Sarah. Remember, she's cut from the same cloth as her mother and grandmother. Things pretty much go the way she decides they go."

"Yeah, I noticed that. I think we all have." Kaitlyn batted her eyes at Chris.

"Don't you have work to do? We'll be opening in a few minutes."

Kaitlyn grinned as she watched Chris disappear into the kitchen. It hadn't taken Sarah long to discover what Kaitlyn had known all her life. Teasing Chris was one of the great pleasures of life. His size and serious demeanor discouraged most people from even thinking about it, but once you discovered how flustered he could become with just a little needling, well, it was just impossible to resist.

"What about you, Miss Olivia?" Juanita had returned from the storeroom and was tying on her apron. "What do you think about having a brand-new aunt?"

Olivia, sitting at the counter eating scrambled eggs, shrugged.

"Are you going to get to be a flower girl or a junior bridesmaid?"

Olivia shrugged again without looking up, but for some reason this breach of manners didn't seem to annoy Juanita as much this morning. She gave Olivia a little rub between her shoulder blades. "I guess it's kind of early in the morning for wedding talk, isn't it? You still waking up?"

Juanita went about her work, talking to the room in general as she usually did, but in a much better mood. Her early morning cheerfulness was as puzzling to Kaitlyn as Olivia's refusal to even acknowledge the upcoming wedding. After all, what little girl didn't dream of dressing up and being in a wedding?

"So, Kaitlyn, I'm sure you're planning on staying at least till the wedding, but what then? With Chris starting his new life with his new wife, I imagine you'll have places to go and things to do. Last Chance must seem duller than ditch water to you."

Ah. That explained Juanita's cheery mood. She was imagining the diner the way it used to be—without the boss's sister hanging around.

"I don't know, Juanita. I haven't thought that far ahead." Kaitlyn suppressed a sigh and turned away to find herself caught in Olivia's anxious gaze.

Kaitlyn's heart caught within her. Was that what was the matter with Olivia? Could she really think her mother had places to go and things to do that didn't include her? Kaitlyn winked at Olivia and walked over to give her a one-armed hug.

"How are you doing here? Need a little more cocoa?"

Olivia just shook her head, and Kaitlyn leaned in and whispered, "Don't you think for one minute I'm ever going anywhere without you again. Got that?"

Olivia didn't look at all reassured and Kaitlyn gave her another squeeze and kissed her forehead. "We'll talk later, but this is something to be happy about, not worried about, okay?"

Chris flipped on the neon Dip 'n' Dine sign and unlocked the front door as the first pickup pulled into the parking lot, and before long the diner was humming with conversation and fragrant with breakfast. Almost everyone had heard the news of the engagement, and those who hadn't were soon brought up to date by Juanita. As most of the early arrivals were men in hard hats and pickups on their way to work, few specifics were requested. They just shook

Chris's hand and said, "Heard the news. Congratulations," before turning to other topics of interest. But Kaitlyn had little doubt that the next wave of diners would want details, and she knew that somehow by then Juanita would have details to give.

—∞—

"You're awful quiet this morning, Livvy. What's up?" The sun was well up but a thin layer of frost still painted the brush in the empty lot next door when Kaitlyn started the engine and put the Jeep in Reverse to drive Olivia to school.

Silence from the backseat.

"Livvy? Did you hear me?"

Kaitlyn glanced in the rearview mirror. Olivia still had nothing to say, and she did not look happy. Kaitlyn shoved the gearshift back to Park and turned off the engine. She turned to look into the backseat.

"Livvy, what is going on? You are very sad, and I want to know why."

Olivia's whole body heaved a sigh. "Mom, why do Uncle Chris and Sarah have to get married, anyway?"

The question took Kaitlyn by surprise. "Well, when people love each other, they want to spend the rest of their lives together, so they get married. Why? I thought you liked Sarah. Don't you want her to be your aunt?"

"I like her to be my teacher. And I like to go to the ranch and ride horses with her. And I like her to come to our house sometimes, but why do they have to get married?"

"I told you why they want to get married, Livvy, and I don't think that's what's bothering you. Now, what's the matter?"

"I don't want things to be different." Olivia's voice was shaky. "I like living with you and Uncle Chris, and there won't be enough rooms if Sarah comes to live with us, and there won't be enough rooms if we go to live with her. And I don't want anyone to go away."

Kaitlyn reached back and gave Olivia's bony knee a squeeze. "Honey, no one's going away. And weddings are happy times. That's when families grow, not get smaller. Wait and see."

Olivia still didn't look thrilled, but she didn't look quite so worried either. Kaitlyn smiled and gave her leg a last pat before turning around, starting the engine again, and heading out of the parking lot.

"Don't a couple of Sarah's nephews go to school with you?"

"Uh-huh. Jacob and Michael James. They're bigger, though. Jacob's a third grader and Michael James is a fourth grader."

"Well, guess what? They're going to be your cousins now. And that means that Miss Elizabeth will be your Gran, I bet."

"And your Gran too?"

"We'll just have to see."

Kaitlyn had no doubt that Olivia would be swept into the heart of the Cooley family. They pretty much saw her as belonging to Chris anyway. But Kaitlyn? Well, they were kind and warm and never made her feel like an outsider, but when you got down to it, wasn't that exactly what she was? Someone who roared in and out of town on a motorcycle, abandoning her daughter on the way, only to come slinking back with her tail tucked? If that thought filled Kaitlyn with disgust and revulsion, what must it do to good, decent people like the Cooleys?

Olivia's voice had brightened with the talk of her expanding family, and by the time they pulled up in front of the school, she was wondering aloud if the impending marriage meant that Meeko and Speed Bump would be cousins as well.

When Olivia unbuckled her seat belt and leaned between the seats to give her mom an awkward hug before climbing out at the curb, Kaitlyn held her just a second longer than usual before sending her off.

"See you at three."

"Mom." Olivia's voice took the tone of a tired teacher. "There's a basketball meeting after school today. Uncle Chris signed that paper, remember? Don't come for me until four."

"Ah, right. Four it is."

Kaitlyn sat a moment watching Olivia head up the walk to the big front doors of the school, her pink backpack bouncing against her narrow back with every step. Olivia raised some good points. What would they do when Chris and Sarah got married? He was still her legal guardian, and as Olivia had pointed out, neither their place nor Sarah's was big enough for the whole family. And even if one of them were, Kaitlyn had not the slightest intention of setting up housekeeping with a couple of newlyweds.

She watched the front doors close behind Olivia as the first bell rang. Olivia was happy here, and doing well. In fact, everyone seemed to have a plan but Kaitlyn. And truthfully? She didn't have a clue. She shook her head as she turned the key in the ignition and headed back to the Dip 'n' Dine. What a mess.

Uncle Joe Jr. was already at the breakfast table when Steven came in the back door. He barely glanced up from his biscuits and sausage gravy.

"Get the stock fed?"

Steven nodded as he pulled off his gloves and stuffed them in his coat pocket before hanging it on a hook by the door. "Yep."

He hung his hat next to his jacket and sat at the table. Joe Jr. wasn't much for idle conversation at any time of day, but at breakfast his words were especially scarce and related almost entirely to ranch work. Wordlessly, he pushed the bowl of scrambled eggs toward Steven, followed by the dish of green chile.

"Thanks." Steven filled his plate and reached for a biscuit. "I'm going into town later this afternoon. Either of you need anything?"

Joe Jr. shook his head without looking up from his breakfast. "Nope."

"I can't think of anything either, right now. But stop in before you head out in case I have a list for you by then." Nancy Jo filled his coffee cup. "You might drop by and see Rita, though. Did she ever get in touch with you?"

Steven took a big bite of eggs and green chile instead of answering.

"She called here yesterday looking for you." His aunt gave him an exasperated look. "She said she'd left any number of messages on your phone, but you hadn't called her back."

Steven looked back at his plate. "Okay, I'll do that, I guess."

"Well, I wish you would. You know she's not going to just give up and say, 'Oh, well.' And I don't blame her. That boarded-up bar is the first thing anyone sees when they drive into town, and it's an eyesore. What are you going to do about it?"

Joe Jr., still intent on his breakfast, forked in his last bite of eggs and sausage and got up. He stopped at the back door and shrugged into his sheepskin jacket and tugged his battered hat down before heading outside. Clearly, Rita and the closed and boarded High Lonesome Saloon were not high on his list of things to worry about this morning.

Steven watched him go. He wished he could dismiss the High

Lonesome that easily, but, man, Rita was persistent. He tried to make sure he stayed out of her way, but every now and then she'd sneak up on him, and he was stuck before he knew it.

Through the window, he could see Uncle Joe Jr. heading for the barn, and Steven quickly scraped up the last of his eggs. As far as his uncle was concerned, breakfast was purely for fueling up for the day's work and shouldn't take more than a few minutes to consume. Steven made a couple sandwiches from sausage, biscuits, and green chile to take with him and got to his feet.

"I need to get going." He reached for his coat.

"Well, what are you going to tell Rita?" Nancy Jo may not have had much say about Joe Jr.'s silent breakfasts, but she clearly had no intention of putting up with that in her nephew. "I have more things to do with my day than try to explain to her why I think you're not answering your phone."

Steven pulled his gloves from his pocket and replaced them with the paper napkin–wrapped sausage sandwiches. "Okay, I'll give her a call. And I'll grab the weed burner before I go into town. If the wind's not up, I can get rid of those weeds in the parking lot. That ought to count for something." He tugged his hat low and stepped out onto the back porch.

The sun had made it over the tops of the mountains to the east but had not yet begun to warm anything, and he turned his collar up. Funny how you either took to this life or you didn't. And Steven definitely had not. He and his brother Ray had worked off and on at the ranch when they were kids, but it hadn't taken Steven long to decide he'd much rather be working with his dad at the High Lonesome than be taking orders from his Uncle Joe Jr. He stepped off the porch and headed for the barn. Maybe that was his problem. Even though a stint in the military had gone a long way toward teaching him to bow to the inevitable, he still didn't like taking orders from anyone.

—‍~‍—

Steven stowed the weed burner in the back of his truck and surveyed the parking lot of the High Lonesome. It didn't look great, but it did look better. Maybe even good enough to keep Rita off his back for a while longer. Because, truthfully? He didn't have a clue what he was going to do with the old bar. Despite all of Rita's efforts, Last Chance wasn't exactly in a growth mode right now, and the only one who had shown any interest in buying the place was some guy from El Paso who wanted to reopen the bar. And Steven already knew that was not going to happen. For one, he didn't have the nerve to face his grandmother with that news. She might lack an inch or so from reaching his shoulder, but no one could get him shaking in his boots like Gran.

He glanced at his watch. Just as he had planned, he had an hour or so before he had to be at school. Just enough time to apply a dose of the old Braden charm to the pretty waitress he kept glancing at through the window of the Dip 'n' Dine across the road. She was a hard one to figure out. One minute she was smiling and happy and having a good time, and the next she was as prickly as a pinecone. Anyone else and he'd just tip his hat and wish her well, but there was something about Kaitlyn Reed that just kept him coming back.

He grabbed a menu from the rack by the front door and chose a booth near the back. He didn't need anyone else listening in on their conversation. When he heard footsteps approaching, he decided he'd keep his eyes on the menu for just a beat longer before peering up at her from under the brim of his hat.

"I see you're finally getting around to doing something about that mess across the road." Juanita. Of course.

Steven looked up to find her holding her order pad and staring in marked disapproval at his hat. He removed it and placed it on the seat next to him.

"Well, it's a start." He glanced around for Kaitlyn. She was serving pie and coffee to a couple ladies across the room.

"Barely. It needs a lot more done than setting fire to a few weeds."

Steven turned his attention back to his menu. Maybe Juanita would take the hint and let it drop. He opened his mouth to order.

Juanita, never known for taking hints, spoke first. "You know, I never did like having a drinking establishment right here at the gateway to Last Chance and was as pleased as anyone when you decided to close it up. But good night, Steven, I never dreamed you were just going to let it turn into a rat palace. What would your father say?"

"There aren't any rats." Steven was offended.

"Well, you couldn't tell it by me. Now, what'll you have?"

Steven briefly considered continuing his defense of his property but decided he'd rather have Juanita just go away. He handed her the menu. "Just a burger with double green chile, some fries, and a strawberry shake."

Juanita wrote it all down and shook her head as she tucked her pencil behind her ear. "I don't know how you kids can eat all that and still stay trim. Well, enjoy it while you can, honey. One of these days you're going to look down and find you're wearing it around your middle. Take my word for it."

She headed off to the kitchen and Steven watched her go. There was a time when he'd have stuck his tongue out at her retreating back, but that was a few years ago. Now he just thought of a few choice words he'd say if he didn't know they'd get back to his grandmother before sundown.

He slumped down in his seat and watched Kaitlyn, who hadn't even glanced his way. Really smooth, sitting in back like this. He felt ridiculous and completely out of sorts. What was even keeping him here in Last Chance, anyway? He was getting nowhere with Kaitlyn, and he might as well admit it. Why not just take off till he had to show up for the academy in April? There were still a lot of places he wanted to see. About the only one who'd miss him would be Gran, but she was used to him taking off, and she had to know he'd come back. Didn't he always?

By the time he finished his lunch, Steven was feeling pretty good. He was practically on his way. There was still the after-school basketball program, but maybe he could get Manny Baca to take that over. Manny was a pretty good player when they were in high school, not tall, but really fast. And if not, well, Mrs. Martinez ought to be able to find somebody.

Kaitlyn finally looked his way when he reached the door of the Dip 'n' Dine. He smiled and tipped his hat. *And all the best to you, Kaitlyn Reed.*

12

It was only about ten minutes past 3:00 when Steven pulled into the parking lot of Last Chance Elementary School, but Mrs. Martinez was waiting out front with the kids who had signed up for basketball, and she didn't look happy. He could only imagine her reaction when he told her she was going to have to find another coach. He had hoped to bring her news of a replacement when he resigned and had stopped by Otero Gas and Oil to talk to Manny on the way to school, which was why he was late in the first place.

Manny hadn't been real busy at the moment, which boded well for Steven's plan, and it wasn't long before he had Manny laughing and reminiscing about their days on the basketball team of Last Chance High School, but when Steven tried to segue from playing basketball in the good old days to coaching elementary school basketball in the here and now, Manny stopped laughing. In the first place, with three kids of his own under four years old, spending what little free time he had with more kids just didn't sound like that much fun. And in the second place, in case Steven hadn't noticed, Manny did have a business to run. Just taking off in the middle of the afternoon wasn't an option.

Mrs. Martinez smiled a tight smile over the heads of the children crowding around her. "Ah, here you are. We were beginning to worry."

Steven started to apologize, but she kept on talking as she handed him a clipboard. "Here's your list of participants. I've checked and everyone is here today. The bag of basketballs is over there. Have a good time, everybody."

Steven nodded and looked around. He hadn't realized there would be quite so many kids. And they all looked pretty energetic too.

"Oh, and Mr. Braden." Mrs. Martinez had stopped on her way back inside, and it took a moment before Steven realized who she was talking to. "Would you mind stopping by my office before you leave, please?"

The door closed behind her, and Steven surveyed the students looking up at him. There was a good group—a glance at his clipboard told him he had just over twenty—and although it comprised mostly boys, a fair number of girls, including Olivia Reed, had turned out as well.

"Okay, team, let's head out to the playground. Michael James, do you want to grab that bag of basketballs over there?" Steven led the way and the kids followed.

"Mr. Braden? Mr. Braden?" The little girl walking next to him had to tug at his jacket to make him realize she was talking to him. "I have a doctor's appointment and my dad's picking me up at 3:30. Is that okay?"

"Sure." Steven stopped under the basketball hoop and raised his hands for silence. "Hey guys, need your attention here. Guys? Quiet down a minute, will you?"

It took a few minutes before the confusion settled, but Steven was finally able to make himself heard. "Guys? All right, we need to get some things straight. First, when I raise my arm like this, it means 'listen up.' So stop what you're doing and gather around—without talking. And next, don't call me Mr. Braden. I'm not going to know who you're talking to if you do."

The girl with the doctor's appointment raised her hand and waited to be called on. "What should we call you?"

"How about my name? Steven."

From the expressions on their faces and the way they looked at each other, it was clear that calling an adult by his first name wasn't something that they were comfortable with. He tried again.

"Okay, what about Coach?"

The name found universal acceptance, and Steven set them to doing drills designed to check the relative athletic ability of his crew. Some were naturals and would be tearing up the court at Last Chance High in a few years. Others, not so much. Steven snagged a ball that had whizzed right past one kid and tossed it back. Olivia Reed was one of the kids who showed some promise. It would have been fun to see what she could do.

The afternoon was warm enough for them to be outside but not so warm that the kids could play without their jackets, and as he walked among them calling out encouragement and instruction, Steven made a mental list: They needed an indoor space if they were going to really play basketball. He'd have to see what he could find. The high school was just across the field. Maybe they could find a time when the gym wasn't in use. And he'd like to leave whoever took over when he left with an assistant. Maybe a high school kid could help out. And a whistle. He had to get a whistle.

After practice, Steven waited with the kids until the last of his team had been picked up and then sighed and headed for the principal's office. Might as well get this over with. At least he could assure Mrs. Martinez that he intended to do everything he could to help her find somebody else before he left.

The halls were empty and the reception area in the office was deserted, but Mrs. Martinez's door was ajar, and he tapped as he stuck his head in. She was on the phone and lifted one finger before indicating with the same hand that he should take a seat.

When she hung up the phone, she turned to him with a smile. "They finally got back to me about using the high school gym. It's ours from 3:00 sharp to 4:00 sharp Mondays and Thursdays. I trust that will work with your schedule."

Steven nodded and opened his mouth to speak, but Mrs. Martinez went right on talking. "That means, in order to make optimum use of our time, that you'll have to have the children ready to go in right at 3:00 since you'll have to have finished and be out by 4:00. I'm afraid that leaves little room for casual punctuality, so you'll need to be here and waiting when the final bell rings at 2:50."

Mrs. Martinez fixed a look on him that made him squirm inside. She had been his fourth-grade teacher before she became his principal, and this was nowhere near the first time Steven had sat measuring the distance between himself and the door. He decided to put off until another time telling her he was not going to be sticking around.

Reminding himself that he was an adult and she couldn't give him detention anymore, he willed casual confidence into his voice. "Sounds like a plan. In fact, I was going to suggest that very thing. The playground isn't the best place for a basketball program in winter."

Mrs. Martinez turned her attention to the file folder open on her desk. "Then we'll see you Thursday at 2:50."

Steven jammed his hat down on his head as he strode through the silent halls. For crying out loud, not only was he not a ten-year-old caught shooting spit wads, but he was doing her a favor by even being here. He paused and looked over his shoulder, considering turning on his heel and marching back into her office and telling her this coaching gig wasn't going to work out for him after all. But after only a few seconds, he picked up his pace again and shoved his way through the big glass front doors of the school. Maybe he should at least try to have another coach lined up before he did that.

A pink backpack, nearly hidden behind a trash can, caught his eye, and he almost left it there. After all, the only other thing he could do with it was take it back to Mrs. Martinez, and he really didn't want to do that right now.

He stopped halfway to his truck and, muttering a few words under his breath, went back and snatched up the backpack. The name tag flopped against his wrist, and his mood immediately improved when he read Olivia's name. Great. He could just drop it off at Gran's.

The closer he got to Gran's, the more he looked forward to it. It hadn't been actually cold standing around on the playground, but it was cool enough to make him look forward to being inside, and Gran would make him some coffee and give him something to eat. Kaitlyn would doubtlessly have gone back to the Dip 'n' Dine, but Olivia would be there. And to Steven's surprise, he was enjoying being around her more and more.

A siren behind him caused him to pull over, and an ambulance shot past, lights flashing. Steven's mild curiosity turned to concern when it turned down the same road he was heading for.

By the time he turned onto Gran's street, the flashing lights had stopped in front of her house and the paramedics were running up her walk. Olivia was standing on the sidewalk near the open door of the Jeep, crying, and Kaitlyn and Sarah were kneeling next to a crumpled heap that, even covered in a purple and lavender afghan, seemed far too small to be his indomitable grandmother.

Steven had barely shoved his gearshift into Park before he vaulted from behind the wheel and raced across the road to Elizabeth's house. The paramedics were bending over Elizabeth, and Kaitlyn had returned to the Jeep and was holding Olivia. Sarah stood just out of the way of the EMTs, pressing her clasped hands against her mouth.

"What happened?" Steven couldn't take his eyes off his grandmother as he came to a stop next to his cousin.

She shook her head. "We don't know. It looks like she may have fallen down the porch steps. Kaitlyn and Olivia found her this way when they got here."

"Is she going to be all right?"

"Steven, I don't know." Sarah sounded almost frantic as she brushed the heel of her hand across her cheek. "I hope so. I pray that she is. She has to be."

Steven slipped an arm around her shoulders. "You've called your mom and dad?"

Sarah nodded. "They're on their way."

While two of the technicians went for the gurney, the third looked up at Sarah and Steven. He addressed Sarah. "You're her relative?"

Sarah nodded again. "She's my grandmother."

"And mine." Steven was not going to be left out of this conversation. It meant too much.

"Is she going to be all right?" Sarah's voice was about to break.

"We're doing what we can. There's something going on with her leg here, but the first thing we need to do is get her body temperature back up. She must have been lying here awhile. We're going to take her to San Ramon General, if you want to follow."

"Can't I ride along?" The paramedics had gently transferred Elizabeth to a gurney, and Sarah took her grandmother's hand and held it to her cheek. "Her fingers are so cold."

"Nope, afraid not." The EMT's smile was gentle. "We're going to be busy taking good care of Grandma for you. We'll see you in San Ramon."

Steven and Sarah followed the gurney down the sidewalk and watched as it was loaded into the ambulance. When it moved on down the street and the siren picked up again, Sarah dug for her keys and headed for her car.

Steven put a hand on her arm. "Let me just tell Kaitlyn what's happening, and then I'll drive. You go ahead and call your folks and tell them we'll meet them at the hospital."

While Sarah made her call, Steven walked over to the Jeep where Kaitlyn sat sideways on the front seat cradling Olivia on her lap. Olivia was hiccupping with sobs, and for her sake, Steven tried to keep his voice light.

"Well, they need to get her warmed up and fix her leg, so they took her to the hospital to do that. Sarah and I are going up there now."

"Is she going to die?" Olivia's voice rose in a wail.

"Gran? Because of a little tumble down the stairs? Nah. Gran's a lot tougher than that." Steven put his hand on Olivia's head and smiled, but when Kaitlyn's eyes met his, he could see his own fear mirrored in them. "Oh, and before I forget, I've got your backpack. You left it at school."

When he retrieved it from his truck, Sarah was already waiting in the passenger seat, talking to someone, probably her mom, on the phone.

"Here you go." Steven opened the back door of the Jeep and tossed the backpack on the seat.

"Call me." Tears shone in Kaitlyn's eyes. "Call me the minute you know *anything*, you hear me?"

"I will." Funny, as desperate as he was to get to the hospital and see that Gran was going to be all right, it just tore him up to leave Kaitlyn here alone trying to comfort her inconsolable child. "I'll call just as soon as I can. And, um, if you could pray for her, that would really be great."

"I will." Kaitlyn rocked Olivia back and forth, resting her cheek on the top of her daughter's head. "I will do that."

—m—

It was nearly midnight before they got to see Elizabeth in her room at the hospital. Her leg was indeed fractured and immobilized, and her temperature was near normal. Something, probably pain medicine for her leg, had made her a bit loopy. In his entire life, Steven had never seen his grandmother loopy, and it was more than a little odd.

"Well, isn't this nice, having everyone here like this. Want some coffee? I bet we can get someone to bring us some coffee. And some chairs. We don't have enough chairs. Steven, see if you can get us some more chairs, will you, hon?"

"No, Mom." Joe Jr. took his mother's hand. "We don't need any coffee. In fact, they're going to run us off here in a minute. They just let us come in for a little bit to see that you're all right and to tell you that we love you."

"Well, I love you too, you sweet thing." Elizabeth beamed up at him.

"Do you remember what happened, Gran?" Sarah stood on the other side of the bed. "How did you happen to fall?"

"Well, of course I remember, Sarah. I just broke my leg; I didn't lose my mind. I thought I'd go out and check the mailbox, and that crazy cat of mine got tangled up in my feet, and the next thing you know, I was down and couldn't get up. Just like those TV ads."

Steven whistled under his breath. Gran started looking for the mail about noon. She had to have been lying on the sidewalk in that light housedress for hours. They were so fortunate that the day had been warm for January. They nearly lost her to the cold as it was.

A nurse came in and injected something into Elizabeth's IV. She smiled at the family gathered around her bed. "This young lady needs to get some sleep now, so say your good-byes, and you can come back tomorrow."

Elizabeth fixed her with a glare. "If you think I'm a young lady, young lady, I don't want you anywhere near me because you are as blind as a bat."

"Mom, she was just trying to be nice." Nancy Jo smoothed the covers and tucked them around Elizabeth. "Now you go on to sleep and don't worry about another thing. We're going to get your room all fixed up for you. We'll even bring that old cat of yours up to the ranch, if you're still speaking to him."

"Why?" Elizabeth's eyes were getting droopy.

"Why what, Mom?"

"Why are you taking Sam to the ranch? I need him."

"Of course you do, Mom. And that's why he's coming. To keep you company."

Elizabeth had almost drifted off to sleep, but she opened her eyes again and looked from her daughter-in-law to her son. "If you think you're getting me back to the ranch over this, you can just think again, buster, because that'll happen when pigs fly. I'm still your mother . . . your mother."

Her voice slowed to a stop as her eyes closed. It took a while longer for her belligerent expression to relax into one of peace.

"Well, that went about like I thought it would." Joe Jr. gazed down at his sleeping mother. "Looking at her now, you wouldn't think she was near that tough, would you?"

"Tough or not, there's no way she can stay by herself and she's just going to have to get used to that idea." Nancy Jo straightened the blankets one last time and bent to kiss her mother-in-law's forehead before picking up the bag that held the clothes Elizabeth had been wearing. "I'm as sorry as I can be that it had to happen this way, but we both know that it was past time for her to come home, anyway."

"Maybe." Joe Jr. covered the gnarled hand lying on the bed with his own before he too bent down to kiss the sleeping face. "I just wish it were her own idea. I hate to see her unhappy."

Steven and Sarah, after whispering good night to their sleeping grandmother, followed Joe Jr. and Nancy Jo out into the hall. Sarah stopped at the nurses' station.

"You have our numbers, right? You'll call if anything changes?"

The nurse looked up from her charts and smiled. "I'm thinking she's going to be just fine tonight, but yes, I do have your numbers."

Steven rested his hand in the small of his cousin's back and guided her to the elevator, where her parents were still discussing Elizabeth's impending move to the ranch.

"Why can't I look after Gran? I'm just two doors down, and I can even spend the nights with her until she gets back on her feet." Sarah clearly didn't like the idea of seeing her grandmother unhappy any more than her dad did.

"Honey, we don't know that she *is* going to get back on her feet." Nancy Jo sounded tired. "The doctor said it was a bad break, and

Gran is nearly ninety years old. Her bones are not likely to heal the way they would have fifty years ago. And besides, you're gone all day. I'm afraid Gran's going to need help 24-7, and that's why the only thing that makes sense is for her to come back to the ranch. She always said she'd wind up back at the ranch one day anyway."

"She meant she'd come back to die." Sarah's voice went up about two octaves as the tears came. "Don't make her go back yet."

"Sweetheart." Nancy Jo gathered her daughter in her arms and held her head against her shoulder. "Coming back to the ranch isn't going to shorten your grandmother's life one day. If anything, our good care will give her even more time with us, so just blow your nose and get hold of yourself here. There's a whole lot in life that we don't want to see happen, but it happens anyway, and falling apart never has changed that."

With a *ping*, the elevator doors slid open, and they stepped inside. Steven couldn't help noticing that the entire conversation about Elizabeth's future and welfare had been among the three Cooleys present. Maybe it was completely coincidental; maybe it was because as a Braden, he was not in the line of family authority; or maybe—and Steven had to admit to himself that this was the most likely case—it was because when a crisis occurred, Steven Braden was the last person anyone would turn to for a solution.

The temperature had dropped to near freezing, and stars glittered like ice against the midnight sky when they walked out into the nearly empty parking lot.

"You know, I think I'll stay at Gran's tonight." Steven stopped at his uncle's truck. "I need to get Sarah home anyway, and I'll just check to make sure everything's okay. Find her cat and see that it gets fed. She'll want to know all that tomorrow when we see her. I'll get up to the ranch first thing in the morning."

Joe Jr. nodded as he climbed into the cab of his truck. "Okay, but don't be too late. We got way behind today."

"I'll be there first thing. You can count on it." And Steven was surprised to realize that "you can count on it" was exactly what he meant.

13

Have you heard anything?" As usual, Juanita was talking as she came through the doors of the Dip 'n' Dine.

"Nope, at least nothing new." Chris didn't bother looking pointedly at the clock like he usually did. Juanita never seemed to care anyway.

"I called up to the hospital first thing this morning—that's the good thing about hospitals; someone's always awake—but they just said she had rested through the night. Well, of course she rested. What else is she going to do? Handsprings down the hall at 3:00 a.m.? I pointed out that Elizabeth Cooley and I have been friends for nearly sixty years and I would appreciate some real information, but they just said that was all they could tell me."

She huffed in exasperation as she tied on her apron. "And there you have the bad thing about hospitals. It's not bricks and mortar that hold up the roof. It's rules. And if they bend just one, the whole thing will come crashing down. At least that's what they seem to think."

For once, Kaitlyn welcomed Juanita's nonstop chatter. She never seemed too concerned about whether anyone was listening, and that left Kaitlyn to her own concerns, which centered on her daughter. It would always rip at Kaitlyn's heart, but Elizabeth had been one of the first people in Olivia's short life to draw her in and just delight in her, and when they found Elizabeth cold and unresponsive on the sidewalk, Olivia had been beside herself.

Chris, of course, had gone up to San Ramon and the hospital as soon as he closed the Dip 'n' Dine, and he had stayed until the family had been assured that, barring the unforeseen, Elizabeth would recover. But even that news hadn't cheered Olivia. All she knew was that Elizabeth was not in the little house Olivia had come to feel so safe in and would not be there for a long time. Kaitlyn crossed the room to where Olivia sat stabbing at a plate of pancakes and slipped an arm around her shoulders.

"How're you doing?"

Olivia shrugged and didn't look up.

"Miss Elizabeth's going to be fine. You heard Uncle Chris." Kaitlyn gave the skinny shoulders a squeeze.

"Here's another early bird." Juanita drew their attention to the front window as the lights from an SUV cut across the back wall of the Dip 'n' Dine. "I declare, they just keep coming earlier and earlier. We might as well not even have an opening time posted. What do you think, Chris? Should we let him in, or have him wait?"

"Might as well let him in. It's cold out there." Chris had turned to go back to the kitchen but stopped when the driver stepped into the parking lot and dug his hands deep in his coat pockets. "Isn't that Steven?"

"Why, yes, it is." Juanita had already reached the front door and opened it. "You come in here. Are you on your way to the hospital? How's your grandmother?"

"She was doing pretty good last night." Steven took off his hat when the door closed behind him. "She had everyone up there marching double time. I think Aunt Nancy Jo's planning on going up this morning, but I'm not sure when today I'll get back. That's up to Uncle Joe Jr. I'm heading back to the ranch right now, in fact. I just stopped in for a real quick breakfast on my way."

"You didn't spend the night at the hospital, did you?" Juanita was trying to direct Steven to a booth, but he took a stool at the counter next to Olivia before he ordered his eggs and sausage.

"Nope. I spent the night at Gran's. We left in such a hurry that I thought I'd better make sure everything was okay at her house." Steven looked down at Olivia. "But everything was just the way Gran would have wanted to leave it. Sam was even inside and fed. Did you do that?"

Olivia nodded. "Mom and I did. Sam was meowing on the porch and I knew he was wondering what was happening, so I told him Miss Elizabeth had to go to the hospital, but I wouldn't let anything happen to him. Then we took him inside and fed him. Mom said he'd be just fine by himself and we'd go by every day to check on him and feed him."

"Well, that will make Gran feel much better. I know she was worried about him."

"Is she really going to be okay?"

"That's what they tell us."

"Can I go see her? And bring Sam?"

"I'm afraid not, sweetie." He held his cup up as Kaitlyn approached with the coffeepot. "They have rules about kids and pets at the hospital."

"And that is just what I'm talking about." Juanita never stayed out of any conversation that interested her for long. "Rules for the sake of rules. What's wrong with Olivia visiting Elizabeth for a few minutes? It's not like she's going to run up and down the halls screaming. Although they may have a point about the cat. That probably wouldn't be a good idea."

"I'll tell you what you can do, though, other than look after Sam for her." Steven poured a big dollop of cream in his coffee and gave it a stir. "You can draw some pictures for her hospital room. It's really bare now, and some of your pictures would make the room seem more like home."

"I could draw a picture of Sam so she wouldn't miss him so much. And maybe one of her house." Kaitlyn could almost see the wheels turning as Olivia planned her artwork.

"And draw some of you. And of your mom." Steven smiled at Kaitlyn as she set his plate and a dish of chopped, roasted green chile in front of him. "Thank you, ma'am."

Kaitlyn returned the smile. Really, she could have hugged him. With just a few calm words, Steven had managed to accomplish what Kaitlyn had been struggling so unsuccessfully to do since yesterday—give Olivia some peace and a reason to believe everything was going to be okay. Despite the tough little exterior she presented, her daughter's world was fragile as spun glass.

And whose fault is that? Always, always that contemptuous inner voice whispered that no matter what she tried to do, she could never atone for Olivia's first seven years. Kaitlyn turned away as she felt the smile fade from her face.

"I'll get you some more coffee."

"Nope. Don't bother. I have about five minutes to eat this and then I've got to get going. I promised Uncle Joe Jr. I'd be home first thing this morning, and what he considers first thing, most other folks call the middle of the night." He spooned green chile over his eggs and picked up his fork as he turned back to Olivia. "I'll stop by here on my way to the hospital to see if you have any pictures for me."

Olivia started to push her plate away. "I'm all done. I'll make one now."

"No rush. Finish your breakfast. I won't be back till late this afternoon." He really was making short work of his breakfast, and Kaitlyn was pretty sure Elizabeth would have had something to say about it had she been there.

As he had said, within five minutes Steven had eaten his breakfast and paid his check and was jamming his hat back on his head as he headed out to his truck. The neon Dip 'n' Dine sign was still gray against the window, and the sky hadn't even begun to lighten.

"Well, I don't know if Joe Jr. was finally able to get a fire lit under that boy, or what." Juanita stood watching through the window, hands on hips, as Steven's truck pulled out of the parking lot and disappeared down the deserted road. "But I don't believe I've ever seen him in such a hurry to get to work, not when the alternative was sitting around drinking coffee and talking."

No one responded to Juanita's comment, but since most of her comments seemed to be delivered to the universe at large, folks rarely did, and that did not seem to bother her at all. Chris crossed the room to flip the neon sign on, and Kaitlyn followed him back to his desk in the kitchen.

"Hey, brought you a cup of coffee." She smiled as she placed the mug on his desk.

"Thanks." He barely looked up as he switched his computer on.

"We haven't had more than a minute to talk since yesterday."

"And I don't have much time now either. I need to get this taken care of before the breakfast crowd turns up."

"Look, it's about Olivia."

With a sigh he pushed back from his desk and looked up at her. "Okay."

Kaitlyn glanced through the window into the dining room where Olivia sat at the counter coloring on a placemat and lowered her voice to just above a whisper. "I'm really worried about her. You should have seen her when we drove up and found Elizabeth. I didn't know who to deal with first. If Sarah hadn't practically followed us down the street, I don't know what I would have done."

"Yeah, that had to have been rough. So what do you think we should do?"

It did not escape Kaitlyn's notice that her brother had asked her opinion in a matter that concerned Olivia. That had not happened since Kaitlyn returned to Last Chance, and truthfully, not even Kaitlyn had expected him to.

"For one thing, I want to be with her after school. After I pick her up, we'll go by Elizabeth's to check on Sam, and then go on home. Not much happens here after three anyway." She smiled. "I can help her with her homework, and maybe we can even have dinner ready for you when you get home."

"Stop talking about me." Kaitlyn looked through the window to the dining room to find Olivia, crayon poised over the placemat she was drawing on, glaring at her.

"Sure, sounds like a good idea. Now, I really have to get to this." Chris shook his head as he returned to his computer. "Man, the acoustics in here are something else. No wonder everyone says there are no secrets in Last Chance."

Kaitlyn walked back into the dining room and sat on a stool next to Olivia. "Tell me about your picture."

Olivia didn't look up. "That's Sam and he has a lizard. And Miss Elizabeth is saying, 'Not in here, buster.' How do you spell *buster*?"

"B-u-s-t-e-r." Kaitlyn waited until Olivia had painstakingly printed each letter before giving her the next. "I know you overheard Uncle Chris and me talking. What do you think of our plan?"

"Okay, I guess. Just until Miss Elizabeth gets home from the hospital, though. I help her and read her stories and we crochet and cook stuff."

"We could do those things." Kaitlyn tried to keep her voice light. Truthfully, she had hoped for a little more enthusiasm on Olivia's part.

"Mom, do you even know how to crochet?" Olivia's patient sigh was way too grown-up for a seven-year-old.

"No, I guess I don't. Maybe you could teach me."

"Well, it's really hard." Olivia returned to her drawing.

"Okay, then we'll just have to do other things. But, Livvy, look at me." Kaitlyn waited until Olivia, with another heavy sigh, looked up. "Miss Elizabeth might be in the hospital quite a while. And even after that, it will probably take a long time for her to get strong again."

She had intended to begin to prepare Olivia for the real possibility that her after-school hours at Miss Elizabeth's were likely over, but at the stricken look that filled Olivia's face, she decided to let it go. "But we'll sure go see her as soon as she gets home." She swept Olivia into a hug, which her daughter endured for about three seconds before starting to struggle.

"Mom, you're going to make me mess up."

"All right." Kaitlyn ended the hug with a kiss on the top of Olivia's head, inhaling the sweet fragrance of her hair. "Draw your pictures. I'll give you about a fifteen-minute warning before we have to leave for school so you can finish the one you're working on then."

As she picked up Olivia's breakfast dishes to return to the

kitchen, Kaitlyn could hear Juanita discussing Elizabeth's fall with a table of breakfasters. Briefly, she considered asking Juanita to remember how upset Olivia was, but she gave that idea up. In the first place, Juanita would insist that she was practically whispering and no one but her intended audience could hear her anyway. And in the second place, this was Last Chance. Short of Kaitlyn taking Olivia home and keeping her there, there was no way Olivia was going to avoid hearing people talking about her beloved Miss Elizabeth's brush with eternity.

It was beginning to get light, but it was still quite a while before the sun would make it over the mountain peaks when Steven walked up the steps of the back porch and opened the kitchen door. Nancy Jo and Joe Jr. sat at the table cradling mugs of coffee in their hands, and from their expressions, they were deep in serious conversation.

His aunt smiled and moved to get up. "Wow. You did get here early. Need some breakfast?"

"Nope. Just a cup of coffee." Steven waved her back in her seat as he poured himself a cup and joined them. "Is there any news about Gran?"

"Not a whole lot." Joe Jr. leaned back in his chair. "Called up there a little while ago and she was still asleep."

"Just as soon as I get things under control here this morning, I'm going to stop by her place, gather up some of her things, and head on up to San Ramon." Nancy Jo got up and started clearing the dishes. "I want to talk to her doctors, and then I'm going to check on what kind of modifications we're going to have to make to the house here. You know, ramps and railings and such. We might as well get started on that."

"Why?" Joe Jr. leaned forward and planted his elbows on the table. "Don't you think we should at least see how she's going to be before we start redoing the whole house?"

"You know as well as I do that as old as your mom is, this is not going to be an easy row for her to hoe. She'll likely wind up using a walker, and even if she eventually gets down to just a cane, those steps outside are going to be just too much for her." Nancy Jo's voice softened a bit, and she rested her hand on her husband's shoulder. "I know seeing her this way is hard on you too. But we need to think about Mom. She's coming home, like she always said she would. And we need to make this house as easy for her to get around in as we can."

"I think you're both underestimating Gran."

Joe Jr. and Nancy Jo looked at Steven as if Speed Bump had piped up from her bed in the corner.

"Seriously." Steven looked from one startled face to the other. "This is Gran we're talking about. And she made it more than clear that she's not going anywhere but home. Her home. That needs to be where our plans start."

Nancy Jo finally broke the silence left by Steven's outburst. Her smile was kind. "I know. It's hard on all of us seeing our tough old Gran get feeble, but honey, that's just part of life. She's had a great life. She'd be the first to say so."

"And you talk like it's over." Steven could feel the heat spread through his chest and head for his ears. "Did you even hear Gran in the hospital last night? *Feeble* is the last word anyone would use to describe her, even with a broken leg. And if you think you're going to just run roughshod over what she says she wants, well, all I can say is good luck with that."

"All right, son." Uncle Joe Jr.'s voice left little doubt that Steven was skating on thin ice. "We all love Gran, and we appreciate your concern. Now, why don't you go on out and get started. I'll be out directly."

From the silence that followed his uncle's slow drawl, Steven knew that the conversation, at least any that would include him, was over. And from the set of Uncle Joe Jr.'s jaw, he knew that heading out to the barn would probably be a good plan. He got up and went for his sheepskin jacket and his hat. At the door, he took a deep breath and turned to face his aunt and uncle.

"Okay, do what you think you have to. But I'm going to get Gran's house ready for her."

"Steven." Aunt Nancy Jo sank down in her chair in exasperation. "There's just no point—"

"That's all right, Nancy Jo." From Uncle Joe Jr.'s expression, Steven knew he was still skating on thin ice, but he hadn't fallen through quite yet. "Don't see how it could do any harm. And what's done can be undone if we have to sell."

"But it's just a waste of money." Aunt Nancy Jo was clearly not ready to let this go.

Steven thought about reminding her that it was his money that would be wasted but decided that he had pushed Uncle Joe Jr. about as far as a man with any sense at all would push him. He put his hat on and let himself out onto the back porch. Through the kitchen window he could see that the conversation had resumed. And Aunt Nancy Jo was doing all the talking. He turned his collar up against the cold and jammed his hands in his pockets as he stepped off the porch. Speed Bump, who had been at his side since he left the table, followed close at his heel. The anger that had been burning in his chest flared again, and his hands, deep in his coat pockets, balled into fists. Dang! That was his grandmother they were making decisions for back there. His mom may have been just Uncle Joe Jr.'s baby sister, and his dad may have been a rodeo bum who never quite made it to the family's inner circle, but Elizabeth was *his* grandmother just as surely as she was Sarah's or any of his other cousins'. And he'd be blamed if he'd let anyone just brush him aside like some pesky fly.

14

Did Steven come get my pictures?" Olivia wasted no time when she threw her backpack into the backseat and climbed in after it.

"Yes, he did. Just as I was leaving." Kaitlyn waited for the seat belt click before joining the line of cars snaking out of the school parking lot. "I imagine he's almost to the hospital with them by now."

"Did you show him the one of Speed Bump and Sam making friends?"

"Honey, I didn't have time to do more than just hand him the pictures and run out the door. He'll see them when he shows them to Miss Elizabeth. Now, what do you say we go see how Sam's doing? I'll bet he could use some company."

Sam was sitting on the welcome mat when they stopped in front of Elizabeth's house, and he chirruped as he trotted down the walk toward them, tail held high.

"Sam! How did you get outside?" Olivia tried to carry him back to the house, hugging him around his rib cage, but his hind feet barely cleared the sidewalk, and he protested with a low moan.

"Put him down, Livvy. He's too big. He'll come with us."

Kaitlyn walked up the steps and tried the front door. It seemed strange to find it locked. From what she had heard, most people in Last Chance didn't even know where their house key was until they were going to leave for some extended period of time. Sarah, or someone, must have locked up when they let Sam out. She gave the door another little rattle.

"It's locked."

"I can see that, Livvy." Kaitlyn glanced at her watch. Sarah probably wouldn't be home for another hour. She supposed they could come back later, but getting Olivia to leave Sam alone and locked out, even for an hour, was probably going to involve some drama.

"Here." Olivia nudged her off the welcome mat and turned back the corner, exposing a key. She picked it up and handed it to her mother.

"Well, there you go." Kaitlyn fitted the key in the lock and opened the front door. "How did you know there was a key there?"

"I saw it when me and Miss Elizabeth were sweeping the porch." Sam led the way inside, but Olivia stopped just inside the front door. "It's cold in here and it's dark."

"I guess someone turned down the heat since no one's home." Kaitlyn turned on a lamp and headed for the kitchen. "Come on. I'll bet Sam's ready for his dinner."

"And it smells funny too." Olivia still stood in the middle of the living room. And she didn't look happy.

Kaitlyn sniffed. "I don't smell anything."

"Well, it doesn't usually smell like this."

"Sweetie, I know it's different. Miss Elizabeth isn't here." Kaitlyn began to wonder if bringing Olivia over was the good idea she thought it was. Far from finding comfort in the familiar surroundings, all Olivia could see was the dark, the cold, and the absence of her friend. "Come on. I'll bet Miss Elizabeth wouldn't mind if we had a cup of tea while Sam eats his dinner. I'll make the tea. You feed Sam."

A few minutes later as they sat at the table sipping tea and Sam was crouched over his food dish, tail wrapped around his body, they heard the front door open.

"Hello?" Nancy Jo appeared in the kitchen doorway. "I thought that was Chris's Jeep outside." Her smile was friendly, but she was clearly waiting for an explanation for their presence in Elizabeth's deserted house.

"We, um, just stopped by to look after Sam." Kaitlyn tried to shake the feeling that she had been caught doing something wrong. "We thought it would make Olivia feel a little better. Steven seemed to think it would be okay. Didn't he mention it?"

"Oh, Steven." Nancy Jo flapped an indifferent hand. "He probably meant to. He's just, well, Steven. But I think it sounds like a great plan. Sam could probably use the attention. He is one spoiled kitty."

"I hope it's okay that we made some tea. Elizabeth and Olivia always have a cup after school."

"Of course it's okay." Nancy Jo's warm smile put Kaitlyn at ease. "In fact, having someone spend a little time here every day is probably a good idea. And with everybody as busy as they are, it likely wouldn't happen without you, so come on in, have tea, play with the cat, and make yourself at home. I'm sure Mom will be glad to hear of it."

"How is she?"

"Oh, fine as we can expect, I guess. It's going to be a long road." She shook her head and settled her bag more firmly on her shoulder. "Well, I need to get home and start supper. I've been at the hospital all day. Just stopped by for the mail. Be sure to close up tight when you leave, okay?"

"Sure thing." Kaitlyn returned Nancy Jo's smile and a few seconds later heard the front door open and close. She was pretty sure that if anyone else had asked—Sarah, say, or maybe even Juanita—the hospital report would have been much more detailed. But the outsider got the quick-and-easy, thanks-for-asking version. Harder to understand, though, was Nancy Jo's dismissive attitude toward Steven. Kaitlyn somehow knew that Nancy Jo wouldn't have told him much either.

Olivia drained her teacup and went to sit on the floor by Sam, and Kaitlyn took another sip of her own tea as she watched her daughter stroke the big tabby while he ate. Everyone had told her that Steven was the black sheep of the Cooley family, but even if they hadn't, she would have known. She knew all the signs well. There was the cocky attitude, of course, and the your-rules-aren't-my-rules swagger. But beyond the bluster and even, in Steven's case, the charm, there were the eyes. And his eyes looked so lost.

"She asleep?" Chris looked up from the computer on his lap when Kaitlyn came back into the living room.

"Pretty close. I got the usual fuss about her early bedtime, but she settled down pretty quick." Kaitlyn settled into a corner of the sofa.

"Yeah, well, a 4:30 wake-up call will do that to you." He tossed the remote into her lap. "Watch what you like. I've got about an hour of work I have to finish."

"You know, Chris." Kaitlyn flipped idly through the channels. "If I stayed home in the mornings, Livvy wouldn't have to get up so early. I could come over after I dropped her off at school."

"How? You don't have a car." Chris didn't look up from his screen.

"Well, I could run you over to the Dip 'n' Dine real quick. I'd be back in maybe ten minutes."

"And leave Livvy alone?" This time Chris did look up, and from his expression, Kaitlyn realized she had failed another mom test.

"It would just be for a couple minutes . . ." Her voice trailed away. Parenting seemed to be filled with these pop quizzes. And how come Chris always seemed to have the right answer when she did not?

With a shake of his head, he went back to his computer, and Kaitlyn hit another button on the remote. On the screen, someone was solemnly being told they had not made the cut and would henceforth no longer be part of the group. She gave the remote another punch and settled into watching an old movie. Who needed to watch reality when you lived it?

Chris had just closed his computer and stretched when they heard the sound of a car crunching up the gravel drive.

"Who could that be? And why would anyone be coming by this late?" Chris checked his watch.

"Good grief, Chris, it's 8:30. Someone around here needs to get a life."

"Got one, Kait. It just starts way early in the morning." Chris got up and headed for the door.

Kaitlyn hadn't even realized she had been thinking about Steven, but seeing him on the porch gave her a little start, almost as if she had conjured him up.

"Hey." Steven took off his hat as he stepped inside. "I'm on the way back to the ranch and took a chance Livvy might still be up. I have something for her."

"She's been out for over an hour; we go to roost pretty early around here. But we'd be happy to pass something along for you." Chris's smile may have softened his message a bit, but Kaitlyn noticed he didn't ask Steven to sit down either.

"Oh, it's no big deal." Steven put his hat back on and grinned. "I just took some pictures of Gran looking at her drawings. I can show her some other time."

"She will love that. Can I see?" Kaitlyn held out her hand for the phone Steven held.

Chris had not budged from his spot near the front door, still hinting he would be glad to show Steven out. Kaitlyn could have slugged him.

"Are you hungry? I know you can't have eaten at the hospital." Kaitlyn ignored Chris, but Steven clearly caught the incredulous look he directed her way.

"I'm good. I'll just grab something out of the refrigerator when I get back to the ranch. You guys need to get to bed."

"Don't be silly." Kaitlyn got off the couch and motioned him to follow her into the kitchen. "I'll heat you up some spaghetti. I did the cooking tonight, so don't expect much."

Steven stood where he was, looking from brother to sister. Kaitlyn smiled. "Come on."

Chris gave up. "I've got to get to bed. Do what you want, but remember that alarm's going off awfully early." With a wave at Steven, he ambled down the hall to his room.

Steven still hadn't moved. "Really, I guess it is later than I thought. I should head on back."

"Don't mind Chris. He's really old." Kaitlyn raised her voice to make sure Chris could hear her before turning back to Steven with a grin. "I give him a hard time, but as brothers go, he's not too bad. Just really, really conscientious."

"Sounds like my brother Ray." Steven followed her into the kitchen and dropped into the chair she indicated at the kitchen table. "On the one hand, I've looked up to him and admired him all my life, but on the other, I knew there was no way I was ever going to measure up, so why try?"

"We don't have the same brother, do we?" Kaitlyn put a saucepan on the stove and reached into the refrigerator for the leftover spaghetti.

"I hope not." There was that dimple again. "I haven't exactly thought of you as a sister."

"Maybe you better not think of me at all." Kaitlyn put the leftovers on to heat and turned to face Steven. "Or maybe just as a waitress at the Dip 'n' Dine, or Olivia's mom, or something. I'm trying to avoid complications right now, not find new ones."

"Hey, I'm not complicated. Ask anyone." Steven didn't seem ready to give up, but that smile didn't seem as assured as Kaitlyn had seen it.

She turned back to the stove and didn't speak again until she had put the dish of spaghetti in front of him and taken the chair across from him.

"Steven? Do you ever get tired of it?"

"Tired of what?" Steven's fork stopped midway to his mouth. "Tired of trying to get to know someone better? It's not like I hide in the bushes waiting to leap out at every woman who passes by, you know."

Kaitlyn almost smiled. "No. That's not what I was asking. I imagine you'll be hitting on the nurses when you're in the home. I meant, do you mind being the screwup?" She stopped when she saw all the teasing animation drain from his face. "I phrased that wrong. I mean, do you get tired of people just expecting it from you, of never even noticing when you're doing it right because they're still remembering the last time you messed up, or waiting for the next time?"

Steven still hadn't said anything, and Kaitlyn felt tears sting her eyes. She blinked them away and cleared her throat. "I'm sorry. I'm making a lot of assumptions here that I have no right to make. Forgive me . . . and eat your spaghetti. I'll even get you a glass of milk to wash it down. Chris, as you know, is the cook in the family. I'm just . . . well, we already covered my place in the family."

"Yeah, you're right." Steven finally spoke, and Kaitlyn stopped in midpour.

"Right about what? My role as family disaster, or how bad the spaghetti is?" Since she was the one who brought it up, Kaitlyn knew she didn't have the right to be offended, but that didn't change the fact that she was.

"Neither." Steven's grin was back. "The spaghetti is outstanding, by the way. I'd eat it any day. No, I meant you're right about me being sick and tired of everyone just assuming I'm about one step away from planting my boot in another cow pie. Sometimes I think it would just be easier on us all if I just gave them what they expect."

"Well, that would solve everything, wouldn't it? And what's stopping you from that astoundingly mature course of action?"

"Gran, I guess." Steven looked up at Kaitlyn. "She's the one who never stopped believing I was better than I was. Actually, that's not quite right. She knew me exactly as I was but never stopped believing I had it in me to be a better person than I was letting on. I finally got tired of disappointing her."

"Is she going to be okay?"

"I think so. I hope so. I can't imagine a world without Gran in it."

"Let me see the pictures." Kaitlyn held out her hand for his phone. She smiled as she scrolled through them. "Olivia will love these. Your grandmother looks just like herself. You'd never dream she went through what she did yesterday."

"Well, I tried to keep as much of the hospital stuff out of the pictures as I could. The point was to cheer Livvy up, not upset her more. And, of course, Gran wouldn't let me anywhere near her with a camera until she'd fixed her hair and put on lipstick."

"Sounds like her." Kaitlyn handed the phone back. "Thanks for doing this. It will mean a lot to Livvy."

"Glad to do it, and thanks for the dinner too." Steven pushed back from the table and grinned at Kaitlyn. "Now, I should get going and let you get to bed. I understand you all get up real early around here."

Kaitlyn rolled her eyes. "Oh, Chris. He means well, but he still thinks I'm Livvy's age."

Steven laughed as he got to his feet and shoved his phone back in his pocket before heading through the living room, picking up his hat on the way. "Well, I need to be getting on home, anyway. We start things pretty early at the ranch too. Sorry I missed Livvy, though. I know Gran wanted her to see how pleased she was with the pictures."

"I'm sure we'll find a time. If not before, you'll see her at basketball practice Thursday." Kaitlyn stopped at the door and smiled up at him. As tall as she was, there weren't many men, outside of Chris, who she looked up at. And truthfully? It was kind of nice.

"Hey, why don't I send them to you, and you can show them to her?" He pulled out his phone again. "What's your number?"

"Okay, it's 5—" She stopped. "Are you just trying to get my number?"

"A little full of ourselves, aren't we?" Steven raised an eyebrow. "I just want to send you some pictures to comfort your child, and you make it all about you."

Kaitlyn gave him a look. He may have intended to look disapproving, but the smile he was trying so unsuccessfully to hide gave him away.

"You think you are one smooth dude, don't you?" But she gave him her number.

"Got it." He winked as he shoved his phone back into his pocket and opened the front door. And just before he jammed his hat back on his head and shut the door behind him, he bent down and left the lightest of kisses on her lips.

Kaitlyn listened to his steps cross the porch and crunch across the gravel, too surprised—and face it, unsettled—to do more than stand there. When was the last time she had been caught off guard like that? And who did he think he was anyway? Had she not made it clear—every time they had met, in fact—that she was not interested?

She drew a deep breath and flipped off the porch light. It was late, as Chris had been pointing out for the last hour. And morning would come early. He had mentioned that too. She checked on Olivia one last time, drawing the kicked-off covers over her sleeping daughter, and floated through the house switching off lights, turning down the thermostat, and doing all the little late-night tasks that prepared the house for the night. Finally, she slipped into her coat and ran around to her own little trailer in the back. And through it all, she could still feel Steven's kiss, as light as it was, like a whisper on her lips.

Steven had second thoughts about the kiss almost as soon as he heard the latch click, and if he had thought about it for two seconds before he did it, he might not have kissed her at all. If it had been anyone else, he probably would have planned things a little better. But with Kaitlyn, he always seemed to be acting before he thought, and with disastrous results, he had noticed.

"You need to get a grip, Braden." He started the truck and headed for the road. "Either start being a little more cool or move on, because you are making no headway with this woman at all. In fact, every time you are with her, you wind up worse off than you were before."

He turned onto the highway. Way ahead down the road, he could see the taillights of what was probably an eighteen-wheeler. Other than that, he was the only one on the road. Maybe moving on was the best idea. Last Chance really wasn't his kind of place. Never had been. He and Kaitlyn had joked about Chris thinking 8:30 was late, but he sure wasn't the only one. Everyone in Last Chance seemed to roll up their sidewalks at sundown. Everyone but Gran.

Steven smiled to himself as he thought of his grandmother. She was a real night owl, crocheting and watching endless reruns of *Perry Mason* way into the night. And she was in the hospital. And when she left there, it would be to go back to the ranch, whether she wanted to or not. Well, that wasn't going to happen. Gran had never stopped fighting for him, and now it was his turn. He'd see to it that she went back to her own home, or die trying. And then—then he'd move on.

15

"Well, we got some good news and some not so good news this morning." Aunt Nancy Jo already had lunch on the table when Steven and Joe Jr. came in at noon. "The good news is that Mom is doing really well. I talked to her this morning, and while we were on the phone, her doctor came in, so I got to talk to him too. He says Mom's not going to need surgery after all, and she'll be ready to leave the hospital for the convalescent home in a few days. He said if she were younger, she might even already be home by now, but since she's so old, they need to be extra careful so she doesn't fall and break something else. I have to tell you, when he said that, I'd have given anything to see Mom's face. And I would love to have been a mouse in the corner when we hung up. You can bet she had something to say about him talking about how old she was."

"And the bad news?" Years of experience had enabled Joe Jr. to sift through his wife's ramblings for the nuggets that interested him while ignoring the rest.

"Oh. It's not that it's bad news. In fact, it's really good news in the long run, I guess."

"Nancy Jo, get to the point." Joe Jr.'s patience did have a limit.

"Well, I talked to Lainie this morning too. She and Ray are coming back to Last Chance."

"And that's bad news? How?" Steven must have sounded a little defensive, because his uncle's hooded gaze rested on him for a long moment before he returned his attention to his lunch.

"It's not their coming that has me so put out; you know how tickled I am at the thought of Lainie and Ray living right here in Last Chance. It's *why* they're coming." Nancy Jo looked from one to the other, clearly waiting for the predictable question. When neither her husband nor Steven seemed inclined to ask it, she answered it anyway. "They want to move in with Mom when she comes home and take care of her. At her house."

"Well, since Gran wants to live in her own house, and you said she needs someone with her all the time, I still don't see the problem." Steven's defense of Ray was automatic. No one, not even his aunt, could so much as hint criticism of his brother and get away with it. Truthfully, though? Steven felt a familiar knot of frustration settle in his gut. He had wanted to make sure his grandmother got what she wanted, and was ready to take on the entire Cooley clan, in fact, if he had to. And then here came Ray on his white charger to save the day while his hopeless younger brother stood by and watched. Of course.

"The problem, Steven, is that Gran needs to be here where I can look after her." Aunt Nancy Jo sat back and planted her fists on her hips. "I know Ray means well, but he and that sweet wife of his need to worry about their own lives. They're practically newlyweds, for Pete's sake. The last thing they need to do is pull up stakes again and come back here to take care of an old woman."

"You're talking about Gran?" Steven's voice was as cold and expressionless as stone.

"Of course I'm talking about Gran." His aunt puffed her exasperation. "I know you love her; we all do. But that doesn't change the fact that she's staring ninety in the face and has just suffered an accident that will likely leave her needing someone looking after her every day for the rest of her life. And I might as well just say it. I think Ray has more than earned the right to think of his own plans for a while."

And there it was. The never mentioned but always just under the surface charge that Steven had allowed his brother to give up years of his life to keep that bar open for him while Steven was away in the service, only to have him walk away from it when he got home.

He pushed away from the table. "You know, I'm not real hungry. And since I'm going into San Ramon this afternoon to see about getting Gran's house fitted out for her, I'd better finish what I started out there."

"Steven, hang on there a minute." Steven had just picked up his hat and reached for the door when his uncle's voice stopped him. "I'll have a word with you on the porch before you head out."

Jamming his hat on his head and giving the brim an extra tug over his eyes, Steven stepped out on the porch to wait for his uncle. Joe Jr. never raised his voice or quickened his step, but on the ranch, and even in town, all he had to do was clear his throat and everyone stopped to see what he had to say.

His uncle wasn't wearing either his hat or his jacket when he joined Steven on the porch, and if he even noticed the blast of winter wind that had Steven hunched into his own sheepskin jacket, he gave no indication of it.

"Listen, son." Joe Jr. had to look up to meet Steven's eyes, but Steven didn't feel he had the advantage. At all. "I know that after your mother passed, Gran all but raised you, so I'm going to cut you a little more slack than you probably have coming to you, but we need to get some things straight." He looked out toward the mountains, and Steven followed his gaze. "See that? As far as you can see, that's Cooley land. Including my grandchildren, six generations of Cooleys have lived on it. It belongs to all of us, including you. But see that?" He jerked a thumb over his shoulder. "That house belongs to one person only, and she's in there cleaning up a lunch you wouldn't eat. And anyone who walks through that door is going to show her the respect she deserves. Are we clear on that?"

"Yes, sir." What else could he say?

"Good." Joe Jr. reached for the door. "Then before you sit at her table again, she'll have your apology, right?"

"Yes, sir." Steven's teeth were gritted, but he got the words said, and that seemed to be all that his uncle was looking for.

"I'll tell her she can look for it." He gave Steven another long look before letting himself back into the house.

Steven took a few deep breaths to calm the rage burning in his chest before shoving his hands deep in his jacket pockets and stepping off the porch. Speed Bump, who had slipped out when Joe Jr. went in, trotted at his side as he headed for the barn.

This, *this* was why he left Last Chance in the first place. This was why he was in no hurry to come back, and this was why that highway was taking him out of here the minute he could manage it. He was sorry he had let his temper show when Aunt Nancy Jo had alluded to Ray's sacrifice on his behalf. And he was sorry Ray put his own life on hold to run the High Lonesome Saloon for him. But, dang it, he hadn't asked for that. He hadn't even been consulted. First he heard of it was at Dad's funeral when Ray told him it had been their father's dying wish that the bar would be waiting for Steven when he got out of the service.

"I told him then not to do it." Steven stopped and looked down at the dog at his feet. Speed Bump gazed up at him with solemn attentiveness. "I told him he should just stick to his painting, but he said all Dad could talk about before he got real bad was how he and I had planned to run the bar together someday, and he was doing it for Dad. Never mind that I was fourteen when we made those plans."

He paused, almost expecting the little dog to say something. Speed Bump remained silent, but she did look concerned. "And here I am, trying to carry on a conversation with a dog. At least you listen, don't you, Speed Bump?"

Steven clamped his hat to his head as a gust of wind tried to lift it, and he picked up his pace as he headed to the barn. Speed Bump had to move from a trot to a lope, but she never left his side.

—∾—

"Chris, I was thinking." Kaitlyn shouldered her way into the kitchen carrying a bin of dirty dishes. "Do you think it would be all right if I took off early this afternoon and ran up to San Ramon to visit Elizabeth before I pick Olivia up? She was in such bad shape the last time I saw her. I'd just like to see for myself that she's doing okay."

Her brother pushed back from his computer and looked up. "Yeah, I guess so. It's pretty quiet today. You might want to run the idea past Juanita, though, since she's here by herself now when you have Olivia in the afternoons."

Kaitlyn sighed and looked back through the window into the dining room. Juanita was standing at one of the three occupied tables talking to the diners sitting there. This was not going to go well. She just knew it. Juanita didn't say much anymore when

Kaitlyn left to take Olivia to school or to pick her up, but her pinched mouth and huffy sighs said all she needed to say. Kaitlyn could never quite understand how Juanita managed to convey her annoyance at both Kaitlyn's presence in and absence from the Dip 'n' Dine, but it was pretty clear that Kaitlyn got on her last nerve just by breathing the same air Juanita did.

"Um, Juanita, do you have a minute?" Kaitlyn intercepted Juanita at the coffee machine.

Juanita barely glanced at her as she began making another pot of coffee. Her brisk movements conveyed the clear message that unlike some people, she had more pressing things to do than stand around chatting. "What is it?"

Kaitlyn let her gaze fall on the table where Juanita had spent the last few minutes visiting with the customers while she gathered her courage. Taking a deep breath, she plunged in. "I'd like to leave early this afternoon and run up to San Ramon to see Elizabeth before I pick Livvy up. It's really the only time I can go, and I've been so worried about her. Chris said since you were the one picking up the extra slack, I should check with you."

There. She hated the fact that she sounded like a five-year-old asking if she could go out to play, but when you got down to it, a lot of her conversations with Juanita seemed to take that tone.

"Oh, for Pete's sake, Kaitlyn." Juanita probably thought she was keeping her voice low, but even the diners in the furthest booth looked over to see what was wrong. "It's not that I can't manage without you. Chris and I did just fine before you got here. But you're treating this more like a hobby than a job. Do you work here or don't you?"

Kaitlyn bit back the answer that flew to her lips. Juanita wasn't really looking for a response, and that was probably a good thing.

Because truthfully, if Kaitlyn allowed herself to say what she thought, who knows where it might end? Not with a visit with Elizabeth, she was pretty sure about that.

After a second or two, Juanita snatched up a full coffeepot and turned back to the dining room. "Oh, go ahead. Give her a hug from me and tell her that Russ and I will be up to see her sometime soon." She paused for emphasis. "*After* work."

Kaitlyn took a few deep breaths, trying to calm down enough to wait on customers, but gave up and slammed into the kitchen.

Chris stopped her with a raised hand as she opened her mouth. "I heard. Everybody heard. Just grab your coat and go. I'll talk to Juanita after we close."

"But—"

"Here." He tossed her the keys to his Jeep. "I'll give you a call when I need you to come get me."

Kaitlyn still had so much to say, but when she tried, Chris stopped her again.

"Just let it go for now. Wait here. I'll go get your coat and you can leave by the back door. The customers have had enough entertainment for one day."

Kaitlyn watched him move through the dining room on his way to the storage room where they left their things. He seemed so relaxed and easy as he stopped to exchange a few words with this table or that. Even Juanita seemed in better spirits as she shared a joke with some friends of hers at a window booth. The diner was the perfect picture of a friendly, hometown eating establishment. The only piece that didn't fit was her.

"Am I the cause of all the drama around here, or am I just imagining it?" Kaitlyn turned to Carlos who was ladling green chile sauce over a plate of chile rellenos.

"Nope, it's pretty much all about you." Carlos deftly wiped the edge of the plate and set it on the shelf.

This was not the response Kaitlyn was expecting. "Hey, you're supposed to be my friend."

"I am your friend, *chica*." He reached for another plate. "Look, I've lived here in Last Chance all my life, so I've never been the outsider, but I've seen a few trying to make their way here. And they wind up falling into one of three groups. They make the effort to fit in, or they stay an outsider, or they leave. Come to think of it, there's only two groups—those that make an effort and those who leave. It wasn't easy for your brother when he first got here, but he's part of Last Chance now. So what are you going to do?"

Kaitlyn swallowed. She had gone to Carlos for some sympathy, not a lecture. "I guess I don't know."

He shrugged and went back to his stove. "Well, it's up to you, but I don't think you'll find folks more willing to meet you halfway than the folks here in Last Chance."

"Here's your stuff." Chris came back through the kitchen door. "And don't worry about anything. Just enjoy your afternoon and we'll talk when I get home."

Kaitlyn could still smell the spicy aroma of chile and corn when she let herself out the back door, but the sights and sounds of the Dip 'n' Dine were replaced by the gold and gray and distant blue of the desert. A sudden gust of wind caught her as she walked around the building to the parking lot in front, causing her to pull her coat closer around her. Carlos made a good point, even if she couldn't agree that she was the source of all the drama. But leaving Juanita aside, what was she going to do? If it were just her, it would be a no-brainer. Last Chance would be so far behind her she'd never be able to find it again. But it wasn't just her. There was Olivia. And for the first time in her young life, Olivia seemed at peace, and at home, and happy.

Kaitlyn shook her head as she buckled herself into the front seat of the Jeep. Funny how just a few months ago, thinking about Olivia safe and happy in Last Chance had cleared her conscience to stay away. Now it was the only thing that kept her anchored to this forsaken place.

—✻—

Elizabeth looked up when Kaitlyn tapped lightly at her door, and the pain lines between her eyes and around her mouth disappeared into a warm smile.

"Well, look who's here!" She switched off the TV with a punch at her remote. "Come in here and sit down."

"It's so nice to see you looking so well." Kaitlyn bent over to kiss her cheek. "You sure had us worried."

"Well, I am just so sorry I caused such a fuss. I never will get over getting all tangled up and falling down my own front steps. And then that ambulance! I suppose everybody in town heard it. And now they all have something new to talk about, I guess."

Kaitlyn smiled. "Well, everyone's worried about you, that's for sure. How are you feeling?"

"I have felt better. I'll be honest about that. This leg hurts like the very dickens. They keep trying to push painkillers on me, but I have no intention of becoming a drug addict at this stage of the game."

"Elizabeth, you are the least likely person I've ever met to become an addict. Just take them as they're prescribed and you'll be fine. And your leg will feel better too."

"Maybe." Elizabeth brushed the subject away with her hand

like it was a pesky fly. "Now tell me about that precious daughter of yours. Oh, how I miss Livvy. Did Steven tell her how much I love her drawings? You can see how they've brightened up the room."

"Well, I brought you some more. And your crocheting—that was Livvy's idea too. And I brought some pictures to show you of her taking care of Sam and sitting in your recliner crocheting. I hope you don't mind that we go over there for a little while every afternoon to take care of Sam. It makes her feel a little better."

"Honey, that pleases me to no end. The first thing I thought of when I could finally do some thinking was that Sam was home wondering where I was. Let me see those pictures." She held out her hand for the phone Kaitlyn had dug out of her purse.

Kaitlyn smiled as she watched her scroll through the photos. Elizabeth saw no reason to own her own cell phone, but this clearly wasn't the first one she had held. "You know, I'm going to have to take some more of you to show Livvy. She'll be waiting."

Elizabeth's delighted smile faded as she handed the phone back. "Oh, no, darlin'. I am such a mess. My hair is as straight and flat in the back as a tile and I don't have a speck of makeup on. A picture would just scare that poor child to death."

"Just seeing you smile into the camera would be enough for Livvy, but as a woman, I know how you feel. Do you have any makeup here?"

"Just a lipstick that Nancy Jo brought me. She doesn't worry much about makeup herself and didn't think to bring much when she brought me my things."

"Well, let me run down to the gift shop and see what they have there. I'll give you a little makeover. It'll make you feel better." Kaitlyn picked up her purse and stood up.

"Oh, honey, don't . . ." Clearly, Elizabeth was used to being the servant, not the served, and her protest was almost automatic, but right in the middle, she stopped and smiled. "You know, I would just love that. They tell me I had a close call, but every time I look in the mirror, I think I didn't make it after all."

16

Elizabeth held the hand mirror and looked into it as Kaitlyn picked up the brush and began pulling it through the white hair with long strokes. "You know, I feel like I should go dancing. I just look like a movie star. You are so gifted."

"It's what I do, remember?" Kaitlyn smiled and continued brushing. "Or, it's what I used to do. Now I serve green chile stew and pour iced tea."

Elizabeth's eyes, which had been drifting shut, opened again and she adjusted her mirror so she could meet Kaitlyn's eyes. "And is all that serving and pouring what you like doing?"

Kaitlyn made a face without answering.

"Then why do you do it?" Elizabeth let the mirror drop to her lap and closed her eyes as Kaitlyn put the brush down and began massaging her scalp with her fingertips.

"Because it's a job. And I don't really have a lot of options." Kaitlyn gently kneaded the muscles of Elizabeth's neck and shoulders. "There, does that feel good?"

"Kaitlyn." Elizabeth reached up for Kaitlyn's hand and pulled her around so she could look in her face. "I know that when you're as young as you are, you look at an old woman like me and think you have a hundred long years stretching out to try every last thing you want to do. But let me tell you, when you look at life from my view, you are just astounded at how fast it all went by, and at the number of things you always thought you'd do that are never going to get done. So promise me this." She gave Kaitlyn's hand a little shake. "Promise me you'll never again say you don't have any options. Because you do. No matter what you think now, life is just way too short to waste a minute of it."

Kaitlyn dropped her gaze from Elizabeth's piercing blue eyes to the freckled, blue-veined hand grasping hers. It was hard to imagine Elizabeth having regrets; she always seemed so content and at peace.

"I'm talking to you, Miss Kaitlyn." Elizabeth gave her hand another little shake. "Are you going to promise me?"

Kaitlyn took in a breath and let it go with a long, slow sigh. "Yes, I'll promise."

"That's what I want to hear. And when you go to thinking about all those options that you do have, the best place to start is by asking the Lord what he has in store for you. Because believe me, darlin', he has something wonderful planned for you. I know that as sure as I'm sitting here. You just watch for it."

"Watch for what? If it's me, here I am." Steven grinned as he appeared in the doorway. He gave a low whistle when Elizabeth turned her smile on him. "Hey, beautiful."

"It is most certainly not you, Steven Braden, but you can come give me a kiss anyway." Elizabeth held her arms out to her grandson. "I'm so glad to see you, honey."

"So if it's not me, what are you watching for?" Steven bent to kiss his grandmother's cheek and stood to look from her to Kaitlyn.

"What I need to be watching is the time." Kaitlyn looked at her watch. "I have to be back in Last Chance by 3:00 to pick Livvy up. I should go."

"Oh, you don't have to go yet, do you?" Elizabeth took her hand again. "You have lots of time. Sit down a minute. Steven, grab that chair over there and pull it up so you can sit down too. Now, tell me all the news."

"Well, I guess the big news is that Lainie and Ray are coming back." Steven set the beige vinyl chair next to Elizabeth's bed and plopped down in it.

"You don't mean it. To stay?" Elizabeth's eyes sparkled.

"It looks that way. And there's more. Unless you want to move back to the ranch, they want to stay with you."

"Of course I'm not moving back to the ranch. Not yet, anyway. I thought I set your Uncle Joe Jr. and your Aunt Nancy Jo straight on that. But that doesn't mean I need a babysitter if I stay in town, you know. I'm perfectly capable of taking care of myself."

"I'm sure you are." Steven managed to exchange a glance with Kaitlyn without Elizabeth noticing. "And it will be even easier after I get that ramp to the porch built and the grab bars put in your bathroom. I'm starting on that today. But Lainie and Ray have to live somewhere, and I think Lainie kind of thinks of your place as home. But I can tell them it's not convenient if you want me to."

"You'll do no such thing. Of course they're going to stay with me. Where else are they going to go? Do they know I'm not going to be home for a while? They're fixing to send me off to some convalescent home for who knows how long."

"They know, and it will give them some time to close things up in Santa Fe and get moved."

"Lainie and Ray back in Last Chance." Elizabeth sat back against her pillow and beamed. "That's just more than I could have hoped for. The Lord is so good."

"You know Ray and Lainie, right? Didn't you meet them when they were here at Christmas?" Steven looked across the bed at Kaitlyn.

She nodded. "Yeah, I really liked them too. Especially Lainie. I'm glad they're coming back."

As far as Kaitlyn knew, Lainie Braden was the only woman she had met since she got to Last Chance with a past as patchy as her own. And everyone knew her story, and everyone loved her. Kaitlyn had even heard Juanita speak fondly of Lainie. Maybe she could get Lainie to share her secret.

"I really do have to go." Kaitlyn picked up her purse and stood up. "I have barely enough time to get to school to get Olivia now. And if there's any traffic, I'll be late."

"Oh, honey, you're not in the big city now. There won't be any traffic." Elizabeth reached for her hand again. "You'll be fine. And just because Ray and Lainie will be with me does not mean that Olivia is not to come to me after school every day, you hear? And you tell her that for me."

Kaitlyn smiled. "Well, maybe you can do that when you come home."

Truthfully, she had doubts that Elizabeth would be able to continue with Olivia, but there was no point in going into that now, just as there was no point in letting Olivia get her hopes up.

"I do need to get some pictures before I go, though." Kaitlyn dug for her phone. "Livvy's going to be mad enough that I got to come see you and she can't."

She took photos of Elizabeth smiling as she crocheted, smiling as she blew kisses, and glaring sideways in startled irritation as Steven threw his arm around her and leaned into the shot at the last instant.

"Steven, what in this world are you doing?" Elizabeth slapped at his shoulder. "You scared the life out of me."

He laughed and gave her a squeeze before standing up again. "Sorry, Gran. I thought you might like a picture of the two of us."

"Not with me sitting in a hospital bed, I don't." Elizabeth still looked miffed. "Those pictures were for Livvy only."

"Don't worry. It's already deleted." Kaitlyn settled her bag on her shoulder and blew a kiss from the doorway. "Bye, now. I'm really going this time."

"Wait. I'll walk you to the elevator." Steven caught up with her just outside Elizabeth's door and fell in beside her. "Did you fix Gran up like that? She really looks nice."

Kaitlyn nodded. "A little blush and mascara can go a long way toward making someone feel more like herself. And then her personality did the rest."

"Well, whatever you did, it worked. She really looks happy. Thanks for being so nice to my grandmother."

"My pleasure. And I mean that." They stopped in front of the elevator and the Down button glowed yellow when Kaitlyn pushed it. "She has been so good to Livvy, and Chris, and even me from the day any of us got to Last Chance. I'd do anything for her."

"Then how about going out with her favorite grandson?" Steven leaned against the wall and flashed his dimple.

"What? Where did that come from? No. Just no. We've gone over all this before. No."

The elevator arrived and Kaitlyn stepped inside. As the doors slid shut, Steven stood in the corridor with his hands shoved deep in his pockets, grinning at her. Just before he disappeared from view and the elevator began its descent, he gave her a long, slow wink.

Kaitlyn shook her head in disbelief. Who goes from showing such tender concern for their grandmother to hitting on someone without taking a breath? The question answered itself, of course. Steven. She found herself almost smiling as the elevator opened again and she walked through the lobby toward the parking lot. He really was as much of a mess as everyone warned her he was, no doubt about that. But there was another side she kept seeing as well. She had heard about him taking on his aunt and uncle to keep Elizabeth in her own home. And he had thought to take pictures of Elizabeth to show Olivia she was going to be all right. And then there was that ridiculous little white dog he had rescued and took with him everywhere. The teasing she had seen him take over the boot-sized dog didn't seem to faze him a bit. He'd just pull his hat a little lower over his eyes and say, "Careful now, you don't want to get her riled."

She giggled at the image as she walked across the hospital porch, causing a couple heading inside with a vase of flowers and a balloon to look at her with mild alarm. She smiled, wished them a good day, squared her shoulders, and headed out across the parking lot.

She was still smiling when she reached the Jeep and climbed in. And her good mood went beyond Steven and his foolishness. Truthfully, she had forgotten what fun it was to see someone's eyes light up when she handed them a mirror to view her handiwork. In the exclusive salons where Kaitlyn had worked in Scottsdale, the clients were much more likely to scowl slightly and demand this little change or that before they finally nodded their approval and left. Not since cosmetology school when she would go to the nursing home to do hair had she seen such appreciation. Okay, to be honest, when she gave Juanita her perm, Juanita had been delighted and had even bragged about her in the Dip 'n' Dine. Too bad that hadn't lasted.

She pulled out onto the highway and headed for Last Chance. Maybe that was the whole problem, though. Maybe she was a great hairdresser but a lousy waitress. She'd have to think about that. In fact, she had a lot of things to think about now. The image of Steven standing in the doorway of the elevator giving her that long wink came unbidden to her mind, and she smiled. He was *so* cocky. But she was beginning to suspect that there was more to Steven than attitude. And maybe it was time to find out just what that was.

Steven checked the measurements on the scrap of paper he had pulled from his pocket as he wandered down aisles stacked high with four-by-fours and sheets of pressure-treated plywood at the building supply store. Building the ramp for Gran's front steps was going to be a little more complicated than he had thought, but it was still doable. Carpentry was nothing new. He had handled a hammer since he was old enough to lift one and had spent a summer before he was even out of high school helping his brother build the cabin that now served as Ray's local studio.

Nope, building Gran's ramp wasn't the problem. And now that they had told him Gran was going to get better and he had seen for himself that she was as unsinkable as ever, Gran wasn't even the problem. The problem was Kaitlyn Reed, and coming to grips with the inescapable fact that she was just not into him. And furthermore, she showed no signs whatsoever that she could ever be into him.

It wasn't that he hadn't tried. He had, in fact, pulled out every surefire, never-fail, hundred-percent-guaranteed play in the playbook, and not only was every last pass incomplete, it didn't even bounce. It just landed with a thud and laid there on the field like a brick. Finally today, when the elevator closed on her looking at him like he was a lunatic, he heard the final whistle blow. It was over.

And that was really too bad. Because somewhere along the line, it had stopped being a game. He had begun to look for excuses to run into Kaitlyn, to talk to her, to try to make her laugh. He had even found himself wondering what a life with Kaitlyn and Olivia might be like. And he had never gone there before.

"Earth to Steven. Hello?"

It took a minute to realize someone was talking to him, but eventually he noticed the laughing brunette standing right in front of him.

"Hey, Jen. Sorry. I was a little distracted here. How are you?"

She laughed again and tipped her head to look up at him. "I'll say you were distracted. I called your name three times. What are you building? A hideout? You look so grim."

"Nah, just a wheelchair ramp for my grandmother. I was concentrating, I guess. Sorry." He blew out a breath and smiled. *Shake it off, Braden.*

"So . . . you never called." She peeked up at him through her lashes. "Lose my number?"

"Oh, wow, yeah, I guess I must have. Sorry." He grinned and tipped his hat back with one finger. "How many 'sorrys' does that make? Three?"

"Well, you should be sorry." Jen looked adorable when she pouted, and Steven knew she knew that. "I think you need to make it up to me, don't you?"

"I guess I do, at that." Steven shoved the paper with his notes in his back pocket. The ramp could wait. "What do you have in mind?"

"Well, first you can come home with me and put up these new towel racks I'm buying. And then you can take me out to eat."

"I think I can do that."

"And then you have to promise to come with me to a party on Saturday."

"Saturday too, huh? I really did get myself in trouble by losing that phone number, didn't I?"

"You have no idea." There was that pout again. "And I'm not sure that your coming with me Saturday will get you completely off the hook either."

"Well, all I can do is try." He draped his arm around her shoulder as they walked to the front of the store to pay for her towel racks. He and Jen had been good friends in high school, though they had never gone out. Maybe it was time to change that.

The line in front of the school was down to the last few cars when Kaitlyn took her place at the end. Ahead, she could see Olivia with her pink backpack waiting for her.

"I thought you were going to be late." Olivia threw her backpack ahead of her and climbed in the backseat.

"Nope. I'm right on time." Kaitlyn waited for the seat belt click before pulling away from the curb.

"But you were almost late."

"There's no such thing as 'almost late.' You're either late or on time, and I, my dear, was on time." Kaitlyn glanced at Olivia in the rearview mirror. Her daughter seemed content to let the topic drop and gazed out the side window humming to herself.

When Chris had turned the afternoon pickup over to Kaitlyn shortly after she arrived in Last Chance, Olivia's distress had been loud and unrelenting. And truthfully? Kaitlyn didn't blame her then. Why would Olivia think her mother would be there for her? Kaitlyn didn't even believe it herself. Finally, Chris had dropped to one knee so he could look in Olivia's face and told her she could count on it. Her mother would be there every day when she came out those front doors.

And she had been, watching the frantic expression Olivia wore as she searched the line of cars turn to one of almost palpable relief as she spotted the Jeep waiting by the curb. Today was the first time Olivia had to wait a few minutes, but it looked like she was finally ready to believe her mom wouldn't let her down. Kaitlyn felt like singing. It had been a good day—after she left the Dip 'n' Dine, that is.

"I saw Elizabeth today." Kaitlyn turned onto Elizabeth's street.

"When's she coming home?" Olivia was only interested in one aspect of Elizabeth's hospital stay.

"Oh, honey, it's going to be a while. After she leaves the hospital, she has to go to another place where they'll help her learn to walk with a broken leg so she won't fall again."

"But that will take too long." This was clearly not the news Olivia was looking for.

"I know. But the good news is that you can visit the new place, and she'll be there in a few days. We'll go after school." Kaitlyn brought the Jeep to a stop in front of Elizabeth's house.

"Every day? And take Sam too?"

Kaitlyn laughed as she and Olivia got out of the Jeep and joined Sam, who was waiting on the sidewalk. "You are something else, kiddo. But no, we won't go every day. Elizabeth has work to do. That's why she's there. And you have basketball practice on Mondays and Thursdays, remember?"

"And Sam? Can he come with us?"

"We'll check on that. Sometimes pets can come visit. But don't say anything to Sam yet, okay? We don't want to get his hopes up."

"Mom, he's standing right there." The look of patience pushed to the brink that Olivia gave her made Kaitlyn laugh again. "And he's not deaf."

A few minutes later as Sam crouched over his food bowl and they sat at the kitchen table with their cups of tea, Kaitlyn let Olivia scroll through the pictures she had taken at the hospital.

"She was really happy to get her crocheting. She told me to thank you for thinking of it. No one else did."

Olivia nodded without looking up. "Well, her and me crochet a lot."

"She and I." The correction was automatic and completely ignored by Olivia as she kept scrolling.

"Whose arm is that?"

Kaitlyn took a look. "Oh, that's Steven. He was there too."

Olivia nodded. "I like Steven. I used to think he was dumb, but he's nice. And I like Speed Bump too."

"I know what you mean." Kaitlyn took a sip of tea. "He does kind of grow on you. In fact, I was thinking. Uncle Chris is going out with Sarah Saturday night. What would you think of inviting Steven over for dinner and a movie?"

Olivia shrugged. "Okay, I guess."

"All right, then I'll ask him. What do you think I should fix?"

Olivia looked away from the phone while she considered. "I guess the best thing you fix is macaroni and cheese with hot dogs in it. And then maybe we can watch *Pocahontas*."

"Sounds like a perfect evening." Kaitlyn laughed. If Steven wanted to be part of her life, it was best he knew exactly what he was letting himself in for. "I'll give him a call this evening and ask him."

17

Russ and I went up to see Elizabeth last night." Juanita, as usual, was talking as she came in the front door the next morning. Chris glanced at the clock to remind her of the time, as he did every morning, and Juanita ignored him, as she always did. "My, she looked pretty. I was expecting the poor thing to look like something the cat didn't want. She's not that far from ninety, after all, and we nearly lost her. But there she was, sitting up in bed looking as fresh and pink-cheeked as a berry, crocheting and watching *Perry Mason*. I didn't even know *Perry Mason* was still on."

Chris gave up and went back in the kitchen, but Kaitlyn just smiled a greeting and went on filling the napkin dispensers. Juanita rarely needed a vocal participant to have a conversation.

"She said you fixed her up. And it took you about two minutes flat. Is that right?" Juanita stopped on her way to the storage room, her coat and purse over her arm.

It took a second for Kaitlyn to realize Juanita was waiting for a response. "Oh. I just used a little mascara and blush and lip gloss. They don't have a lot to choose from in the hospital gift shop. I think just feeling better is what made the real change."

"Well, whatever it was, she looked the picture of health." Juanita talked all the way back to the storeroom to put her things away and was still talking when she came back into the dining room. "And she acted that way too. I half expected her to get up and walk us to the door when we left."

Juanita continued her monologue, occasionally raising her voice to include Chris or Carlos in the kitchen as they prepared the diner for the breakfast crowd, and even though Kaitlyn only half listened, Juanita didn't seem to notice. Truthfully, since her conversation at the hospital the day before, Kaitlyn had been thinking about the options Elizabeth made her promise she'd consider, and for the first time in months, she began to feel alive. She hadn't quite got around to talking them over with the Lord, another of Elizabeth's suggestions. But then, she hadn't talked anything over with the Lord for a long, long, *long* time.

"So, Kaitlyn, I was wondering." At the sound of her name, Kaitlyn became aware that Juanita was actually talking to her. "Russ's sister and her husband are having a fiftieth wedding anniversary celebration at the Elk's Lodge over in Deming Saturday night. Do you think you could fix me up a little bit? You know, do my makeup, fix my hair?"

"I'd love to, Juanita, if you think we'd have time." Actually, giving Juanita a makeover did sound like fun. "I may have plans for Saturday night too, so we'd have to squeeze it in right after we close. Could you come to my house? I don't think I'd have time to go out to yours."

"Yeah, Steven is coming over for macaroni and cheese and to watch *Pocahontas* with us." Olivia looked up from her scrambled eggs long enough to send a dark look Juanita's way.

"Really." Juanita cocked her head and raised her eyebrows.

"Livvy!" Kaitlyn sent a warning frown her daughter's way before turning back to a very attentive Juanita. "Oh, we just thought it might be nice to have some company since Chris is going out. But it's super tentative. I haven't even talked to him yet."

"You said you were going to call him last night." Olivia's tone accused Kaitlyn of fibbing, even if her words did not.

"Well, I tried, but he didn't answer and I didn't leave a message, okay?" Kaitlyn felt heat prickles move up her neck and into her scalp. She was desperate to get the subject changed. "Now. Juanita. Yes, let's plan on my doing your hair and makeup Saturday. I'll come out to your house. We'll have Steven over another time."

"Mo-o-om!"

"No, I wouldn't think of having you change your plans on my account." Juanita flapped a hand at her. "I've got this all figured out. I'll just bring all my stuff with me Saturday, and Russ can pick me up on the way out of town. There's that shower in the employee restroom; I'll use that."

"You're not doing hair in my restaurant." Chris appeared in the window to the kitchen, offended astonishment written all over his face. "Are you out of your minds?"

"Oh, for Pete's sake, Chris, settle down. We won't get past the storage room, and probably not even that far. More than likely, I'll just sit there on the john in the bathroom and let Kaitlyn work on me in there."

Chris turned back to the kitchen. "I don't even want to think about that."

"Well then, don't. It doesn't concern you anyway. Besides, here comes company."

Juanita went to unlock the door as an extended cab pickup came to a stop in the parking lot and two men in heavy jackets got out. The early morning sky was still a thick winter black, and as they made their way to the front door, the puffs of their breath went before them like tiny clouds.

"Good morning, gentlemen. Sit anywhere you'd like." Juanita was already on her way to get the coffeepot. "Let me guess. Coffee first, and then menus."

"You got that right."

The men slid in on either side of a booth by the window and held their cups up for Juanita. She filled each cup with a quick twist of her wrist. "Need any cream?"

"Nope, I'll take it as hot and strong and black as you've got it."

Kaitlyn watched Juanita's easy conversation with the customers as she handed them their menus and talked about the daily specials. Now that Kaitlyn had made the conscious decision to stop looking at Juanita as the enemy, she saw an easy proficiency that she had been feeling way too sorry for herself to notice before. Juanita did know her job. Of course, she also knew everyone else's job, or thought she did, and had no problem critiquing the performance of that job. But that was another issue.

Juanita breezed by on her way to the kitchen with the order. "Kaitlyn, don't just stand there like Lot's wife. Get to work. It looks like Olivia's finished her breakfast. You can clear her place, and then you can roll some more silverware until we get more folks in here."

Kaitlyn felt the familiar flash of resentment start in her chest and head for her mouth. This time, though, she clamped her teeth on the retort and took a deep breath before answering.

"Sorry, Juanita, you caught me daydreaming. I'll get right to it."

Juanita froze in midstep for a brief second. Kaitlyn smiled. Apparently not quite convinced that Kaitlyn wasn't being sarcastic, Juanita scowled at Kaitlyn for another moment. Finally, her brow smoothed and she gave a quick nod before continuing to the kitchen.

"Good."

Kaitlyn cleared Olivia's dishes and then settled in a back booth with the napkins and silverware. She had only intended to change her attitude toward Juanita and the Dip 'n' Dine because it needed changing. It was holding her back and dragging her down. But in her heart of hearts, she had to admit that seeing Juanita thrown for a loop and at a loss for words, even for a second, was an added bonus.

It was nearly 3:00 before the lunch crowd finally thinned out and Kaitlyn was able to grab a cup of coffee and slide into her favorite booth in the back. Just a little more than an hour left and basketball practice would be over and she could go get Olivia. She leaned back and closed her eyes. She was glad her brother had found his dream in this place, she really was. But with every order she took, with every cup she poured, Kaitlyn was more convinced than ever that this was not for her. And while willing a better attitude might go a long way toward making the day go more smoothly, it didn't change the fact that she *hated* her job.

"My goodness, this day was busy." Kaitlyn opened her eyes as Juanita slid in across from her, holding her own cup. "If it had been like this yesterday when you were gone, I would have just run my feet right off."

Kaitlyn leaned forward, cradling her cup in her hands. "Juanita, can I ask you a question?"

"Sure, as long as it doesn't have anything to do with my age or my hair color."

"No, it's not that." Kaitlyn smiled. "Do you like working here? I mean really."

"Well, it's not easy work, I'll give you that. But sure, I like it. I like the people and seeing folks have a good time in here. I even like that good tired feeling that comes from doing a solid day's work. And when I go home and Russ starts talking chile at me, why, I can tell him all about my day too. Why?"

Kaitlyn reached across the table and clutched Juanita's arm. "Because I hate it. I hate it so much."

Juanita tossed a worried glance toward the kitchen and lowered her voice to as near a whisper as she could go. "Sshh. Chris'll hear you. I'm here to tell you that boy has ears like a hawk."

"I'm not hearing anything I don't already know." The voice floated from the kitchen.

"See? I told you," Juanita hissed before raising her voice and turning toward the kitchen. "Although hearing is one thing and listening is another. I've talked to you about eavesdropping before, Chris Reed."

Chris appeared in the window. "And I've told *you* that everything you say can be heard in every corner of this restaurant. I'm just glad there weren't any customers in here to hear that."

"Now, if there were customers, would we be sitting here drinking coffee? You need to lighten up a little bit, I think."

The phone in Kaitlyn's apron pocket vibrated, and she left Juanita and her brother to their discussion of acoustics.

"Hey, sorry I missed your call last night." It was Steven.

"Oh, it was nothing important. I just wanted to ask you something."

Juanita must have figured out who she was talking to, because she immediately left off lecturing Chris on eavesdropping and turned her rapt attention to Kaitlyn.

"I can't talk right now. I just got to school for basketball practice and Mrs. Martinez is waiting with the kids. I guess I'm a little late.

Tell you what, I'll bring Olivia to the Dip 'n' Dine after practice for you. We can talk then, okay?"

"Wait—" But he was gone before she could say anything, and Kaitlyn slipped her phone back in her pocket.

"Well, that didn't take long. Did he hang up on you?" Juanita stirred a little more sugar into her coffee.

"No, he just couldn't talk now."

"Then why did he even call? That's just plain silly."

"He just called to tell me that he'd bring Olivia here after practice."

"Oh, well, that's nice of him. Save you a trip."

"Not really." Kaitlyn took the last sip of her coffee and slid out of the booth. If it was impossible to have a private phone call in the Dip 'n' Dine, she could probably sell tickets to a face-to-face conversation. "Livvy and I have to go take care of Elizabeth's cat anyway. I'll just go on over and wait for practice to be over. Save *him* a trip."

She was on her way to the kitchen with her empty mug when Chris came through the door putting on his jacket. "If Steven's bringing Livvy over, I'm going to run up to San Ramon real quick. I need to take care of some business, but I can never seem to get out of here before everything closes. I shouldn't be gone more than an hour, but at least Livvy won't be stranded if I'm held up."

Kaitlyn watched him head out the door and climb in his Jeep. Her conversation with Steven had taken maybe fifteen seconds, and everyone in the diner seemed to think it involved them somehow. Unbelievable.

"Hey, Carlos, we haven't heard from you yet." She continued into the kitchen with her mug. "Don't you have anything to add?"

"Nope." He was taking advantage of the empty diner to begin

cleaning and didn't look up. "Except it's a sin to invite someone to dinner and then serve them that mac and cheese. You need to learn to cook, girl."

—m—

Kaitlyn kept an eye on the clock, willing Chris to get back in time for her to meet Olivia and Steven at school. She did not want to talk to Steven about Saturday with Juanita and Chris and Carlos and who knows, maybe some customers, hanging on her every word. It was just an invitation for him to come hang out with her and Olivia Saturday, but even so, a little privacy would be nice. And privacy was hard to come by at the Dip 'n' Dine.

At 4:00 on the nose, she saw the Jeep turn off the highway and stop in Chris's usual spot near the door. Great. Too late to go get Olivia, but in time to add one more person to her audience.

In the next fifteen minutes, Lurlene Porter and Evelyn Watson came in for coffee and pie, Rita Sandoval came in needing to see Chris about something, and a public service company truck brought four men in hardhats looking for a late lunch. Kaitlyn was sure someone had to be out on the highway with a flag, waving folks into the Dip 'n' Dine.

"There they are." Juanita nudged her as she went by, drawing Kaitlyn's attention to Olivia and Steven getting out of Steven's truck.

"Hey, Mom, guess what? Steven lets me ride in the front seat." Olivia burst through the door ahead of Steven.

"So I see."

"I'm not supposed to?" Steven glanced at Olivia as he took off his hat and hung it on the rack by the door.

"No, it's safer in the back, and she knows that." Kaitlyn put her arm around her daughter and gave a squeeze. "I think she was just seeing what she could get away with."

"Is that how you're playing it?" Steven turned back to Olivia. "That could cost you that cup of cocoa we were talking about."

"But you promised. And you told me it was okay if I sat in the front. I asked, remember?" Olivia had changed so much since she had been in Last Chance, but she still knew how to work things to her advantage. That was another thing Steven would have to learn if he was going to spend much time with them.

"I guess you got me. You go ahead and grab a booth. I'll be there in a sec." He turned to Kaitlyn with a rueful grin. "So is there anything else I need to know?"

"Well, it's usually a good idea to check with a kid's parents before you offer them things to eat or drink, especially this close to dinner."

"Man, I'm striking out all over the place." Steven ran his hand through his hair. "I guess it's a little late, but is the cocoa okay?"

Kaitlyn smiled. "It's fine. Don't worry about it."

He returned the smile, and somehow it was his eyes, the same clear blue of Elizabeth's eyes, that caught her attention. That dimple that he loved to flash couldn't hold a candle to his eyes. "So what was the phone call about?"

Kaitlyn looked around. The ladies eating their pie had been watching their conversation with unabashed interest since Steven came in, and Juanita, while not actually staring, had arranged to be close enough to hear everything that was said. She took a deep breath. "Oh, nothing important. I'll give you a call later."

He looked puzzled. "Why? What did you need?"

"Seriously, it's not anything we need to talk about right now. I'll call you tonight."

"Okay." Doubt still clouded his face, but he began to edge toward the booth where Olivia waited.

"We want you to come have dinner with us Saturday and watch a movie." Olivia might not have actually yelled, but the sound seemed to Kaitlyn to reverberate from the rafters. Certainly everyone else in the diner looked up to see what was going on.

Steven jerked his head around to look at Kaitlyn, and she threw up her hands and laughed. "Well, there you have it. If you don't have anything going on, Livvy and I'd love to have you come over Saturday. Nothing major. Livvy thought we could have mac and cheese with hot dogs and watch *Pocahontas*. Sound like an evening you can't pass up?"

Steven opened his mouth and closed it again. But words were not necessary. Kaitlyn had only to look at his stricken expression to know. Right there in the middle of the diner, with everyone looking on, he was going to turn her down.

Steven pounded the side of his fist against the steering wheel. *Where did that come from?* How many times and in how many different ways had she told him she was not interested? She had said no at least three times by the elevator at the hospital before the door could even close, and that was just one incident.

Then the one time, the *one time*, he decides to spend an evening with a very lovely young woman—a woman who, by the way, he had once rejected in favor of Kaitlyn—Kaitlyn suddenly decides to let bygones be bygones and invites him to dinner. Steven shook his head to clear it, but it didn't help.

It couldn't have been long, maybe a second or two, between the time she asked him and the moment she threw up her hand to ward off his fumbling explanation, saying, "It's no big deal, really. Just a thought." But it sure seemed like a long time. Why had he insisted on going on, telling her if he had only known he never would have made plans, begging her for a rain check, when she clearly just wanted him to shut up? If he hadn't already promised Olivia that cup of cocoa, he would have got himself out of there right then, but no, he had to go sit with her and talk about basketball and her cat and pretend nothing had happened. Kaitlyn brought them their cocoa and smiled as if nothing had happened, and everyone else in the diner went back to their meals as if nothing had happened. And it was all as awkward as a calf on ice.

A tumbleweed the size of a small boulder blew across the highway in front of him, and he braked slightly to keep it from getting caught in his grill. For maybe the fiftieth time since he had returned to Last Chance, he let himself think about what it would be like to just keep going. To the west, the sun was about to slip below the horizon. It looked like it might still be shining on California, and if he got on Interstate 10 and headed that direction, he could be in San Diego before it came up again. He leaned back against his seat and smiled. Really, what was holding him here? He was going to have to report to the academy in April, but until then? Nothing.

Of course, he'd have to go back to the ranch for his stuff and his dog. Uncle Joe Jr. was expecting him soon to help with the evening chores, so he'd have to at least wait till they were done before he left. Might as well stay till after dinner. That would give him time to line up someone to pick up the basketball jerseys he had ordered for the kids. There was Gran's house to finish up, of course, but maybe if he really cranked it, he could get most of it done in the next week or so.

He drew in a deep breath and blew it out with a gust. Every

one of those things was something he would have shoved off on someone else without a second thought only a few weeks ago. What was going on here?

He turned off the highway and bumped over the cattle guard onto the dirt road that led to the ranch house. "Face it, Braden. You're getting old."

18

Kaitlyn came back into the living room after tucking Olivia in bed and curled up in a corner of the sofa. Chris looked up from his computer with a sympathetic smile.

"Rough day, huh?"

Kaitlyn fell over sideways and buried her face in a sofa cushion. "The worst."

He reached over and put his hand on her head. "I didn't understand what you said, but I'm betting you weren't disagreeing with me."

Bringing the cushion with her, she sat up and hugged it to her chest. "Why, Chris, why does a simple phone call that involves only two people become the property of the whole blessed town? Why?"

"Well, that's Last Chance. They're not nosy; they just care."

"Baloney. They're nosy, and you know it."

"Well, maybe they are a little nosy." Chris grinned. "But they do care. When you're not used to having anyone really care about your life, it does take some getting used to. I know. I had a problem with it too when I first got here."

"Personally, I can do without so much caring. I'm sure by breakfast all of Last Chance will be caring deeply that Steven Braden, of all people, shut me down in the middle of the Dip 'n' Dine."

"Oh, come on. He just said he already had plans for this Saturday. It happens. He did say he'd like to come another time."

"Yeah, right. That's going to happen."

"Suit yourself." Chris went back to his computer. After a few minutes he closed it and set it on the coffee table. "There's something else I want to talk to you about, though."

Kaitlyn just looked at him.

"That conversation you had with Juanita this afternoon, when you told her how much you hated working at the Dip 'n' Dine?"

"Oh, Chris, do we have to talk about that now? I'm so not in the mood. It couldn't have come as a surprise."

"No, it didn't. I knew you didn't want to come to work there, but I hoped once you settled in, you might like it a little better."

"Sorry." She buried her face again in the pillow she held.

"We need to figure something out then, Kaitlyn. In the first place, as your brother, I hate to see you so unhappy. But as the owner of the Dip 'n' Dine, I don't want employees who hate working there. It shows, and it's bad for business."

Kaitlyn looked up at Chris. It hadn't occurred to her that he might think she was bad for his business. He was her big brother. He had to make a place for her, even if she didn't want it.

"Got any ideas?" He raised an eyebrow. "There are just not a whole lot of options here in Last Chance, you know."

She smiled. "Funny you should mention options. That's exactly what Elizabeth and I talked about yesterday."

"Oh? Come to any conclusions?"

"She seemed to think that there *were* a lot of options and that I should start praying about them."

"She is a wise woman."

"Since then, I've been thinking I might want to get my New Mexico cosmetology license."

"Really. Then open a shop here in Last Chance?"

"I wouldn't go that far, but who knows? I guess that's one of the things I need to pray about." The words sounded so odd to Kaitlyn's ears, but right nonetheless.

"I'll pray too." Chris reached for his computer again. "Meanwhile, let's see what it would take to get your New Mexico license."

Kaitlyn scooted next to him so she could see the screen too. There was a time in her life when she had prayed, but that had been long ago. And she had the feeling that when she did start praying, there was a whole lot she was going to be talking over with the Lord before she even got to the subject of her salon.

Actually, the next day went a lot better than Kaitlyn was afraid it might. It only took until about 10:00 to convince Juanita that she did *not* want to talk about Steven, his plans, or anything that happened the day before and only until around 1:00 for Juanita to get over being miffed about that. After that, things went smoothly until it was time to go get Olivia.

"Do you want to do something Saturday? It's just going to be the two of us now." Kaitlyn sat at the kitchen table at Elizabeth's house watching Olivia try to interest Sam in a piece of yarn she was dragging across the floor.

Olivia looked up. "Like what?"

"Oh, we could go out for pizza, or a hamburger. Maybe see a movie."

"Could we go to that place we went to with Steven? The one where you put the quarters in for music?"

"Oh, Livvy, really?"

Suddenly going to San Ramon for the evening didn't sound like such a good idea after all. She hadn't thought about bumping into people.

"But I like that place." Olivia drew the words out in a long whine.

"How about this?" Kaitlyn tried to keep her voice light. Olivia's days started before 5:00 a.m.; she was entitled to be a little tired and cranky this late in the day. "Let's go ahead and make the mac and cheese with hot dogs together like we planned. We can even eat it on the coffee table while we watch *Pocahontas*. Then we'll give each other manicures and pedicures."

"Sounds like fun. Can I come?"

Kaitlyn jumped as Sarah walked into the kitchen. "Hey there. Didn't hear you come in."

Sarah grinned. "I learned where all the squeaky boards were when I lived here during high school. Gran is a very light sleeper."

Olivia scrambled to her feet and threw her arms around Sarah's waist. "Sure, you can come. I've got blue sparkle polish and purple sparkle polish. You can pick."

"Sarah's going out with Uncle Chris Saturday, remember? That's why we're having our girls' night."

"Oh, right." Olivia dropped her hands, clearly disappointed. "Well, why did you ask if you could come then?"

"I guess I was wishing I could come. It sounds like you're going to have so much fun." Sarah gave her a quick squeeze before dropping into a chair across the table from Kaitlyn. "How're you doing? Seems like I hardly ever get to see you."

Kaitlyn sighed. "I'm doing fine. I'm doing just great, thanks. I don't know if Chris sent you to check on me, or if you thought of it on your own. But believe me, I'll survive."

Sarah looked at her in puzzled silence for a moment before bursting into laughter. "Oh, you think I came in to pat your poor hand and commiserate because my dumb cousin has other plans Saturday? Like that's a surprise? No, Gran's moving to the rehab center tomorrow, and I've come to pack her a suitcase. She gets to wear her own clothes. Yay. Besides, why would I think you're falling apart over Steven, anyway? You've got way more sense than that."

"Steven's not dumb." Olivia, who had gone back to trying to entice Sam with the yarn, glared up at them. "Calling people dumb isn't nice anyway."

"You're right, Livvy. Words do hurt. Thanks for reminding me." Sarah turned back to Kaitlyn with a weary smile. "There you have teaching in a small town. You're never away from the classroom."

"Yeah, I'm learning all about life in a small town. Who told you about Steven and his plans, anyway?"

"Chris, of course. We may not see each other a lot during the week, but we do talk. He says, 'How was your day?' I say, 'How was yours?'"

"Oh." Kaitlyn was beginning to feel a little silly. Maybe she was making just a little more out of this than it warranted.

"But I'm much more interested in the news that you're thinking about getting your New Mexico beauty license. Is that true? Say yes." Sarah grabbed Kaitlyn's arm and gave it a little shake.

"Maybe. I just started thinking about it."

"Well, when you finish thinking about it, do it! Then open a salon right here in Last Chance. Please, please, please. You have to."

Kaitlyn grinned and shook her head. Sarah Cooley's enthusiasm was hard to say no to. No wonder her brother was toast.

"I don't know. That's jumping way, way ahead. But it would be easy to transfer my license. The requirements for both states are identical, so all I need to do is prove my Arizona license is valid, and it's done. Then I could maybe get a job at a salon in San Ramon, or even volunteer up at that convalescent home where Elizabeth is staying. It's kind of exciting to think about."

"Well, I love it, so keep thinking about it. But don't go work in San Ramon. Open a place here in Last Chance." The phone Sarah had placed on the table vibrated, and she picked it up and smiled at the screen. "Excuse me, would you? He only calls from work when he has something to say."

"Go ahead." Kaitlyn watched her head down the hall, cradling her phone to her ear. She was happy Sarah and Chris had found each other, really she was. If anyone deserved the outright adoration that lit Sarah's face when she saw him, it was Chris, and he more than returned the devotion. But if she were honest with herself, Kaitlyn had to admit that seeing them together, or even hearing them speak about the other, sometimes made her feel so alone that she thought she might break in half.

"You'll never guess." Sarah came back in the kitchen, tucking her phone back in her pocket. "Your mom just called Chris and invited him and me up to Scottsdale next weekend. Sounded kind of like a royal command."

"Yeah, that's Mom. She probably shuffled some stuff around on her calendar and inked you in. Announcing your engagement got you on the priority list. After all, she has to meet you if she's going to start telling everyone how adorable Chris's fiancée is."

"What if she doesn't think I'm all that adorable?"

Sarah really did sound worried, and Kaitlyn gave an airy wave of her hand. "Oh, you'll be adorable by definition. You're going to be her daughter-in-law, and everything concerning her is top-notch. Except me."

"If that was supposed to make me feel better, it didn't." Sarah's forehead puckered in a frown. "Now I'm really worried."

Kaitlyn looked over at Olivia. "Livvy, honey, we're going to have to be leaving in a minute. Go put that yarn back in the sewing room, would you please? Be sure to wind it back up in a ball."

When Olivia left, she turned back to Sarah. "Don't be worried, but let me give you some advice. First of all, do not try to impress her or act like you need her approval. She can smell that like a shark smells blood in the water, and she'll forever hold it just out of your reach. Be yourself, and let her tell everyone how adorable you are. Second, remember that when the weekend's over, she's staying in Scottsdale, and you're coming back to Last Chance with Chris."

Sarah did not look at all comforted. "Good grief, Kaitlyn, now I'm terrified. Don't ever try to talk anyone off a ledge. It would end in disaster."

Kaitlyn laughed as they stood up and enveloped Sarah in a hug. "Don't be. I mean that. I'm just saying be yourself without worrying too much about what Mom thinks, that's all. The rest of us, including my dad, think you're great. Especially Chris, and he's besotted."

"He is not. What's besotted?" Olivia had rejoined them.

Kaitlyn handed Olivia her backpack and jacket. "It means he's crazy about Sarah. Come on, we need to get home."

"Oh, that." Olivia didn't seem inclined to pursue that line of conversation and headed for the front door. "Bye, Sam, see you tomorrow."

Kaitlyn followed. At the front door, she turned and smiled at

Sarah. "Seriously, do not worry one way or the other about making a good impression on Mom. You'll do fine."

"Yeah. Right. Thanks."

Sarah's smile did not reach her eyes, and Kaitlyn felt a twinge of conscience as she followed Olivia to the Jeep. Maybe she should have stayed out of it. Certainly, when Chris heard about the conversation, as Kaitlyn was sure he would, that would be his strongly vocalized opinion. But she could not let Sarah go in there expecting to find warm acceptance, expecting to be loved, only to find that no matter what she did, she would never quite measure up to Brooke Reed's standards. That just hurt too much.

No one made a conscious decision Sunday morning to leave Elizabeth's place on the aisle vacant, but when they all sat down, there it was. In the few months she had been in Last Chance, Kaitlyn had never seen that spot empty, and she had a feeling that if asked, most of the people who came every Sunday would give a similar answer. But Chris and Sarah had gone to see her at the convalescent home last night after she got settled in and said she was ready to get to work, so maybe it wouldn't be long till she was back where she belonged. Kaitlyn hoped so. She had come to church under protest in the beginning only because Chris wanted her to and because he said he always took Olivia. But Elizabeth had been so delighted at her presence, and had made her feel so welcome, that she didn't protest quite so much the next time. Now, just a couple months later, Sunday worship services with the family were as much a part of her life as weekdays in the diner. She wasn't quite ready to give Chris the satisfaction of telling him, but she was beginning to look forward to going.

Lurlene took her place on the podium and nodded to the pianist. As the music filled the church and the choir filed in, Kaitlyn felt a movement at her left elbow and turned to find Steven sliding in next to her. She glanced up at him, he smiled, and she turned back to the front. Lurlene announced the first hymn, and he picked the hymnbook up, found the place, and held it out for her to share. She took it—it would have been rude not to—but she didn't look at him. Steven had a nice tenor voice, and he sang harmony to her soprano. With Chris's strong baritone, Elizabeth's family pew sounded pretty good. Of course, there was Sarah, who never quite hit the key, but she sang with joy and gusto anyway. Elizabeth would have been proud.

Although she did her best to ignore him, Kaitlyn found, to her annoyance, that throughout the service, she was increasingly aware of Steven sitting next to her. It wasn't that he did anything to draw attention to himself. He just sat there listening, occasionally shifting position or clearing his throat, chuckling when Brother Parker made a joke, leaning over to read from the Bible Chris had given her when a Scripture reference was given—even flipping through the minor prophets to help her find the book of Micah as if he had the whole thing memorized.

By the time the final hymn was sung, she was thoroughly rattled, furious at herself for allowing him to rattle her, and ready to make a run for the door. But stuck as she was between Chris and Steven, she didn't have much choice but to stand there and wait for someone to move.

"Hey." He gave her a crooked smile. "I've been hoping we could talk. Are you busy this afternoon?"

Kaitlyn shrugged. "I don't know. Why?"

Steven ran his fingers through his hair. The smile was gone.

"Because every time I try to talk to you, something goes south, and you wind up mad at me again. I hate that. Especially since it usually involves a misunderstanding of some kind. What do you say? Can we go somewhere and just talk?" He grinned again and gestured with his chin at Chris and Sarah, moving down the aisle hand in hand. "I mean, we're going to be kin, or close to it, pretty soon. Don't you think we should at least be on speaking terms?"

Kaitlyn watched Chris and Sarah head into the vestibule before looking back at Steven. Just a few days ago, she had been ready to get to know Steven a little better, and when you got down to it, the only crime he had committed was having prior plans. Not exactly a capital offense. She looked back at him and smiled. "Okay, I guess we can talk. I have to go get Livvy from Sunday school, but Chris and Sarah have already promised to take her to San Ramon for ice cream. I wasn't going to go with them anyway. Shall I go tell Chris I won't need a ride home after all?"

A real smile broke through. "Yeah. I'll go with you."

Steven looked over at Kaitlyn as he left the church parking lot. Man, she was so pretty, and whatever the outcome of the day, he really hoped that they could be friends. Olivia had wanted to come with them instead of Chris and Sarah, but fortunately, when she found that their plans did not include ice cream, she decided to go on with Chris and Sarah. It wasn't that Steven didn't like having Olivia around. He did. But today he just wanted to be with Olivia's mom.

They rode in silence as Last Chance disappeared behind them and the desert took them in. Steven had so much he wanted to say, but he just didn't know how to begin. Kaitlyn didn't seem to mind, though. He kept taking little glances her way, and she leaned her head against the headrest and gazed to the side. Finally she caught him looking.

"What?" She smiled an easy smile.

"Truthfully? I'm afraid of blowing it again."

"Blowing it? How?"

"Oh, you know, saying the wrong thing. Seeing you close up, shut me out."

There, like that. Steven turned back to the road. Maybe he *should* give up. This really was going nowhere.

He heard her gusty sigh and looked back over at her. When she turned to him, she smiled. Or tried to.

"I'm sorry. I know I'm prickly. I don't mean to be, really. I even try not to let things get to me, but I can't help it. I just keep looking for that barb beneath the surface."

"Well, you won't find any barbs with me. I promise you that. I don't know. Depending on how well we get to know each other, we might disagree about stuff, even argue. But I'll always be straightforward with you. You can count on it."

"Thank you." This time she did smile.

"Okay, since we've got that settled, I think we should clear the air. I know you've heard some things about me, likely from my own dear grandmother and cousin, so is there anything you'd like to know? Ask anything you want. Go ahead, I'm game."

He waited, determined to be honest, no matter what she asked.

"Okay, I do have a question."

"Shoot."

"Did you have a good time last night?"

He gave her an injured look, which she returned with a sweet smile. He wasn't expecting to talk about last night.

"Well, you said I could ask anything." An angel couldn't have sounded more innocent.

"No, I did not. I had a rotten time, thanks for asking."

"I'm sorry." She really did sound concerned. "I was just teasing you a little. What happened?"

Steven took a deep breath. "Well, I went to a party with a friend from high school—Jen, you met her, remember? I knew just about everyone there, and it was like every other party I'd been to since high school. The same people were drinking just to be drinking, partying just to be partying, pretending it all meant they were having a good time, and suddenly I was so bored I knew I'd go nuts if I didn't get out of there. Jen didn't want to leave, so she got someone else to take her home, and I was back at the ranch by 9:00."

"I am sorry, really." Kaitlyn reached across the seat and put her hand on his arm. "That sounds pretty rough."

"Do you know the worst of it?"

"What?"

"I kept thinking, 'I gave up mac and cheese with hot dogs and *Pocahontas* for *this*!'"

19

It was already getting dark and Venus hung bright in the still-glowing western sky when Steven's truck found its way back to Last Chance.

He reached for her hand and glanced over with a tender smile. "How are you holding up?"

Kaitlyn swiped at her nose with the balled-up tissue she held in her other hand and sniffed. "Well, my eyes feel like sandpaper, my head is still stuffed up, and the rest of me feels so tired and kind of empty. Like I've been hollowed out. Thanks for the fun afternoon. We'll have to do this again sometime."

They hadn't done much but drive, stopping for hamburgers that they ate in the car. And with no interruptions, no distractions, and no place to stomp off if anyone got mad, they talked.

Steven told her what it was like growing up in Last Chance, not quite a Cooley, never quite able to measure up to the bar his older brother set.

"See, since the ranch is the Rocking JC, all the boys have names that start with J, so there'll always be a JC running the ranch. My middle name is John. But of course, Braden doesn't start with C, and I've known all my life that after Uncle Joe Jr., my cousin Justin will run the ranch."

"Wow. Sounds like the royal family." Kaitlyn had been impressed. "Did you even want to run the ranch?"

"No, not really. But still, growing up, I felt a little on the edges of the family. While my mom was alive, it was different. She had been born on that ranch and grew up there, and there was never a question that she belonged there. Since we were her kids, so did Ray and I. She was kind of like Sarah in that way. She just expected people to want to do things her way." He paused then and looked straight ahead with a little half smile while the pavement disappeared beneath them. After a few seconds, he cleared his throat and continued. "And then there was Dad. I don't know which came first, the family's disapproval of him or his cocky disregard of them, but those two things fed on each other until they barely spoke."

"And you decided to take after your dad?" Kaitlyn smiled.

"Yeah, I guess I did. It wasn't all that hard since I'm an awful lot like him anyway. I liked approval as much as the next guy, but if anyone wanted to look down their nose, well, I was happy to give them something to disapprove of."

"I think I know that story. Then when you add an older brother who never gets anything but approval, the ending writes itself."

Steven glanced over at her. "Yep, that's about it. But if you ever think about joining the military, you might want to leave that attitude at home. I'm here to tell you it's not going to fly. I was a different man when I came home, or thought I was. But the minute I got back in Last Chance, it was all the same ol', same ol'. I was hit with all these expectations, and conflicting expectations at that. My dad's dying wish had been for me to take over that bar. Gran and the rest of the Cooleys still thought of it as Satan's own stronghold brought into Last Chance by my dad for the specific purpose of disgracing them. Poor Ray was caught in the middle, hating the bar and yet honoring my dad by putting his own life on hold to run it till I got home. Everybody was looking at me to do something about it, so I did what I do best. I took off."

Kaitlyn watched him drive in silence for a while. She could only imagine what he might be thinking as he clenched his jaw and stared through the windshield.

"But you came back." Her voice was gentle.

Steven's laugh was more of a bark. "Yeah, I came back, and I can't tell you the number of times since I've been back that I've had to force myself to turn onto the ranch road instead of just heading on down the highway."

"But you haven't gone. You're still here."

It was a long moment before he spoke. "Yeah, I'm still here."

"Tomorrow?"

"I'll be here. I've got Gran's house to get ready for her, for one thing. And I need to settle things with Ray when he and Lainie come back to Last Chance. We've talked of course, and I saw him at Christmas, but the bar is one subject we've avoided. That's got to change."

"What about the Law Enforcement Academy?"

"That's not till April. Of course, after that I'll have to go where I'm assigned, but I'm beginning to think being here in the southwestern part of the state wouldn't be all that bad." He smiled.

Kaitlyn smiled back, and when Steven looked back at the road, she turned her eyes to the wintry desert sweeping past the side window. She knew Steven wouldn't push the issue, probably wouldn't even ask questions, but she wanted to tell him her story, just as he had opened up to her. Actually, on the surface, their stories looked pretty similar. Both had grown up in the shadow of a model older brother, had families with high expectations, and had systematically set about disappointing those expectations as soon and as thoroughly as they could. But where Steven ran, Kaitlyn made excuses. Nothing was ever her fault. She closed her eyes against the stab of pain that greeted that realization.

"You okay?" Steven must have caught her expression.

She nodded. "Just thinking. So, is it my turn?"

"Only if you want."

For a while, Kaitlyn was able to keep things pretty matter-of-fact as she told him of a rebellion that began about the time she entered middle school.

"My parents have their own business and have always worked long, long hours. They depended on poor Chris to keep me in line, and I found I could get back at all of them by doing exactly what I wanted to do. When I realized they wouldn't actually kill me, and I had seen the worst they could do to me, there was no stopping me. I probably missed as much school as I attended."

"How did you manage to stay in school?"

"I don't know. I think my parents spent more time at school than I did. But it was a losing proposition. I don't think I would have made it, even if Danny hadn't entered the picture."

"Ah, Danny."

"Yep. Olivia's father. He was super smart. He managed to cut class *and* ace his AP classes. When we found out Livvy was on the way, he and his parents freaked out. He had plans, you see. His parents shipped him off to live with his grandparents, and the last time I heard anything about him, he had been accepted to Stanford medical school."

"He doesn't have anything to do with Livvy?" Steven seemed to be putting an awful lot of effort into keeping his voice neutral.

"Nope. His parents offered a pretty good sum of money to, I

don't know, buy off any responsibility he might have, I guess. But my parents, bless them, told them to keep it. Not exactly in those words, but you get the idea."

"The little twerp."

"Twerp is a good word. Anyway, my parents didn't want me to have the baby, but when I told them I was going to have her and that was all there was to it, they had to accept it. But they laid down the law. The baby and I could live with them until I got on my feet, but I was going to get my GED and some kind of education so I could support her. For once, I was scared enough to listen. So Livvy was born, and I went to cosmetology school."

"How long did you and Livvy live with your folks?"

"I was about twenty and Livvy was nearly three when we got our first place."

"That's kind of young to be on your own with a kid to support."

Kaitlyn didn't say anything for a while. She had been able to hold it together just fine until she started talking about Olivia as a baby. Now it felt as if a vise was tightening around her chest. Her breath came in short gasps.

"I was young. I was so young. I couldn't take care of myself, let alone a baby."

"Hey, it's okay." Steven had stopped in the parking lot of a hamburger stand and reached for her hand. "Livvy's a great kid. Whatever happened then, she came through it."

Kaitlyn pulled her hand away and shook her head. "No, she deserved so much more, and I did not deserve her."

She went on with her story, making no excuses, taking all the blame, her breath coming in hiccups, while Steven looked on with gathering concern. When she got to the part about leaving Olivia behind with Chris and heading off across the country on a motorcycle, she could go no further, and her face contorted in sobs.

Steven leaned across the console and, unsnapping her seat belt, pulled her to him, cradling her against his chest, holding her until she had no more tears.

—∞—

"Mom, you were gone so long." Olivia looked up from a game of Sorry she was playing with Sarah and frowned when Kaitlyn and Steven came in. "What's wrong?"

"Nothing's wrong, sweetie." Kaitlyn tried to look extra cheerful. "Did you have a good time getting ice cream?"

"But you've been crying." Olivia scrambled to her feet and came to take Kaitlyn's hand. She glared at Steven.

"Honey, I'm fine. Really. Steven and I were talking and I remembered something that made me sad, but it happened a long time ago. It's okay. I'm happy now."

Olivia didn't look at all convinced, but neither did Sarah, still sitting in front of the Sorry board. Or Chris, who also gave Steven a hard stare as he looked up from the computer opened on his lap.

Kaitlyn sighed. "Really, you guys, I had a moment, that's all. Nothing's wrong. I'm fine. What I really want to know is, who's cooking? I'm ready for dinner."

Chris went back to his computer. "Give me a minute here. I'm fixing omelets. You staying, Steven?"

"Sure. Love to." Clearly choosing to ignore Chris's less than welcoming tone of voice, Steven went over to the Sorry game on the coffee table and sat cross-legged on the floor. "So, who's winning and can I get in on the next game?"

"Livvy just won her third game. You can take my place, but be warned. You will lose." Sarah got to her feet and cornered Kaitlyn in the bathroom where she had gone in search of a tissue. "Seriously, what's wrong? Did Steven say something? Or do something? You look like you've been crying for days."

"Pretty much since lunch, off and on." Kaitlyn blew her nose. "But not because of anything Steven did. He was great, as a matter of fact. I'm over it now, so don't get me started again."

Kaitlyn could see the worry in Sarah's face. She could also see that Sarah didn't want to leave the bathroom without finding out what had made Kaitlyn cry, but frankly, Kaitlyn had nothing more to say about it. Not now, and maybe not ever again.

"Come on." Kaitlyn led the way out of the bathroom and Sarah followed. "Let's go tell Chris he needs to put that computer away and fix us some omelets."

Later, after Olivia had gone to bed and Chris had gone to take Sarah home, Kaitlyn joined Steven on the sofa in the living room. She kicked off her shoes, stretched her legs out so her feet were on the coffee table, and let her head fall against the back of the sofa.

"What a day." She closed her eyes.

Steven stretched his arm across the back of the sofa and traced her cheek with one finger. "Yeah, I feel kind of wrung out myself. But I do feel like I know you a little better now. And I like what I know."

She opened her eyes to find him smiling at her. "Now that I can't figure out. I'd think you'd be disgusted."

"Nope. I'd like to mess up that Danny so bad it would take the entire Stanford medical school to sort him out, but I think you're amazing. I think Olivia is a lucky little girl to have you for her mom."

Tears welled up in Kaitlyn's eyes, and she dug in her pocket and pulled out a wad of tissue. "Good grief. I didn't know I had any tears left."

With two fingers, he turned her face toward him, and she felt his lips gently brush her cheeks, just under each eye. "Mmm, salty."

His forehead touched hers, and she felt his breath warm on her face. Her eyes drifted closed again, and she felt his next kiss land gently in her hair as he slipped his arm around her and drew her head to his shoulder.

She tucked her feet under her and curled into the shelter of his arm. A peace she had not known for longer than she could remember filled her to her fingertips. Everyone she had met since she came to Last Chance had warned her against this man, and she might yet find they were right. But right now she felt safe, and safe felt good.

The crunch of gravel outside signaled Chris's return. With a sigh, Kaitlyn sat upright and slipped her shoes back on.

"That didn't take long." Steven looked at his watch. "What does he do? Slow down to twenty and boot her out as he drives by?"

"Not quite, but it is a work night, and whether he's over there Sunday evening or Sarah's over here, he's usually home by about 9:00."

"Think he'll throw me out?"

"He'll probably try."

On cue, the front door opened, and Chris came in.

"Hey, Steven. Still here, huh? Saw your rig outside."

"Just leaving." Steven winked at Kaitlyn and got to his feet. He extended his hand to Chris. "Thanks for the hospitality and the omelets. It's been a pleasure."

Kaitlyn walked him to the door, and as she closed it behind him, she turned on her brother.

"Really, Chris? Could you have been ruder? Why didn't you just grab him by the collar and seat of his pants and give him the old 'heave ho'?"

"What? It's late. He's been here all evening, and morning—"

"Don't." Kaitlyn cut him off. "If you tell me morning comes mighty early around here one more time, I'm liable to throw something heavy at you."

"What's the matter with you? In fact, what was the matter with you when you got here tonight? You'd been crying, and crying hard. I want to know why. Sarah told me you said Steven didn't have anything to do with it, but since you'd been with him since church was out, I don't buy it, so what's going on?"

"Don't you need to get to bed? After all, morning comes—"

"Stop it, Kaitlyn." Chris's eyes narrowed as he interrupted her. "It's not funny. You're getting your life squared away here. Watching you with Livvy, I see a completely different girl—woman—than you were even a couple months ago, and when one afternoon with Steven Braden turns you into such a blubbering mess, I get worried."

"Blubbering mess?" Kaitlyn couldn't help smiling. "That bad, huh?"

Chris folded his arms. He did not smile.

Kaitlyn folded her arms too and stared back.

"Still not funny, Kaitlyn." He hadn't budged.

Finally, Kaitlyn sighed. The thing about Chris she loved most was that he was there for her every moment of her life. The thing that drove her the craziest was that he was there for her *every* moment of her life.

"Okay, if you get that ferocious look off your face, I'll tell you."

She could tell he tried to soften his expression, but he wasn't very successful.

"We talked, that's all. We drove for miles and miles and talked. He told me what it was like for him growing up here in Last Chance with a dad the family disapproved of, and I told him about my life. About Danny, and trying to take care of Olivia and doing such an awful job of it. Of course, he already knew about me dropping Livvy off with you and taking off with Jase, but we talked about that too. He listened, and he let me cry, and that's all."

Chris still didn't look happy. "You didn't have to talk about that. That's ancient history. It's all behind you."

She shook her head. "No, it's not. I live with it every day. For Pete's sake, Chris, I'm not even the guardian of my own daughter. Even if you wanted to hand the guardianship back right now, I'd be so afraid I'd mess up her life, I don't think I could take it."

Chris took the few steps to where she stood and pulled her into a hug. Of course, when she felt his strong arms around her, she started to cry again.

"Shh. It's okay." He rocked her slightly as he held her. "You're not going to mess up anyone's life. Not your own, and certainly not Livvy's. You need to believe that."

She nodded against his shoulder and felt the scratchy wool of his sweater against her cheek. "I'm trying. Before today, I'm not sure it even occurred to me that I didn't have to go through my life moving from one failure to the next. I mean, it's not like I planned it that way or anything. It's just that even when things were going well at the moment, there was always this little voice in the back of my head that said, 'Give it time; you're going to find a way to mess this up too.' But today, talking with Steven, for the first time I began to see, to really see, that it didn't have to be that way."

Kaitlyn felt Chris's shoulders stiffen ever so slightly, and looking up into his face, she saw she had hurt him. He was tall, but so was she, and she didn't have to rise very far on her toes to kiss his cheek. "I know. Steven wasn't the first one to tell me that. It's not that I didn't want to believe you. But you have to admit, the evidence didn't really support your claims. In our world, I kept messing up, and you never messed up. I didn't see a lot of life changing going on. But with Steven, I do. I've heard all the stories about him, but the guy I was with today is facing down his past, and because I believe he can change, I believe I can change. Can you see that?"

"I guess that makes sense. As long as you remember that I never stopped believing in you." He looked tired as he patted her shoulder. "I turned the heater on in your trailer before I took Sarah home. I guess we should get to bed. Morning comes . . . Well, good night."

"Good night, and thanks."

As he ambled down the hall toward his room, Kaitlyn was filled with a wave of love for this bear of a brother who so steadfastly tried to put himself between her and anything that might hurt her.

"You know, Chris, when Livvy heard that you and Sarah were getting married, she didn't see why you had to mess things up." He turned around at her voice. "She thought things were going so well the way they were that there really wasn't any reason to change. I'm beginning to think she might have a point."

Chris just turned back to his room without saying anything, but from his raised eyebrow and that funny little smile, she could tell he wasn't ready to go that far.

20

No question about it, Steven knew he was going to have to talk to Chris. Once, in high school, he had actually had a girl's dad sit in the living room cleaning his shotgun when Steven was over. Chris hadn't done that, but Steven had the feeling that it was only because he didn't own a shotgun. Chris just glowered. He glowered when Kaitlyn and Steven went out. He glowered when they stayed in. He even glowered when Steven came into the Dip 'n' Dine for lunch, and as far as Steven could tell, no other customer, either from Last Chance or just passing through, ever got glowered at.

A few weeks earlier, when Chris and Sarah had gone to Scottsdale for the weekend to meet Chris's folks, Chris had suddenly decided that he didn't want Kaitlyn staying behind in Last Chance without him and tried to get her and Olivia to come along. No one liked that idea. Olivia didn't want to miss her riding lesson, Sarah tried diplomatically to point out that the invitation had just included the two of them, and Kaitlyn had told him he was flat out of his mind. In the end, Chris and Sarah had gone alone. From what he had heard from Kaitlyn, she had made the right decision, because the weekend had been a disaster, although the word was that Brooke was telling all her friends that Chris's fiancée was absolutely darling—in a fresh, unspoiled, country way. And whether it was Kaitlyn staying behind where Steven was or the disastrous trip to Scottsdale, Chris left Last Chance glowering and had pretty much glowered nonstop since he got back.

He stopped his truck in front of the Dip 'n' Dine and shut off the engine. For a moment he just sat there. In one bound, Speed Bump cleared the console and stood on his lap with her front paws on the door, looking out. He put her back where she was.

"Sorry, dog. You're staying in the truck. I'll be back soon." He got out and headed for the door. Kaitlyn had already gone to get Olivia, and there were only a few tables filled this late in the day.

"Hey, Steven. Grab a seat anywhere. I'll be with you in a minute." Juanita breezed past with a couple plates of enchiladas.

He sat on a stool at the counter and put his hat on the stool next to him. Through the window into the kitchen, he could see Chris sitting at his desk, computer open.

"Now, then. What can I get you? Do you need a menu, or do you already know what you want? " Juanita appeared on the other side of the counter and pulled her order pad out of her pocket.

"Nope, don't need a menu." Steven saw Chris look up briefly at the sound of his voice before going back to what he was doing. "I smelled the enchiladas as soon as I got out of the truck, and seeing them go by didn't change my mind any. I'll have the cheese enchiladas, red, with an egg over easy on top. With some iced tea."

"You got it." She wrote down the order and then reached behind her to clip it to the rack in the window. "So, how are things going at Elizabeth's? We went up to see her Sunday afternoon, and she seemed to be coming along really well."

"Yep. She can really move on that walker now. Of course, she's not going to be happy until she's down to a cane, or walking on her own. You know Gran."

"Oh, my, do I. How is the house coming?" Juanita poured his iced tea with a quick twist of her wrist.

"Pretty near finished. I put the grab bars in last weekend, and the ramp is about done. It'll be ready when she is."

"Well, we pray that's soon." Juanita looked up as the front door opened. "Oops, more customers. Give her my love when you talk to her again."

Steven turned around on his stool and leaned back, elbows resting on the counter. Through the front window, he could see Speed Bump, now up on the dashboard, staring at him. She still liked being wherever he was best, but Speed Bump and Aunt Nancy Jo were becoming real buddies, and he had no doubt that when he left for the academy, his dog would have a home. That was one less thing he had to worry about.

Juanita was still busy with the new customers, one of whom apparently had just returned from a trip to Galveston, when Steven's enchiladas were ready, so Chris brought the plate out and set it in front of him.

"Here you go. Anything else I can get for you?" Chris smiled, but it was brief and professional.

"Nope. This looks great."

"Well, enjoy." Chris turned to go back to the kitchen.

"Chris, wait." Steven tried to keep his voice low to keep from alerting Juanita. Chris stopped and looked at him. "We need to talk. I can tell there are some things you need to say, and when you get down to it, I have things to say too. I can't think of a place in Last Chance where we can just talk and know we're not going to be interrupted, so let me pick you up after you close, and we can grab a burger or something in San Ramon."

After a long moment, Chris slowly nodded. "Yeah, okay, I could do that."

"Great." Steven picked up his fork. He had to talk fast as Juanita had noticed the murmured conversation and was clearly trying to wind things up on the Galveston front so she could come see what was going on. "After all, we're going to be relatives, and we need to get the air cleared."

Chris stopped as if he'd walked into a wall and, wheeling around, nailed Steven with a look that should have melted his face.

Steven just shook his head. "You're marrying my cousin, bro. Chill."

The big neon sign showing donuts lowering into a coffee cup that gave the Dip 'n' Dine its name was dark against the window when Steven pulled back into the parking lot, and most of the lights inside were out. Chris must have been watching for him, because he came right out and was locking the front door by the time Steven brought the truck to a stop.

"Been waiting long?" Steven shifted into Reverse when Chris got in.

"Nope. Juanita left about a half hour ago, and Carlos just left. Timing's perfect."

"Great." Steven pulled out onto the highway and headed toward San Ramon. "Burger okay? Or do you have something else in mind?"

"No preference whatsoever. Whatever you choose is good."

Chris looked a little more relaxed than Steven had seen in a while, and he hoped that meant the evening would go well.

"Ever been to El Guapo?"

"Nope. I don't think I've even heard of it."

"That doesn't surprise me too much. It's in kind of a seedy part of town and looks like a real dive from the outside. It looks like a dive on the inside too, for that matter, but the food is worth the drive. They serve local beef—ours, as a matter of fact—and the chile comes from Russ and Juanita's farm, so you know it's good."

"Sounds like a good choice. I'm looking forward to it." Chris really did look interested, and Steven was glad he thought of El Guapo. It also had the added bonus of being rather dark and always busy. They could find a corner and talk as long as they wanted.

The parking lot was nearly full, but Steven found a spot in the back and led the way inside.

"Hey, Steven! Where've you been?" A waitress in jeans and a peasant blouse threw her arm around his neck and kissed his cheek.

"We need a booth in the back, Celia. Got anything for us?"

"Yep, there's that one right in the back. Just cleaned it." She raised her voice to attract the attention of a couple who had just spotted it themselves. "Excuse me! Sorry, that table's reserved."

On their way back to their table, the bartender also called a welcome to Steven, and he wound up stopping at two or three tables to speak to folks who reached out with a smile to shake his hand as he passed by.

"Been here before, I take it." Chris's face was hard to read as he slid into the booth across from Steven.

"Yeah, a time or two." Steven was beginning to second-guess the wisdom of bringing Chris to his favorite watering hole. He had a feeling it wasn't helping his case much.

"Long time, no see, Steven." Celia appeared at their table with glasses of water. She turned her smile on Chris. "Who's your friend?"

"This is Chris Reed. He's the new owner of the Dip 'n' Dine."

"Oh, I've heard about you." She beamed as she extended her

hand. "Everyone's talking about the new owner of the Dip 'n' Dine. Welcome to El Guapo."

"He's engaged to my cousin Sarah."

Celia was all business again. "Well, congratulations. Know what you want, or do you need a little more time?"

"I'll have a cheeseburger with green chile and some fries, and a glass of iced tea." Chris handed her his menu.

"All right. How about you?" She looked at Steven.

"I'll have the same."

"Iced tea too?"

"Yep."

"Alrighty." She looked at him as she took his menu. "I'll get those right out."

"You didn't have to get iced tea on my account." Chris leaned back in his seat and looked around the room.

"I didn't." Steven bristled just a little, but Chris didn't seem to notice.

The burgers were served and eaten and the iced tea glasses refilled before Chris pushed his plate out of the way and propped his elbows on the table.

"Okay, this may sound really corny, but I'd really like to know what your intentions are concerning Kaitlyn."

It was all Steven could do to keep from asking Chris if he was joking. Who asked that these days, anyway? But from the look on Chris's face, he knew there was no joke intended.

"It's kind of soon to know where this is going, Chris. I think both Kaitlyn and I have learned the wisdom of taking it slow. But I'll tell you what my intentions are not. I do not intend to hurt, or show disrespect, or let any harm come to her. I want nothing but good things for Kaitlyn."

"Aren't you leaving town?"

"I leave for the Law Enforcement Academy in April with the intention of becoming a New Mexico State Police officer. That's been in the works since before I met you two. But that doesn't mean I won't come back. Last Chance is my home. I've got family here."

"Even your family has told Kaitlyn to steer clear of you. Do you know that?"

"Yes, I know it. Would it surprise you to know that I even understand why? But they're wrong. You are too, if you think I could ever hurt Kaitlyn."

Chris looked away a moment like he was thinking before leaning forward and holding Steven's gaze with his own. "Look, this is my concern. Kaitlyn may try to look tough with those weird haircuts and that attitude of hers, but she's got a soft and tender heart. And I've seen her give it to jerks who took it, mangled it, and then tossed it in the trash on their way out of town. Danny was gone before I even knew what was going on. That Jase character who she took off with last summer left her broke and stranded in Florida. I've seen the happy little girl I watched grow up diminish a little more, hate herself a little more, every time it's happened. And I'm here to tell you, it's not happening again. Not on my watch."

"More iced tea?" Celia with her pitcher smiled down at both of them. Actually, Steven was glad for the interruption. It gave him a moment to collect his thoughts, because, truthfully, he wanted to punch someone. He wanted to punch Danny. He wanted to punch Jase. When you got right down to it, he wasn't too happy with Chris either, for lumping him in with the other two.

He took a deep breath before speaking. "I know how much Kaitlyn means to you, and I know how much she loves you. Any guy who wants to be part of Kaitlyn's life had better know that and be ready for it. I get that. But you need to get that Kaitlyn is not that little girl anymore. She's a grown woman with a child of her own." Chris started to say something, but Steven held up his hand. "Let me finish. I know she's not been the best mom until now. She told me all about it, and she told me how you stepped in and took over. But she's strong now, and getting stronger every day. Haven't you noticed? Haven't you noticed what a good mother she is? How she loves Livvy and cares for her? I've been over at Gran's every afternoon working on that ramp when Kaitlyn and Livvy come by to feed the cat, and the way she talks to Livvy, and listens to her, and the way Livvy responds just blows me away. Kaitlyn's amazing. Haven't you noticed?"

Steven paused so Chris could say what he had on his mind, but when Chris didn't say anything, he went on.

"Look, I don't know what the future holds. Kaitlyn's still figuring out what she wants to do with her life, and I've got the academy coming right up. But I will tell you this. If I could look down the road and see a life with Kaitlyn and Livvy, I would consider myself blessed beyond anything I could have hoped for."

He stopped talking then, and for a while no one said anything. Celia brought the check and Steven picked it up. Finally Chris cleared his throat.

"You know, when they brought Kaitlyn home from the hospital, they put her on my lap and said, 'This is your baby sister, and your job is to take care of her and make sure nothing ever happens to her.' I was about four, and I'm sure they had no idea I would take it as a sacred charge, but I did. She was *my* baby sister, and protecting her was *my* job. Hard to give it up after all these years."

"You're getting married, man." Steven leaned back and grinned.

"It's time. Kaitlyn's doing fine. And between you and me? I think my cousin is pretty incredible herself and deserves a husband with nothing on his mind but her. Don't tell her I said that, though."

"Your secret's safe." Chris began to move out of the booth, but Steven stopped him.

"Wait, I need to say one more thing."

Chris's smile faded at the expression on Steven's face. "Sounds serious."

"It is. I know—all of Last Chance knows—that last year when Kaitlyn was at her lowest point and you were taking care of Livvy, she signed guardianship of Livvy over to you." Steven paused as he saw Chris's jaw tense. "That may have been the best thing for everyone concerned; general consensus is that it was. I don't know. But I do know this: the Kaitlyn of last summer is not the Kaitlyn we both know. The Kaitlyn I know is a good mother, an outstanding mother, and she's never going to be separated from her daughter again. I think she deserves to be the guardian of her own child. If not today, then by the time you get married at the latest."

"And this concerns you . . . *how*?" Chris's voice was cold.

"Kaitlyn concerns me. Her happiness and well-being concern me, and when you get right down to it, I'm concerned about Livvy and her welfare too. I know I don't have any legal right at this stage to stick my two cents in, and that's your point. But all I'm asking is that you see Kaitlyn as the woman she is, not the woman she was, and talk it over with her." He extended his hand across the table.

After a few seconds, Chris's shoulders relaxed and he shook the hand Steven held out to him. "Okay, I can promise that Kaitlyn and I will talk about this sometime before the wedding. But right now, that's all I can promise."

"Fair enough." Steven slid out of the booth and led the way back through El Guapo, lifting his hand in a wave to the bartender, slapping a diner or two on the shoulder as he passed, and finally giving Celia a one-armed hug at the door.

Outside, the winter night had turned even colder, and he turned his collar up as they went out back where the truck was parked. Steven hoisted himself inside and started the engine while Chris climbed in the other side.

Chris didn't say much on the trip back to Last Chance, and Steven could only guess what he might be thinking. He glanced over and in the greenish glow of the dashboard lights, Chris looked pretty grim.

"Thanks for coming with me, man." Steven looked back at the white lines of Last Chance Highway disappearing into the darkness ahead. "I really appreciate the chance to talk with you."

"Yeah. It was good. I appreciate the invitation."

"So were we able to get things cleared up a little? Are you satisfied that my intentions are honorable?" He looked over with a grin that Chris did not return.

"Well, I liked what I heard. I'll give you that. Kaitlyn tends to do what she wants to anyway. But you've got to know, I'll be watching."

"Right." Steven tried to keep his voice even. "Thanks for the heads-up."

He sensed, rather than saw, the quick look Chris shot his way, and hoped he hadn't undone an evening's effort with one cynical comment. But man, Chris was getting under his skin. He could appreciate the fact that Chris was protective of his sister. She had been through a lot, and he'd pretty much been the only one who was there for her. But he wasn't her father, and she wasn't sixteen. Somehow he just didn't get that.

They were driving into Last Chance when Steven spoke again. "Did you tell Kaitlyn where you were going tonight?"

"No, I just told her she didn't need to pick me up because I wouldn't be home for dinner. She probably just assumed I was going to Sarah's."

"Okay, well, unless it involves looking her in the eye and lying through your teeth, I'd appreciate you holding off telling her about our dinner for a day or so until I can tell her myself."

"What are you going to tell her?"

"Just that we had dinner and talked. Of course, I'll tell her what we talked about."

"You're going to tell her what we said? I thought we were having a confidential conversation."

"Well, I'm not going to give her a transcript of our conversation, or quote you, but she certainly has a right to know what we talked about, at least in general terms."

"You're sure about this?"

"Yep, we really needed to talk, and I'm glad we did. But I'm not starting out by hiding things from Kaitlyn, so I'll tell her and take my beating. But you'd better watch out, because when she's done with me, she'll be coming after you."

21

"You *what*?" Kaitlyn had come out to sit in the sun on the front steps and talk to Steven when he came by a few days later to finish Elizabeth's ramp. "You sat around discussing me like I was a prize cow or something? What? Did you ask if you could take me to the prom? Find out what my curfew was?"

"I'd never take a prize cow to the prom, no matter what her curfew was." Steven sat back on his heels and grinned up at her.

If he thought it was funny, Kaitlyn did not. She gave him a look that could have turned him to stone and jumped to her feet, heading for the front door.

"Kaitlyn, wait. I was kidding. It wasn't that way at all. Let me explain. Please?"

She stopped with her hand on the doorknob and glared at him. Standing up, he held out his hand.

"Come sit with me and I'll tell you all about it. Promise, there was no talk of proms or curfews . . . or cows either, for that matter."

"So what did he do? Demand to know what your intentions were?"

Kaitlyn noticed he didn't answer the question as he led her to the top step and sat down beside her, but she decided to let it go. She was already mad enough; no need to look for gasoline to throw on the flames.

"This is what happened." Steven tried to put his arm around her, but she leaned away. "I couldn't help noticing that the more I was around, the quieter Chris got, and the deadlier those looks he kept sending my way were. I figured for a man who wasn't talking, he sure looked like he had a lot to say, so I took him out for dinner and let him say his piece. That's all."

"What'd he say?"

"Pretty much what I expected. He likes me all right, just not for you."

"What business is it of his anyway? Who does he think he is?"

She rubbed her arms. The sun was getting low, and it was not as warm as it had been. Steven pulled her close, and this time she didn't protest.

"He thinks he's your brother, Kaitlyn. Come on. He's seen you hurt bad by men no worse than me and doesn't want to see it happen again."

"Is that what he said? That you're no better than Jase or Danny?" Kaitlyn jerked away again and looked up into Steven's face.

"No, that was my own take. But cut him some slack, Kaitlyn. Remember the first time I met you at the ranch last Christmas? The first thing Sarah said was that you'd steer clear of me if you had any sense. My own grandmother, bless her, who'd take on a grizzly if she thought one was threatening me, told me I needed to leave you alone. Can you blame Chris for being protective?"

"Why are you sticking up for him? He doesn't know you at all." Kaitlyn relaxed against Steven again. It was warmer, for one thing, with his arm around her and with his big hand running absently up and down her arm.

"I guess I've been doing some soul searching myself. I had to admit that if I were Chris, and all I had to go on was what I had heard about this dude who was interested in my sister, I wouldn't like it much either. Besides, I don't want to take up a grudge against Chris. He's your brother, and he's going to be Sarah's husband. I'd like to be friends with the guy, and I don't want to burn any bridges."

"I'm still so mad at him that I could knock him into next week."

"For what? Giving an answer when someone said, 'What's on your mind?' That's not fair."

"Oh, stop it. If I want to be mad at my brother, I'm going to be mad." Kaitlyn bumped him with her shoulder. After a second, she nudged him again. "So, what did you say?"

"What'd I say when?"

"The other night when you were with Chris. Isn't that what we're talking about? You had to have said something."

"Well, I told him I was going to the academy in the spring, but I was coming back. And I told him I thought you were amazing. You're an amazing woman, you're an amazing mom, and the best part of my life is the part I get to spend with you."

"Really? You told him that?" Kaitlyn twisted slightly in his arm and gazed up at him.

"Really." He smiled and brushed a strand of hair from her face with his free hand before tipping her face to meet his. His kiss was gentle, questioning, but when she closed her eyes and raised her arm to caress his neck, he tightened his embrace and claimed her willing mouth.

"Mom? Can I have another cookie?"

Olivia was talking as the front door opened, and Kaitlyn jerked away. From her expression, it was hard to know what or how much

Olivia had seen, but Kaitlyn still felt a flush cover her neck and warm her cheeks.

"I thought you were watching *My Little Pony*."

"It's over."

"Oh. Well, it's a little close to dinnertime. You're going to have to skip the cookie, I'm afraid."

She didn't move or look at Steven. "Are you coming in now?"

Ah. Well, that answers that question.

"Sure. We need to get going anyway." She got to her feet and smiled down at Steven, still sitting on the top step. "You coming in too?"

He looked back at the ramp. "No, I still have about a half hour of light left, and I need to get this done. I haven't had nearly the amount of time to work on it as I thought I would, and Ray and Lainie are coming in this weekend. I want to have everything ready. All I have left is finishing this ramp and moving the twin bed out of the guest room. They're bringing their own."

"I see." And Kaitlyn did. She could see how important it was to Steven that when his brother walked in the door, he would find nothing left to do but bring Gran home. "Tell you what. Livvy and I have pretty much helped ourselves to whatever we wanted these last weeks. Why don't I give the kitchen a real cleaning out tomorrow when I'm here, and then Friday afternoon we can go up to San Ramon and restock it."

"Sounds good." Steven smiled his agreement.

"Can I come, Mom?" Olivia was still standing in the doorway and still hadn't looked at Steven.

"Of course you're coming." Steven got up from the step and went back to his ramp. "You can even pick where we have dinner."

"The place where you put the quarters in and play music."

"That's just what I was hoping you'd say." He winked at Olivia, and she smiled back at him before she danced inside.

Chris never called Kaitlyn to come get him until he was ready to walk out the door, so she found him waiting in front of the locked and darkened Dip 'n' Dine when she and Olivia drove up to the door.

"Whoa, that was one long day." Chris got in the passenger side and reached for his seat belt. He glanced in the backseat. "Hey there, Miss Livvy. How was school?"

"Good."

He looked back at Kaitlyn and grinned. "Same question, same answer, every day. If I didn't ask one day, I wonder if she'd come find me anyway and say, 'Good.'"

"No, I wouldn't. That would be dumb." Olivia's voice floated from the backseat.

Chris laughed.

Kaitlyn didn't say anything.

"Did you start dinner?" Chris rolled his shoulders to ease the muscles.

"Yes."

"What are we having?"

"Chicken."

After they rode a few more blocks in silence, Chris tilted his head to look over at her. "Is something wrong?"

She gave him a long, slow glare before turning back to the road. "You are in so much trouble."

"Ah." Understanding dawned in his voice. "Saw Steven today, did we?"

"Yeah, and they kissed."

"Livvy!" Kaitlyn glanced in the rearview mirror before looking back at Chris. "We'll talk later, but I don't believe you!"

Chris muttered something Kaitlyn didn't quite catch and looked out the side window.

Kaitlyn didn't say anything else till they walked in the front door, and then all she said was, "Livvy, go finish picking up your room. Dinner will be ready in fifteen minutes."

Chris followed her into the kitchen. "Okay, let's have it."

She turned on him. "For starters, why didn't you tell me you were going out with Steven? You let me think Sarah was picking you up, and that's as bad as lying."

He had the grace to look guilty. "You got me there. I went out for dinner with Steven because he asked me, and as for not telling you about it, well, what would have happened if I had told you?"

"You wouldn't have gone! That's what would have happened."

"There you have your answer." He peeked in the oven. "What did you do to that chicken?"

"I poured a couple cans of mushrooms and a jar of spaghetti sauce over it. It's chicken cacciatore. Now, stop trying to change the subject. You had to know I'd find out."

"I knew you'd find out. Steven told me he was going to tell you all about it, and it sure looks like he did. He said you'd rip him up first and then come after me."

"He was right about that."

"Yeah? Well, I can speak for the coming after me part. But as for ripping him up first, from what Livvy said, that's not exactly how it went down. I'd love to know what he told you."

"Oh, you would? Well, he told me he didn't blame you. He said based on what everyone said, including his own grandmother, you had good reason to feel like you did. He said you felt like you did because you didn't want me to get hurt again, and I should cut you some slack."

As Kaitlyn spoke, and almost against her will, she felt the rage she had been nursing begin to drain out of her. Steven was right. All her brother had ever wanted was to stand between her and anything that might cause her pain, and if that sometimes meant that he got in her way, well, that was just who he was.

"He also said he hopes you two can be friends." Kaitlyn leaned against the counter and folded her arms.

Chris crossed the room, put his hands on Kaitlyn's shoulders, and looked down into her face. "This is not about us being friends. I like Steven. Heck, everyone in town likes Steven, and that's in spite of all the stuff he's pulled over the years. This is about you. It's about Livvy too, since everything you do is going to affect her. Steven talks a good game, but from what I hear, talking a good game is what he's always done best."

Kaitlyn felt a wave of sadness wash over her. This wasn't going anywhere. She stepped away from Chris's touch and looked up at him.

"I have a question, and I want you to think carefully and give me an honest answer. Can you do that?"

He frowned. "I can try."

"Okay, here it is. If all you had to go on was what you saw, what would you think of Steven? I mean if Sarah, and Juanita, and everyone else in town hadn't filled you in, and all you knew of Steven was what you saw with your own eyes or heard with your own ears, what would you think?"

Chris looked over her head a moment. He looked back at her and shrugged. "I told you I thought he was a likeable guy. That's not the issue."

"But it is, don't you see? You don't know what it's like to drag your past around with you. You meet someone, and they don't even see you; they're too busy digging through that pile of junk that you're chained to. All I'm asking is that you try to look past all the garbage and try to know the man. That's all."

"What if you get hurt again, baby sister?" Chris looked so helpless.

"I would deal with it. People can change, Chris. Please tell me you believe that."

"People can change." Chris slowly nodded his head. "I know that. I can see it, and you're not the first person this week to remind me of that either."

"Room's clean!" Olivia ran into the kitchen in her stocking feet and slid across the linoleum until she crashed into the cupboard. "Dinner ready?"

—~~—

"You know what I was thinking?" Juanita spoke to the room at large, and since Chris and Kaitlyn were getting the diner ready to open and Olivia was eating her breakfast, nobody answered. "I was thinking that Lainie might be the perfect solution to our problem."

"Problem?" Chris was still preoccupied, but the word *problem* in reference to the Dip 'n' Dine could get his attention.

"Well, yes, you know she was in charge here all the time Fayette was in Albuquerque, and the place ran smooth as cream. Of course, she had a lot of help, myself included, but think about it, Chris—with you, me, and Lainie in here, the Dip 'n' Dine would practically run itself. You could go on that honeymoon and never have a second's worry." She seemed to realize she may have stepped on some toes and looked at Kaitlyn, busy filling saltshakers. "No offense, Kaitlyn."

"None taken." Kaitlyn looked up and smiled. Truth be told, the idea of Juanita, Chris, and Lainie in here with Kaitlyn elsewhere sounded good to her too.

"Ray and Lainie are coming home to help Elizabeth." Chris headed back to the kitchen. "I think her hands are going to be pretty full."

"But that's the beauty of my idea." Juanita followed him, but acoustics in the Dip 'n' Dine being as they were, Kaitlyn could still hear every word. "Don't you see? I'm thinking Kaitlyn would be there in the daytime, while Lainie worked here. Then at night, why, Lainie and Ray would be home with her. Makes perfect sense to me."

Chris came back into the dining room with Juanita right behind him. Finally, cornered by the pie safe, he turned to face her. "Juanita, has it occurred to you that none of this is your concern? Elizabeth has her family to see to her welfare, and the Dip 'n' Dine, and who works here, is my problem. That's what makes sense to me."

He tried to push past her, but pushing past Juanita was never as easy as you thought it was going to be.

"Well, excuse me for living, Chris, but we all know that the hospitality industry is not Kaitlyn's cup of tea, and now that she's got her New Mexico beauty license, she needs to be doing something she's actually good at. No offense, Kaitlyn."

"None taken."

"I can just see her giving the occasional haircut or perm in Elizabeth's kitchen with Elizabeth sitting there enjoying the company." Juanita sucked in air through her nose. She always seemed to expand when she was offended, a practice that never ceased to fascinate Kaitlyn. "And Lainie is a natural in this business if I ever saw one. Not to mention the fact that a little variety in their day might be appreciated by all three of them. But you know best, of course. Now, if you don't mind, I've got work to do."

She turned on her heel and marched off, leaving Chris grinding his teeth. Kaitlyn caught his eye and gave him a sweet smile. He did not return the pleasantry. He stared after Juanita a long moment, then slapped the kitchen door open with the flat of his hand and disappeared inside.

Kaitlyn picked up Olivia's empty breakfast dishes and followed him into the kitchen. He had plopped in his desk chair and was glaring at his computer screen and stabbing at the keys like he was at war with the keyboard. She put a hand on his shoulder and leaned down to murmur in his ear.

"Are you mad because you don't want Juanita's input, or because her idea was a good one?"

He didn't even acknowledge she was there, and Kaitlyn straightened and looked at Carlos with a shrug.

"Do you ever cut guys' hair?" Pete, the nephew who helped Carlos, looked up from the onions he was chopping.

"Sure." She gestured toward Chris. "I've been cutting his hair since I got here. What do you think?"

He looked doubtful. "Is that the only way you can make it look?"

This time Chris did look up, and his expression said he had taken about as much as any man should be expected to. "What's wrong with my hair?"

"It's too short, man. I've got great hair. Look at this." He bent his head so they could see the top. "Hair like this is a work of art."

"Those onions about chopped, Samson?" Carlos set a pan of biscuits, ready for baking, next to the stove.

Pete sent a look his uncle's way that Carlos chose not to see.

Kaitlyn laughed. "I think I can give you a haircut you'd be happy with. You could come over to the house. Just let me know."

Chris dropped his hands to his lap, leaned back, and glared up at Kaitlyn in exasperation. "We're not getting in your way here, are we?"

She smiled and blew him an air kiss. Mouthing "Later" to Pete, she went back into the dining room. Juanita had unlocked the door and was getting coffee for the first customers.

"What in this world is the matter with Chris this morning?" Juanita's whisper carried, as it always did, but fortunately the early diners seemed more interested in their own conversation than in Juanita's. In the kitchen, however, Chris slammed something down on his desk, and Juanita shook her head as she glanced that direction. "He hasn't been this cranky since he first got here and was having such a hard time settling in."

Kaitlyn lowered her voice to a real whisper. "Maybe we should just leave him alone for a while. He's always been sort of an 'everything in its time and place' kind of guy, and he has a lot going on right now." She lowered her voice even more. "But I *love* your idea."

Steven left the ranch that afternoon in time to swing by Gran's house on the way to school and basketball practice. The work was done, but it had been pretty close to dark when he finished up last night, and he wanted to make sure it looked as good as he thought it did by daylight.

Chris's Jeep was parked at the curb, and as he walked up the sidewalk, Kaitlyn came to the door. Her smile made his day.

"The ramp looks great. You did a terrific job." She stepped out onto the front porch.

He stopped and gave the railing a shake. Rock solid. "Yep, I think it will work." He knelt to inspect his handiwork. "What are you doing here now? Isn't Livvy coming to basketball practice?"

"Oh, yes. She wouldn't miss it. But after we talked about getting the kitchen ready for Lainie and Ray and your grandmother, I got to thinking that the whole house could probably stand a cleaning, so I'm taking this time to do that. You know, put fresh sheets on her bed and clean towels in the bathroom, that sort of thing."

"Really? That's such a nice thing to do." He stood up and leaned against his railing.

"Well, I happen to think your Gran is pretty wonderful. After all she's done for us, I'd like to think I can do a little something for her. I'm so glad she gets to come back to her own house, thanks to you."

"Well, it couldn't have happened without Ray and Lainie coming back either. I just got the house ready. They're the ones who'll be here taking care of her."

"Is your aunt any happier about that?"

"Not especially, and I think I'm beginning to wear out my welcome up there. I haven't been around the ranch as much because of the house and basketball and stuff, so Uncle Joe Jr. has been making a pointed comment or two. And Aunt Nancy Jo really wanted Gran to come back to the ranch to live. She and my uncle have ruled the roost for quite a while now, and they don't like having their edicts questioned." He shrugged. "But this is what Gran wants, and I'm glad that Ray and I can give it to her."

"Does that mean you have to leave? They won't throw you out or anything?"

"Nah. I'm done with the house, and Ray will be here in a couple days. I'll work hard and get back in Uncle Joe Jr.'s good graces, and once Aunt Nancy Jo sees that Gran is not only well taken care of but happy, she'll be okay too. It's only a few months till I leave for the academy, anyway."

"Right. Just a few more months." Kaitlyn had a funny look on her face that Steven couldn't quite read, but at least it had a smile attached to it. "Do you have time to come in for a cup of coffee or something?"

"No time; I need to get to school." He started down the walk, then turned around to see her still standing on the porch. "Shall I bring Livvy here after practice?"

"That would be great, thanks."

He lifted his hand in a wave and headed to his truck. Not for the first time, he wondered what it might be like to have her standing on his porch, waving good-bye every morning.

22

By late Saturday afternoon everything was ready. Gran's house was equipped for her new journey, and it was clean and stocked with groceries. Steven opened a bottle of Ray's favorite grape soda and settled on the sofa to watch a golf tournament on TV and wait for Ray and Lainie to arrive.

"Hey you, heard anything yet?" Sarah opened the front door and slipped off her shoes before padding across the carpet to sit cross-legged in Elizabeth's recliner.

"Yep, they called about an hour ago from San Ramon. They were going to stop in and see Gran, and then come on down. Should be here pretty soon."

"Well, Mom called again, and I'm supposed to call her the minute they get here so she can know when to have dinner on the table."

"They're going to love that." Steven picked up the remote and hit the Mute button. A lot of commentary wasn't necessary to follow a golf tournament. "They've been traveling with all their stuff since this morning, and as soon as they get here, it's back in the car for another trip."

"Well, Mom's got her heart set on a family dinner tonight, and the ranch isn't all that far." Sarah looked around. "Everything looks so nice, Steven. You really did a good job here."

"This is all Kaitlyn's doing. Do you really think I'd have thought to put flowers on the coffee table?"

"I'm not just talking about that, I'm talking about all the other stuff you did. You worked so hard. Gran can live here now, and I love you for that."

Steven turned the sound back on. This was getting embarrassing.

"Hey, there they are!" Sarah headed for the door and barely stopped for her shoes before she ran across the porch and down Steven's ramp.

By the time the fully loaded pickup pulling a small trailer had come to a complete stop, she was standing on the curb, reaching for the door handle. Steven followed, using the porch steps, and met his brother as he walked around the truck to the sidewalk.

"Hey, bro." He drew him into a hug. "Welcome home."

"Thanks. It's good to be here." He looked around. "Yep. Santa Fe's a beautiful city. But Last Chance will always be home."

When Sarah let go of Lainie, Steven swooped her up in a hug and planted a kiss on her cheek. "Everyone in town is looking forward to having you back. Maybe even more than him."

"That doesn't surprise me." Ray hoisted a couple suitcases from the back of his pickup and set them on the sidewalk. "I got an earful from a lot of folks when I took her to Santa Fe with me. Maybe they'll start speaking to me again now."

"Did Steven tell you the plans when you called him from San Ramon?" Sarah picked up one of the suitcases.

"What plans?" Ray looked at Steven.

"I didn't know I was supposed to tell them, Sarah." Steven returned Sarah's irritated stare with one of his own. "Why don't you bring them up to speed?"

"What plans?" This time Ray sounded a little irritated himself.

"Well, Mom wants us all to come to the ranch for dinner. She is so looking forward to seeing you. I know it's a real inconvenience after your long trip, but the meal will be worth the trip, promise."

Ray didn't say anything, but Lainie, after only a second, smiled. "Of course we'd love to come. Let's get the truck unloaded, and then we'll take a few minutes to clean up and we'll be ready to go."

Steven looked in the truck bed. "Doesn't look like you brought much."

"No, not much. I have a box or two of kitchen things that I guess I can store back in Elizabeth's garage, but other than that, it's pretty much just our bed and clothes."

"What about the trailer?" Steven gestured at the U-Haul with his chin.

"That's Ray's studio." Lainie huffed a sigh. "Everything I own, you'll notice, is open to the wind and the rain, but Ray's precious paints are tucked away, safe and dry."

"What rain?" Ray looked into the cloudless sky. "Everything in that trailer is what affords you the sumptuous lifestyle to which you have become accustomed, by the way."

"Tell you what." Steven put another suitcase and a couple boxes on the sidewalk. "Why don't Ray and I put the bed together so you'll have someplace to sleep when you get home tonight? You girls can bring in the boxes and just set them aside until later. If any are too heavy, just leave them and we'll get to them when the bed's done."

Steven, with a mattress rail in each hand, nearly ran into Lainie when she stopped just inside the front door.

"Oh, it looks just the same, and it smells the same too." She smiled over her shoulder at Steven. "Isn't it funny how houses have their own smells? All it needs now is Elizabeth sitting right there in that rocker with her crocheting on her lap."

Steven nodded and shifted the rails slightly in his hands. They weren't particularly heavy, but they were each nearly six feet long and a little awkward. They took a few more steps before Lainie stopped again, and Steven was once more forced to pull up short.

"Here's old Sammy!" The big gray tabby had launched off the back of the sofa and landed at her feet with his usual thud. Lainie knelt to scratch his chin and pet him. With every stroke down his back, Sam's tail rose higher and higher until his back feet were practically leaving the ground. "I'm home, Sam, and I've brought us a new roommate too. You'll like him."

"Watch your head." Steven stepped around Lainie and headed down the hall. It looked like this was going to take a while.

Ray, who had managed to get in the front door before Lainie, had propped the headboard against the wall.

"Where's Lainie?" He moved out of the way as Steven put a rail on the floor at each end of the headboard. "We might as well find out exactly where she wants the bed now. Save us the trouble of moving it later."

"I'm right here." Lainie appeared in the doorway, cuddling Sam. "Oh, I'm so glad everything looks the same. I love this room."

"Where do you want the bed?"

Ray stood ready to move the headboard, but Lainie was still basking in her homecoming.

"You know, when Elizabeth first showed me this room, I thought I had never seen anything so beautiful." She put Sam down and ran her hand across the top of the dresser. "I couldn't believe I was going to get to stay here."

"The bed, Lainie. Where do you want the bed?"

Steven left them and went back to the truck for the footboard.

Maybe they'd have it figured out by the time he got back. If not, well, there were still plenty of boxes to bring in, because Sarah wasn't any more help than Lainie. She was on her phone.

"That was Mom." Sarah followed him out the door. "I forgot to call her, so of course she called me. I told her dinner at 6:00. I think we can do that, don't you?"

Steven grabbed a box from the truck, hefted it to determine its weight, and put it in Sarah's arms. "If we get moving, we can."

She put it on the sidewalk and went back to her phone. "I'll give Chris a quick call and tell him when we'll be by for them."

Once they had the bed together and Lainie had completed her detailed inspection of the house, it really did not take long before the last box had been brought in the house or stored in the garage and the truck bed was empty.

"I guess that's it." Ray picked up the last suitcase and headed for the door. "We can leave the trailer. I'll take it up tomorrow and unpack my studio."

"Are you still going to be using your cabin at the ranch for your studio? Seems like a long way to go every day to paint." Steven followed him up the walk.

"It's not ideal, that's for sure. But I don't know what else to do at this point. I sure can't work here. But when you get down to it, I love that cabin. The light's perfect, and I've done some of my best work there."

Sarah was helping Lainie make up the bed when Steven and Ray walked in with the last suitcase. "This takes care of it. I guess we can start the unpacking tomorrow."

Lainie hit the bedspread with a few smoothing strokes and straightened up. "Steven, what happened to the patchwork quilt that was on the bed in here? I love that quilt."

He thought a minute. “I think it’s up in the top of the closet there, isn’t it?”

“Ah, there it is.” She pulled it down. “I’ll just fold it at the foot of the bed.”

“Are we all ready to go get the Reeds and head to the ranch now?” Sarah was the only one who didn’t look tired, but then, why should she?

“Tell you what.” Steven put his hands on her shoulders and steered her toward the hall. “Why don’t you and I go over there now, and you and Chris can come back for Ray and Lainie while Kaitlyn, Livvy, and I head on up to the ranch?” He glanced over his shoulder at his brother. “I’m thinking you two could use a minute or two to unwind.”

“Hey, that sounds good.” Ray smiled his thanks. “Maybe a half hour?”

“You got it.” He gave Sarah a little nudge between her shoulder blades, and she turned around and swatted at his hand. “Come on, you. Let’s go get Chris and Kaitlyn.”

Kaitlyn grabbed the armrest with one hand and braced the other against the ceiling as Steven’s truck hit a pothole on the dirt road from the highway to the ranch house.

Steven didn’t even act like he noticed, but Kaitlyn noticed, all right, and truth be told, she did not remember this road as being so interminably long, or bumpy, or having so many turns.

“It is so dark. I’ve never seen it so dark.” Kaitlyn kept her eyes riveted forward, where the headlights were, in her opinion, doing an entirely inadequate job of illuminating the landscape.

“Yep, nothing but nighttime out here.” Steven terrified Kaitlyn even further by taking his eyes off the road to smile at her.

When they crested the final rise and the ranch house with warm light pouring from the windows appeared before them, Kaitlyn finally released her grip on the armrest and took a breath.

"Here we are." Steven stopped the car in front of the house and cut the engine.

Olivia was already out of the truck and heading for the steps by the time Kaitlyn opened her door and stepped out. The wintry night air, fragrant with piñon smoke, cooled her cheeks and calmed her soul.

Steven came up behind her and slid his arms around her shoulders. "What are you looking at?"

She leaned back against him and pointed across the valley. "Look at that. The sky and all those stars, it seems to go on forever. It's like we're floating up here."

He rested his chin on her shoulder. "Yep, that view will pretty much take your breath away any time of day, or season of the year, you look at it. Come on, let's go on in. Livvy left the door open, and pretty soon someone is going to be asking if we were born in a barn."

Nancy Jo came down the hall from the kitchen as they came in. "Good gracious, it's cold in here. Shut that door, Steven. Were you born in a barn? Hello, Kaitlyn." She gave Kaitlyn a quick kiss on the cheek and looked around. "Where are the others?"

"They'll be here soon. Don't worry, everyone knows dinner is at 6:00."

"Well, take your coats off and come in. Kaitlyn, would you like to give me a hand in the kitchen?"

Steven gave Kaitlyn a knowing wink as he took her coat. Despite the heroic efforts of her daughters, notably Sarah, no one had been able to convince Nancy Jo that meal preparation was not a fun-filled communal activity to be enjoyed by all of the women and none of the men.

"Love to." Kaitlyn followed her back down the hall. Sarah may have been looking for a way out of kitchen duty since she was five, but the kitchen camaraderie that Sarah tried so hard to avoid was something Kaitlyn had never experienced. And honestly? She liked it.

"Something smells wonderful." Kaitlyn accepted the apron Nancy Jo handed her. "Lasagna?"

"Close. It's spaghetti and meatballs. Nothing fancy, but it was Ray's favorite when he was a little boy, and my homemade French bread, which he also loved, and Caesar salad. Oh, and I made a chocolate cake for dessert. It's not Italian, but there you have it." She took a bundle from the crisper in the refrigerator and handed it to Kaitlyn. "Would you wash and dry this romaine? Use the paper towels right there, and then break it up and put it in that salad bowl."

Kaitlyn took the lettuce to the sink and turned on the tap. Conversation on her part wasn't really necessary, other than the occasional murmured response to show she was listening. Nancy Jo carried on very well without her.

"Well, I don't know." Nancy Jo looked at the clock with her hands on her hips. "If I bring that water back to the boil and put the spaghetti on to cook right now, we'll be sitting down to the table at 6:00. But with the others not here yet . . ."

"I think they'll be here in time." Kaitlyn piled the romaine in the salad bowl. "Chris is driving and he is never late. Trust me, I know. And when it comes to respecting another cook's meal, he'd be there even if it meant leaving the others behind."

"I knew I loved that boy." Nancy Jo smiled and tilted her head as the sound of an arriving vehicle reached them. "Speak of angels and you'll hear the flutter of wings. Here they are."

She headed off down the hall and Kaitlyn turned the fire up under the big pot of water on the back of the stove. She was glad Lainie had come back to Last Chance. They had only spent a little time together last Christmas day, right in this kitchen for the most part, but Lainie made her feel at home. It's not that everyone else hadn't gone out of their way to welcome her, because they had. But Lainie let her know, casually and naturally, that she had once been the outsider with the past, and Kaitlyn loved her for that.

"Here they are!" Nancy Jo ushered Sarah and Lainie into the kitchen. "Let's get this dinner on the table and eat."

"Hey there, Kaitlyn. It's so good to see you again!" Lainie opened her arms, and Kaitlyn, who had hung back a little, walked into her embrace.

"Hi. Welcome home." Kaitlyn wondered where the shyness seemed to have sprung from.

"Sarah, honey, will you put ice in the glasses? They're already on the table." Nancy Jo turned from the freezer with a bucket of ice, but Sarah had already taken advantage of the moment and disappeared. Nancy Jo sighed.

"I'll do it." Kaitlyn reached for the bucket.

"I'll help you." Lainie followed her out of the kitchen.

"Sarah, I need you," Nancy Jo hollered down the hall.

"So how does it feel to be back in Last Chance?" Kaitlyn set the ice bucket in the middle of the table and started filling glasses as she moved down one side of the table.

"I'm so happy, I can't even tell you." Lainie took the other side. "I loved Santa Fe too, but Last Chance is my heart's home, if that makes any sense. I guess you could say it's where I stopped hating myself."

Wow. What do you say to something like that? Do tell?

"Of course, the chance to help Elizabeth is one neither Ray nor I could pass up. If not for her, I don't even know if I'd be alive today."

Kaitlyn picked up the ice bucket. "I think I know what you mean. It will be so great to have her back home again."

On their way to the kitchen, they met Nancy Jo and Sarah, each carrying a huge platter of spaghetti and meatballs.

"Lainie, would you go tell the men that dinner's ready? And have Livvy wash her hands. She hasn't put that dog down since she got here." Nancy Jo put her platter at one end of the table. "Kaitlyn, go get the pitcher of tea and fill the glasses, will you please?"

When all were gathered around the table, Joe Jr. reached for Steven's and Lainie's hand, and one by one they all joined hands and bowed their heads. Kaitlyn had noticed that at the Cooley table, the saying of grace was never passed around, and tonight, as he always did, Joe Jr. lifted their thanks and asked God's blessing on the meal and on the hands that prepared it.

As food was passed and the conversation swirled around the topics of Ray's art, the move from Santa Fe, Steven's renovation project, and whether this dry spell was likely to turn into a drought, Kaitlyn found her thoughts drawn back again and again to Lainie's comment. She could sort of see the "hating yourself" part. Even as Kaitlyn had chosen to do everything she did, and would have said she liked doing it, part of her always knew there was something darker there, something that made her feel dead inside. But the thing Kaitlyn couldn't understand was the rest of Lainie's observation—the part where she said Last Chance was where she learned to stop the self-hate. How did she do that?

"Is what I hear true, Miss Kaitlyn?" Nancy Jo pulled her back into the conversation. "Does Last Chance finally have its own hairstylist?"

"I don't know about that." It took Kaitlyn a second or two, but she caught up. "I did get my license transferred, but that's about it so far."

"Kaitlyn, that's tremendous." Lainie beamed at her as she reached for the Parmesan cheese. "Are you going to open your own shop?"

"That's too far out there for me to even think about right now. I have no idea where I would put it, and it would cost way more money than I have. So right now, my only option would be to get a job in San Ramon. Of course, I'll still be happy to do friends' hair in the kitchen." She caught Chris's glare. "Yes, in the kitchen at home, dear brother. It happens all the time."

"I guess you're planning on doing your painting up at your cabin?" Joe Jr. clearly thought enough had been said about hairdos.

"I'm going to give it a try." Ray looked over at his uncle. "I'd sure like to make it work."

"I probably shouldn't say anything, since it all seems to have been decided, but I'm sorry you gave up everything, *again*, to come back here to take care of somebody." Nancy Jo sat back in her chair. "I guess I can see you coming back to take care of your daddy. With Steven away in the service, and your mom, bless her, passed on, there wasn't really anyone your daddy'd want but you. But that's just not the case with Gran. This is her home, and this is where she should be."

"I appreciate your concern, Aunt Nancy Jo." Ray waited a long moment before he answered. "But coming home was something I wanted to do, both to be with dad, and now to be with Gran, for that matter. I admit I didn't get in as much painting as I wanted to before, but I'm not expecting things to be that way now."

"Well, I hope not. You've put your life on hold long enough."

Nancy Jo picked up the platter near her and passed it. "Chris, have some more spaghetti. A growing boy like you needs to eat."

Kaitlyn happened to be looking at Steven when his aunt was talking, and she saw his jaw tighten and his gaze drop to his plate. She was almost sure Nancy Jo hadn't intended it that way, but with one remark she had discounted Steven's efforts to keep his grandmother in her own home and managed to remind everyone at the table that Ray had given years of his life so their dad's bar would be there for him when Steven came home. A bar Steven never wanted in the first place.

23

Elizabeth came home in the middle of a March sandstorm. Steven stood in her front window with his hands shoved deep in his pockets, watching tumbleweeds and the occasional bit of trash bounce down the street in the pale, gritty sunshine. Every now and then an especially violent gust slammed against the house and sandblasted the windows. He checked his watch again.

A fall during rehab in February had delayed Gran's progress, and Steven had expected her to be crushed at coming so close to going home only to be set back, but that wasn't Gran. She never had time to lament what might have been. She set her jaw, narrowed those blue eyes, and worked all the harder, and today she was coming home. He and Ray had wanted to go to San Ramon to get her, but Joe Jr. had said she was his mother and he would go, so they waited at her house.

All morning people had been dropping by with casseroles and Bundt cakes and bowls of Jell-O salad. When Lainie heard that meals would be brought in, she had tried to tell them that she would be doing all the cooking, not Elizabeth, but that made no difference. In Last Chance a hospital stay, whether it resulted in a new baby, a removed gall bladder, or, as in Elizabeth's case, a stint in a convalescent home, meant food, and lots of it.

"Should we go ahead and have lunch? We don't know for sure when they'll get here." Lainie stuck her head in from the kitchen where she had been trying to find places to put everything. "How about some chili-mac? We have lots."

"No thanks. I'm guessing they'll be here soon. I can wait. You?" He looked over his shoulder at Ray, who had taken Gran's old guitar out of the hall closet and was sitting on the piano bench plucking it.

"Nope." He didn't look up. "I'm good."

Steven turned back to the window. After a minute Ray spoke again.

"Saw Rita yesterday."

Steven shook his head and winced. *Of course you did. You really have to be on your toes to avoid seeing that woman.*

"She wonders if we know what we're going to do with the High Lonesome. I told her I haven't given it much thought. What about you? She seems pretty anxious for us to get something decided."

"I know. Boy, do I know. Every time I leave a building in town, I have to throw my hat out first to see if she pounces on it. I think she hides in the bushes and waits."

Ray, still bent over the guitar, chuckled. "Sounds like her. But she does have a point. We can't just leave it sitting there. Has there been any interest in it at all?"

Steven paced the room, finally coming to rest on Gran's recliner where he could still see the street. "Some guy in El Paso asked about it, but he was looking to reopen it as a bar."

Ray looked up. "Do you have the guts to tell Gran that's what we did? I don't."

"Nope. That's why I told him we weren't interested. But it still leaves us with the problem of what to do with the thing." He got to his feet as Nancy Jo's station wagon pulled up to the curb. "There they are. Tell you what. Why don't we go over there this afternoon after everything settles down here? Maybe we can come up with something."

"Sounds good." Ray laid the battered guitar back in its case. "Lainie, they're here."

Elizabeth didn't stop smiling. She used the walker that Joe Jr. took from the back of the station wagon, but her back was straight and her limp was slight as, despite the punishing wind, she walked up the ramp. She looked like Gran.

"Oh, my goodness, I am home." Steven tried to help her, but she lifted her walker over the doorsill with ease as she came in. "Home has never looked so sweet to me."

"Do you want to go lie down and rest?" Nancy Jo followed her in carrying her cosmetic case. "You must be exhausted after this morning."

Elizabeth held up one hand. "Don't fuss. I'm going to sit right here in my own chair and just be home for a minute. My, something smells good."

"Lunch is ready whenever you are. But it can wait too, so just let me know when to dish it up." Lainie leaned over Elizabeth's recliner and gave her a hug. "I'm so glad you're home."

"And I'm glad you're home too, sweet girl. This is the way it ought to be." She must have noticed the hurt expression on Nancy Jo's face because she held her hand out to her daughter-in-law. "Don't be too put out with me because I wanted to come back to my own house instead of back to the ranch. The ranch was my home for more than fifty years, but it's your home now, and that's the way it should be. Enjoy this time you and Joe Jr. have with each other. You don't know how precious it is." She turned back to Lainie with a smile. "Let's have lunch. Knowing Joe Jr., he's chomping at the bit to get back home."

When Lainie called everyone to the table a few minutes later, Steven, Ray, and Joe Jr. all jumped to help Elizabeth up, but she batted them away. "I've spent the last six weeks learning how to get out of a chair. I can do this, thank you very much."

After they were all seated, Elizabeth looked down the table and smiled. "Look at this. Everyone has just outdone themselves. Sue Anderson took the time to make us her chili-mac, and Juanita, bless her heart, brought us her specialty. And if I'm not mistaken, that's Evelyn Watson's applesauce cake on the counter there. God has surely blessed us with good friends and neighbors."

"How did you know who brought what?" Lainie set the sweetener near Elizabeth's glass and sat down.

"Honey, when you've been to as many church potlucks as I have, you not only recognize the food, but you recognize the dishes. Now, Lurlene and Sue both bring chili-mac in Pyrex casseroles, but Lurlene uses a little more chile and a little less tomato, so hers is darker." When everyone had joined hands, she turned her smile on Steven. "Steven, honey, would you offer thanks for this bounty?"

It had been a while since Steven had prayed, and even longer since he had prayed out loud, so he felt a little rusty at first. But once he cleared his throat and ran through a quick "Dear-heavenly-Father-we-thank-you-for-this-food," his heart caught up with his mouth, and he realized how grateful he actually was. He was grateful Gran was home, grateful for family who had supported him with a love so unconditional he couldn't get his head around it, grateful for friends who gathered around to express their affection and concern the best way they knew—with food—and though he didn't mention it in his blessing, he was increasingly grateful for the little family of two who became more important to him with each day. God was so good.

"Think this wind will keep Rita down at the motel?" Steven parked in front of the High Lonesome and cut the engine. "You know that if she thinks we're here she'll be right here with us."

"I'm kind of surprised she doesn't have an idea or two of her own. She's not slipping, is she?"

"Rita? Are you kidding me? Actually, she'd like us to donate the building and the land that it sits on to the town for a visitor center. Of course, that would mean Last Chance taking on the upkeep and the taxes."

"And as long as Russ Sheppard lives and breathes . . ." Ray grinned.

"It's not happening," Steven finished. "Yep. You've got the picture."

Steven pulled a tumbleweed out of the doorway and let the wind take it before he turned the key in the lock and stepped inside. Ray followed. The howling wind, which had made conversation all but impossible outside, was muffled, if not silenced, when Steven shut the door and flipped on a light.

"Wow." Ray, holding his hat in front of him, stopped in the middle of the room and looked around. "I haven't been back in here since the day I packed my truck and headed for Santa Fe."

"Bring back a lot of bad memories?"

The bar had been an unacknowledged barrier between them for too long. It was time to see if they could get that barrier down.

"Not entirely." Ray walked over to the bar and ran his hand down the marred surface. "I met Lainie in here, you know. She came in one night just at closing with a broken down car left in the parking lot. She had the biggest chip on her shoulder you ever saw."

"No love at first sight?"

"Hardly. By the next day I was ready to fix that car myself just to get her out of here, and if I had, I'm pretty sure the first thing she would have done would have been to run me over."

"Looks like you worked things out, though."

"Yeah, we worked things out." Ray wore a half smile as he went over to the jukebox. He dug into his pocket. "This thing still work?"

"Don't think so. I tried it the last time I was in here. I don't know if they even make the parts to fix it anymore."

"Too bad. We danced one night to a Willie Nelson song. Wouldn't mind hearing it again."

"You getting all mushy on me? Do I need to get you back to Lainie?"

"No." Ray did look a little sheepish. "It's funny, though. The day I handed you the keys, I really didn't care if you burned the place down. I'd have even lent you the matches. But now that I'm here, it's the good times I'm remembering."

"You know what I think about when I come in here?" Steven turned a chair around and straddled it. "I remember Dad. I can still see him behind the bar there. Don't tell Gran I said so, but he was made for a place like this. He was what people came for; the drinks were just a sideline. If he hadn't died, things would have been so different."

"That they would have."

"There's something I've got to say, bro, and I hope you hear me out." Steven took a deep breath and blew it out.

Ray leaned against the bar and folded his arms. "Go ahead."

"I guess what I want to say is I'm sorry. I'm sorry Dad asked you to give up your own life to run this place for me. That's just not something you ask of someone. But I shouldn't have let you do it, and for that I apologize. Even if I had known for sure that I wanted this place, I shouldn't have let you do it, and the fact that even before I came home, I was pretty sure I didn't want this bar makes it even more unforgivable. I think I was maybe hoping that once I got here, I'd feel different." He took another deep breath. "But I didn't. I let you keep on, and I was a total jerk, and I am so sorry, Ray. I am so, so sorry."

Ray didn't say anything for a long time. He just leaned against the bar and stared at a line of sunlight that had found its way through the boards on the windows and stretched across the dusty floor. Finally he looked up at Steven.

"Thanks. I appreciate everything you've said more than you know. And of course your apology is accepted. But it wasn't all bad, you know?" He smiled a slow half smile. "Did you hear the one about the California girl with the chip on her shoulder who walks into a bar?"

Steven laughed and got up. Ray met him in the middle of the room and grabbed him in a bear hug. "That's all history now. It's all good."

"So, what do we do about this place?" Steven stepped back and waved his arm. "We can't just leave it alone. I've tried, and Rita tracks you down like a dog."

"Only the one guy has shown any interest?"

"Yep, he's the only one so far." Steven hooked his thumbs in his front pockets and looked around. "Think it might work as a studio for you? You wouldn't have to make that long trip to your cabin."

Ray opened the door and turned to survey the way the room

filled with light. "If I really was stuck, it might work. But the light comes in from the east, which means it changes all day long. I guess I just can't see me giving up the cabin for this. The cabin's too perfect, even if it is a ways away."

"What about a gallery? You know, showcase our local artist?"

Ray grinned. "Thanks for the thought, but my paintings are too big for this room. I'd have to hang them too low, and even then I could only get a couple on each wall. It's just not a good fit."

Just before Ray shut the door again, Steven saw Kaitlyn come out of the Dip 'n' Dine across the street and get in Chris's Jeep. He looked at his watch. Yep, school would be out soon. He turned back to Ray as an idea struck him.

"How do you think it would work as a beauty shop?"

"What? Where did that come from?"

"I just thought of it. I don't know why I didn't think of it before. You know Kaitlyn is a hairdresser, right? So far she just does hair for free out of her kitchen, but if she's going to stay here in Last Chance, she needs a place of her own. How do you think this place would work?"

"I'm the last person who could tell you that, bro. What does Kaitlyn say?"

"I haven't talked to her yet. I told you I just thought of it."

Ray looked around. "It would take a whole lot of work to make this look like a place ladies would want to go. Especially the ladies here in Last Chance. That could get expensive."

"I could do the work myself. Kaitlyn could tell us how she wanted it, and then she could rent it from us."

"Hold it, hoss. I think you might be getting just a little ahead of yourself. In the first place, you don't even know if Kaitlyn wants her own shop or, assuming she does, if she wants it in an old cowboy bar. Lastly, and this is a biggie, where are we going to get the money ourselves to turn this place into a beauty shop? Lainie and I don't have that kind of money right now."

"I've got some savings. It would be an investment. Better than letting this place sit empty."

"Okay, the first thing you need to do is to talk to Kaitlyn. Chris and Sarah are getting married in a few weeks, and you don't even know if Kaitlyn's planning on staying in Last Chance when they do. I don't see a whole lot of difference between owning an empty bar and owning an empty beauty shop."

"Gran would." Steven grinned.

"Yeah, well . . ." Ray didn't finish his thought.

"Okay, your point is taken. I'll talk to Kaitlyn, and meanwhile you keep thinking. We've got about six weeks to get this taken care of before I leave for the academy."

"I just have one question." Ray grabbed his hat as they headed outside and the wind nearly snatched it out of his hand. "You've been back in Last Chance since before Christmas. What have you been doing about the High Lonesome since then?"

Steven clamped his own hat to his head as he locked the door. "Mostly dodging Rita."

Kaitlyn looked up when Elizabeth's front door opened and Steven and Ray practically blew in.

"Kaitlyn! I was hoping to see you." Steven's smile widened at the sight of her.

"We're not staying long. Livvy just had to come by to say 'welcome home' to Miss Elizabeth, but we don't want to make her tired, do we, Livvy?"

Olivia, making a pointed effort to ignore any suggestion that meant leaving, leaned on the arm of Elizabeth's recliner and continued showing her the day's schoolwork.

"Do you have enough time to come with me for a few minutes? I'd like to show you something."

"Man, you don't waste any time, do you?" Ray tossed his hat on the piano.

Kaitlyn looked from one to the other. "What?"

"Just come see." Steven held his hand out. "We should go now while it's still light."

She still made no move to get up. "What's going on?"

"Oh, go ahead and go." Elizabeth slipped her arm around Olivia. "We're doing fine here. I'm not a bit tired. They've had me doing laps around that nursing home nonstop, don't forget. This is the most restful day I've had in weeks."

"Okay." Kaitlyn took the hand Steven held out to her, and he pulled her to her feet. "We can't be gone long, though. Livvy needs to get home and start her homework."

"All right, let's go then." Steven helped her into her coat and ushered her out the front door into the wind.

"Where are we going?" Kaitlyn clutched her coat around her. "Why are you being so mysterious?"

But Steven clearly had said all he was going to say about the excursion and just leered at her.

"You don't look mysterious when you do that. You look creepy."

When Steven stopped the truck in front of the High Lonesome again, Kaitlyn made no effort to get out. "Yes. This is your bar. I work right across the street, remember? I see it every day."

"But you've never seen inside. Come on."

Kaitlyn had no idea why it had suddenly become so important to Steven that she see the inside of the old bar, but she followed him inside. The room was cold and smelled a bit musty. Clearly it had been empty for a while, but there was something about it she liked. It seemed to tell a story.

"So this is the High Lonesome." Some framed photos hung over the booths along one wall, and she crossed the room to look at them. "Who's this?"

"Those are of my dad in his rodeo days. He made quite a name for himself. When I was a kid, every day or so, someone who had seen him compete would come in just to shake his hand."

She turned to him with a smile. "I think I know why you brought me here now."

"You do?"

"You've changed your mind about running this place, and you want to reopen it, right?"

"What? No! This was my dad's dream. Maybe for a while I thought I wanted it, but I'm going into law enforcement."

"All right then, tell me." Kaitlyn was starting to feel a bit exasperated. "Why are we here?"

"Well, as you probably know, it's been sitting here closed up for about a year now, and Rita's really been on my case to do something with it. She says it's an eyesore, and since it's the first building you come to when you enter Last Chance, it gives the wrong impression of the town."

"I've heard her say so, and she may have a point."

"Yeah, well, that's where the problem is. What do I do with it? I know it's not going to be a bar again. Couldn't do that to Gran. But there aren't that many businesses looking to set up shop in such a small town."

Kaitlyn waited. Eventually, she knew, Steven would get around to saying what he wanted to say.

"So, today I thought, what about a beauty shop? Do you think it might work as a beauty shop?"

"A salon here? In the bar?" Kaitlyn looked around the room again.

"No, it wouldn't be a bar, it would be a beauty shop . . . salon."

"Steven, these bits and pieces you're throwing at me aren't making any sense. Now please tell me exactly what you're talking about. And leave Rita and Elizabeth out of it."

"Okay, I'll try. This building needs a tenant, and if you are interested, I would like to make this place over according to your specs and have you and your . . . salon as that tenant. Look, there's plumbing along that wall, and there's a storeroom right through here, and there are restrooms down the hall. I don't know what all you'd need, but I bet we can work it out."

Kaitlyn sat down in the chair Steven had turned around earlier when he and Ray were there. "I don't know what to say. I need to think about it. Maybe talk to Chris. He owns his own business. When do you need to know?"

"Take your time. No rush. If Rita backs me into a corner, I'll send her to talk to you. Kidding. But I only have about six weeks before I go, so the more time I have to work on this, the prettier I can make it for you."

"But what if you make all these changes, and I don't have enough business to support it? Then what?"

"You know, maybe I should be worried about that, but I'm not. You are an amazing woman, and I have every confidence that you can do pretty much everything you put your mind to."

The sun had long since crossed the sky and was dropping into the hills behind the High Lonesome, and the narrow beams that had found their way between the boards on the window faded away. The single light Steven had switched on when they came in left much of the room in shadow, and that was just as well, because at Steven's unswerving faith in her, Kaitlyn's eyes had filled with tears, and she really did not want him to see that.

24

As she often said, when Juanita Sheppard had a good idea, she wasn't about to let it just lie there and die from lack of attention. And after a couple weeks of Lainie spending every day with Elizabeth and Kaitlyn still working at the Dip 'n' Dine, she found the opportunity to take matters into her own hands one afternoon when Lainie and Elizabeth came in for lunch.

"Well, look who's here." Juanita held the door open as Elizabeth maneuvered her walker through. "And hello to you too, Miss Lainie. Come in here and sit down. My gracious, it's good to see you up and about."

"It's good to be up and about." Elizabeth smiled as she made her way across the room. "It's not like I was always on the go before this all happened, but at least it was my choice to stay in or go out. Now it's such an aggravation to get me anywhere, most of the time I just choose to stay home."

"Well, I'm glad you decided to come out today. We miss you." Kaitlyn followed Elizabeth to her favorite booth and waited to take her walker.

It took Lainie a while to get there, though, because at every table someone jumped up to grab her in a big hug and welcome her back to Last Chance. Even Carlos came out of the kitchen to say hello. This time it was Lainie who grabbed him.

"Carlos, I have missed you so much. You know, Santa Fe is known for its restaurants, but I have yet to taste any green chile stew, or chile rellenos, or carne adovada that can hold a candle to yours."

"So what's wrong with my enchiladas?"

"Nothing! They're fabulous." Lainie laughed out loud. "You are the best cook in the whole state. Fayette always said so, and I'm here to swear it's true."

"Are you going to stay this time?"

"I hope so. We thought we were coming down to give Elizabeth a hand, but with all the improvements Steven made to the house, and Elizabeth's stubborn streak, she needs us about as much as you need a cookbook."

"Well, good to see you. Glad you're back." Carlos had a well-known low threshold for chitchat, and apparently he had reached it. He patted her shoulder and headed back to the kitchen.

"Now, see? This is exactly what I was talking about." Juanita spoke to the room at large as she poured Lainie's iced tea.

"What?" Lainie smiled her thanks.

"You are just a natural when it comes to the hospitality industry."

"Juanita." Chris appeared in the kitchen window.

"Be there in a minute, Chris." Juanita didn't turn around. "You and I both know that there is a whole lot more to good service than just throwing food on the table. Not everybody gets that."

"Juanita." Chris spoke a little louder.

"Be there in a minute, Chris." This time Juanita flapped a hand in his direction. "So, what I want to know is, when are you coming back in here where you belong?"

"Oh, I don't know, Juanita. The deal we made with Nancy Jo

and Joe Jr. was that Elizabeth would stay in her own home as long as there was someone there in case she needed anything, and that's my priority these days."

"I may need that contraption over there to get around because of my leg, but I'm far from being an invalid, and my mind, thank the Lord, still seems to work. Despite what Nancy Jo thinks, I do not need a babysitter." Elizabeth unwrapped her napkin and set her flatware on the table with a little clank.

"Of course you don't. Anyone can see that." Juanita waved that idea away. "But what if someone came over just to keep you company? I'm talking about Kaitlyn. That shop Steven is fixing up for her is going to be opening soon, and she needs to be building up her clientele, not trying to figure out how to be a waitress."

Both Elizabeth and Lainie looked confused.

"I'm just saying that if she were over at your house and someone came to get their hair cut, why, you'd get a little company and she'd get a little practice and impress some of the local folk with what a good hairdresser she is, and Lainie, well, Lainie would be doing something she does really well and getting out of the house for a few hours every day while she does it. I think it sounds like a perfect solution."

Kaitlyn couldn't believe her life was being discussed so thoroughly within her hearing and without her being involved in the conversation at all. The other diners, however, apparently thought Juanita had a good idea. They were unabashedly listening, occasionally nodding their approval.

"Excuse me." Chris brushed past her on his way to Elizabeth's table.

Juanita barely glanced his way when he loomed up beside her.

"Hey there, Lainie, Miss Elizabeth. It's good to see you out. Have you had a chance to order?"

When he turned to motion her over, Kaitlyn could see that his smile was barely hanging on by a thread, and by the time she hurried to the table, he had turned his attention to Juanita.

"I don't know if you heard me call you," he began.

"Of course I heard you, Chris. I said I'd be right there. What do you need?"

"I need to talk to you." His voice was carefully controlled and even, almost pleasant. "And I think we'd have a little more privacy in the kitchen, so would you come with me?"

Juanita rolled her eyes. "Oh, good night, nurse, Chris. Are we going to go through this again? Are you going to fuss at me about a conversation that you weren't even part of but you listened in on anyway?"

He didn't answer, but indicated the kitchen with his hand. Juanita flounced off with Chris right behind her. In a few seconds, Kaitlyn saw, through the window to the kitchen, the back door open and close again.

She turned back to Elizabeth and Lainie with her order pad in hand and smiled. "Do you know what you want? Or do you still need a little more time?"

Lainie was still looking toward the kitchen. A little scowl creased her forehead. "I hope we didn't cause problems for Juanita."

"The only one who causes problems for Juanita is Juanita." Elizabeth handed Kaitlyn her menu. "I think I'll just have a bowl of posole and some flour tortillas, if you please."

"I'll have the chile rellenos. My mouth's been watering since Carlos and I talked about them." Lainie also handed over her menu. "But I think Chris was mad. I hope everything's going to be okay."

"Everything's going to be okay. Strange as it seems, this is pretty standard procedure around here. Every couple weeks, there's a bit of a tussle over who the boss is. Chris has won every time so far, but who knows? She may be wearing him down." Kaitlyn smiled. "I'll go put your order in."

A few minutes later, the back door opened again, and Juanita, followed by Chris, came back in the dining room. Kaitlyn watched them for some sense of what might have happened on the back porch. Chris was always hard to read in the restaurant; his demeanor was unfailingly congenial and professional. But Juanita, who could be moody, was as cheerful as ever as she went from table to table, taking orders and serving meals. Kaitlyn did notice, however, that Juanita left Elizabeth and Lainie's table to her.

After their lunch, Lainie and Elizabeth left with more hugs all around and compliments called out to Carlos, but later that afternoon, Lainie came back.

"Elizabeth's watching one of her shows, so I thought I'd run over for a minute." She climbed on a stool at the counter and looked around. "Where's Juanita?"

"In the storage room, looking for coffee filters, I think." Kaitlyn finished dishing up a slice of chocolate cream pie.

"Good." She leaned forward across the counter like she had a secret to tell, and Kaitlyn leaned to meet her. "Quick! What do you think of her idea? Me working here and you staying with Elizabeth?"

"Love it!" Kaitlyn widened her eyes.

"That's all I need to know." She slipped off her stool as Juanita came back in with the coffee filters, then tapped on the kitchen door while she pushed it open. "Chris? Do you have a minute? Maybe we could use your back porch office."

On an afternoon a week or so later, Rita Sandoval, draped in a nylon cape, sat on a high step stool in Elizabeth's kitchen while Kaitlyn cut her hair.

"I stuck my head in the High Lonesome yesterday to see how it's coming along, and it doesn't even look like the same place."

"Yes, Steven's really working hard." Kaitlyn stepped back, cocked her head as she examined her work, and snipped a little more off the left side.

"He told me all the things you're going to be doing in there. I guess I thought since it's in an old bar, you'd go with the rustic, cowboy look. You know, some calico curtains, maybe some dried flowers in a milk bottle. But it's going to be real swanky, like some fancy Scottsdale salon. Think that will go over here?"

"I'm counting on it. I want to make everyone who comes in feel special. Like they deserve this. If I make them feel welcome, and my prices aren't any higher, and they like the way they look, well, hopefully they'll come back." Kaitlyn drew a comb through Rita's hair to check the length. "Since I'm going to have to get folks from San Ramon down here in order to make a go of it, I need to give them something they can't find in San Ramon."

"My goodness, what are you going to be doing?" Elizabeth was sitting at the table doing some handwork on a pile of gauzy, white fabric that was slowly becoming Sarah's wedding dress. "It sounds quite spectacular."

"I don't know about spectacular, but I'm excited about it. The decorator calls it 'desert chic.'"

"You have a decorator too? Good gracious, Kaitlyn, now I am starting to get worried. I don't think a decorator has set foot in Last Chance since I've been here, and I've been here all my life." Rita fluffed her curls with her fingers and nodded as she examined her haircut in the mirror Kaitlyn held up for her. "I want your shop to succeed almost as much as you do. It's good for Last Chance. But if folks get the idea we're just not good enough for you, well, they'll just keep right on going to San Ramon, and we'll be stuck with another closed-up business."

"Well, that's just the silliest thing I've ever heard, Rita." Elizabeth looked up from her sewing. "If I've heard anything from you, even before you got elected mayor, it's that we should be promoting Last Chance, and here's Kaitlyn fixing to bring the traffic to Last Chance from San Ramon, instead of the other way round. I'd think you'd be cheering her on, instead of throwing cold water all over everything."

"Well, I do wish you well, Kaitlyn. I really do, and I hope my worrying didn't upset you. I didn't mean for it to." She reached for her purse. "Here. This is for you."

Kaitlyn's eyes widened as she looked at the check Rita handed her. "What's this for?"

"It's for anything you might want to spend it on. Everyone whose hair or makeup you've done has chipped in. I know you call what you're doing here building goodwill, but I call it working for free, and that's just not right." She raised a hand to ward off Kaitlyn's protest. "I know, I know. You can't charge until you have a designated workspace. But you've saved a lot of trips to San Ramon and made us all look good in the bargain, so just think of this as a big thank-you."

"I don't know what to say." Kaitlyn still looked at the check like she didn't know what it was.

"You don't need to say a thing, darlin', except 'you're welcome.' Now, if you're going to have a grand opening, and I surely hope you are, I'd love to help you plan it. We really need to make this big."

After she left, Kaitlyn went back into the kitchen where Elizabeth still sat working on Kaitlyn's dress. "Did you know about this?"

"I did." Elizabeth smiled up at her. "And I can't tell you how much pleasure it gave me to get to take part. Now, why don't you put the kettle on for us, and then sit right down here and tell me all about what you're doing with your salon? You have no idea what an answer to prayer it is to see that benighted place turn into something beautiful."

"Oh, it is going to be beautiful, Elizabeth." Kaitlyn tucked the check in her purse and turned with a smile as she felt the excitement bubble up inside her. "I can't wait for you to see the job Steven's doing. I had no idea he was such a craftsman."

"To tell you the truth, I didn't either. But he's just been full of surprises lately." Elizabeth knotted her thread and bit it off. "Now tell me, what's desert chic, and where did you find a decorator? I know it wasn't here, and I wasn't even aware there were decorators in San Ramon."

"This one's from Scottsdale. My mother knows her. In fact, my mother's paying for her services. She's really excited about my salon, and it's kind of weird. She hasn't been really interested in the things I've done before."

The teakettle whistled, and Kaitlyn went to pour boiling water over the leaves in the pot.

"I wonder what made the difference."

"Maybe because it's my business. She's a business owner, you know. She and my dad have their own real estate firm, and she handles the commercial side. I guess the idea of a new business space really gets the wheels turning. Plus she knows a whole lot about salons. Her three places to be are work, the gym, or the salon."

Elizabeth laughed. "It sounds like she'd be the perfect advisor then. I'm glad to see it. I had the idea that the two of you weren't particularly close."

Kaitlyn poured the tea and set a cup where Elizabeth could reach it.

"No, we haven't been, and I really would like that to change. Maybe this will do it." She looked at the little china clock hanging on Elizabeth's wall and took a quick gulp of her tea. "Oh, I shouldn't have poured this. I need to go get Olivia."

"Why don't you just put the cozy on the pot so it will stay warm till you get back. She always likes a cup with lots of milk after school."

"Hey, how're you doing?" Kaitlyn stuck her head in the door of the High Lonesome and looked around.

"Hey, yourself." Steven put his crowbar down and gave her a one-armed hug. "Don't want to get too close. I'm covered in dust. What do you think?"

"It already looks so different, so much bigger."

"Well, I've about got the demo done, and without the booths over there, and the bar over here, it does look bigger. When we get your things in here, it'll probably look a little smaller. Rita dropped by, and I kind of filled her in on all your plans. Hope that was okay."

"She told me. You got the paint samples then?"

"Yep, and a detailed map of the place showing what colors go where, and the information I need to order the light fixtures. Nothing's left to chance, that's for sure."

"Do you mind my mother getting a decorator involved? Are we stepping on your toes?"

"Heck no. I'm good with a hammer, and I can paint. But when it comes to colors, I'm strictly a brown and blue guy. You are getting 'Desert Bluff' and 'Glacier,' among others. Did you know that?"

"I did not. It sounds gorgeous, though."

"I'm sure it will be." He slid his arms around her.

"Mom, Miss Elizabeth is waiting for me. I have to take her for a walk so she can get her exercise."

"Okay, Livvy. In a minute." Kaitlyn remained a moment longer before reluctantly pulling away. He had strong arms, and she liked the way she felt when they were around her. "I guess I do need to get back. I told your grandmother I wouldn't be gone long, but I had to stop by and see how things were coming along."

Olivia, who had already headed out to the car, came back in again. "Mom, are we going, or what?"

Kaitlyn raised an eyebrow. "You can drop the 'or what' when you ask me a question, Olivia. Would you like to try again?"

Olivia heaved a sigh. "Are we going now?"

"Yes, we are. Go get in the car and put your seat belt on." She turned back to Steven as Olivia stomped out. "I should go."

"How long will you be at Gran's?"

"Not long. It's a school night and we have things we have to do."

"Shoot. I thought I might see you if I dropped by later." He took a quick peek through the door to see if Olivia was watching, then pulled her to him for a quick kiss. And she didn't even mind the dust.

Steven took Kaitlyn's hand and walked her out to the car. Olivia was already belted into the backseat, and he stuck his head in the door when Kaitlyn opened it to get in.

"Hey, Liv. I didn't get a chance to say hi. How's it going?"

Olivia would not look at him.

"Livvy? What's wrong? Are you mad?"

Olivia looked at her mother. "We have to go. Miss Elizabeth is waiting."

"Livvy! Don't be rude." Kaitlyn turned around to glare at her daughter, but Steven put his hand on her arm.

"It's okay." He opened the back door and leaned in. "Okay, Livvy. What's up? We've been friends for a long time and I think it's only fair that you tell me what I've done. Because I really don't know."

She stared straight ahead for a while, but when it began to look like Steven wasn't going anywhere until she answered, she looked at him.

"Do you want to be my mom's boyfriend?"

"What would you think if I said yes?"

"I would hate it!" Olivia almost shouted, and Steven heard the tears threatening in her voice.

"Why, Liv? I thought the three of us made a pretty good team."

"Because you don't want to be a team. You just want to be my mom's boyfriend. You just pretend to be my friend, but when Mom starts being your girlfriend, you won't care about me anymore. You'll just go off with her all the time and I'll be alone."

"Oh, Livvy." Kaitlyn's voice came almost as a whisper, and she pressed her hands against her cheeks.

"Is that what's happened before?

She nodded without looking at him.

"Well, that's not going to happen again, Livvy, and do you know why?" Steven waited until Olivia looked at him again. "Because that's not how your mom and I do things. I really like being with you. I really like going to movies or out to eat or just hanging at your house playing with Meeko and playing Sorry, even if you beat me every time. I really think you're great, and I'd think that even if I didn't know your mom. Sometimes maybe your mom and I might go out alone, but most times it's going to be the three of us, unless it's just you and your mom. As for your mom, I think I can say that no one in the world is more important to her than you are. And that's the way I like it. What do you think about that?"

Olivia still looked at her shoes, but there was no more fury in her face.

"Livvy? What do you think about that?" Steven could wait as long as it took.

Finally, Olivia heaved a sigh. "I think it's fine. Now can we go? Miss Elizabeth is waiting for me."

"Friends?" He held out his fist.

She gave him a little smile and bumped it with her own. "I guess."

25

Chris carried a carton from his room and set it among the others in the living room. He dusted off his hands and looked around.

"Well, I guess that about does it." It was hard to read his expression. There was, of course, the happiness and eager anticipation tempered by a little nervousness that you'd expect to see on the face of any bridegroom, but there was something else too—not exactly sadness, but wistfulness, maybe.

"All packed up?" Kaitlyn had to admit she was feeling a little wistful herself.

"Yup. Except for what I'm wearing tomorrow and the suitcase I packed for the honeymoon, everything is in these boxes."

"Okay, we'll haul them over to Sarah's while you're gone, and when you get back everything will be waiting at your new home."

His nod seemed a little distracted. "Right. Just leave the ones marked 'kitchen' in the kitchen."

"Got it. And the ones marked 'bedroom'? What do we do with those?"

He actually looked at her for the first time then, with the blank expression of someone who was just waking up. Kaitlyn laughed and walked over to put her arms around his waist.

"How're you holding up?" She smiled up into his face.

"Fine, I guess." He ran his fingers through his short hair, causing it to stand up even more. "Where's Livvy?"

"Out on the driveway waiting for Mom and Dad."

Brooke and David Reed had wanted to host the rehearsal dinner, and much discussion had gone into where. Brooke was especially distraught that there was nothing within a hundred miles of Last Chance, including the Dip 'n' Dine, that she would even consider gracing with one of her events. She kept saying, "If only this were in Scottsdale," until Chris ended one lengthy phone call by saying, "Mom. It's not. Deal with it." Finally it was agreed that since the rehearsal was actually taking place at the ranch, the dinner would be held there as well, with Carlos's family doing the catering. But Brooke was not happy.

Chris looked at his watch. "Think we should go out there and wait for them too? We're supposed to be there by 4:00."

"Wait. Before we go, I want to say something, and I don't know when I might get another chance." She swallowed the lump that filled her throat as she looked up at her brother. "I just want to say thank you, that's all. Thank you for being there for me every day of my life. Thank you for being there for Livvy when no one else was. Thank you for all you've done for both Livvy and me here in Last Chance. Just thank you."

Kaitlyn was so afraid he was going to trivialize everything and say, "Aw, shucks," or "It was nothing," or something like that, but he just said, "You're welcome. I'd do it again in a heartbeat. Because you have become an incredible mom, and I got to watch."

He stopped talking, and Kaitlyn followed his gaze out the front window to where Olivia was hopping around by the driveway, hitting at tufts of sagebrush with a stick, hoping to scare out a lizard. When he turned back to Kaitlyn, his eyes looked a little misty.

"Right after I get back, we'll start the process of getting Livvy's guardianship back to you. I should have started it earlier. I all but promised Steven I would, but it was a lot harder to think about than I thought it would be. Selfish, I guess."

Simultaneously, Brooke and David Reed's car turned off the road into the long driveway, Olivia made a break for the front door, and Kaitlyn burst into tears. She grabbed the tissue box as Olivia erupted through the front door. This was going to be a multi-tissue evening. She could tell that already.

"They're here!" Olivia stopped when she saw Kaitlyn. "What's wrong, Mom?"

"Happy tears, Livvy. These are happy tears."

Olivia took a close look at her mother's face and must have been satisfied by the size of her smile that all was indeed well, because she threw her arms around Kaitlyn's waist for a quick hug and then dashed back outside to greet her grandparents.

Brooke and David had, of course, called Sarah's parents when the engagement was announced, and Brooke had spent so much time on the phone going over every detail of the rehearsal dinner that Sarah confided to Kaitlyn that her mother wondered if Brooke might in some way be related to Rita. But they had never met in person, and Brooke and David had never been on the ranch.

"All of this belongs to Sarah's family?" Brooke kept exclaiming the same thing over and over as the Jeep bounced along the dirt road leading to the ranch house. "How much land do they have?"

"Don't know, Mom." Chris kept his eyes on the road. "But

when we get there, I'll tell Sarah's dad you're curious. I'm sure he can tell you."

"Don't you dare. It's not at all important. But my goodness, how much land do they have?"

Nancy Jo waited on the front porch, as she always did, but today she wasn't wearing an apron over slacks. She had on a softly swirling broomstick skirt and blouse of deep purple with heavy turquoise and silver jewelry around her neck and encircling her wrist.

"My word, she's wearing a fortune in Navajo jewelry, and if I'm not mistaken, it's nineteenth century," Brooke muttered under her breath as the Jeep came to a stop.

Sarah ran past her mother down the steps and opened the door so Brooke could emerge.

"Hello, Sarah, dear." Brooke offered her cheek for a kiss. "It's lovely to see you again. This must be your mother?"

Nancy Jo came down the porch steps, smiling and holding both hands out to Brooke. "Come in this house. We have been waiting so long to meet you."

Kaitlyn stood back as the rest of the introductions were made and the wedding party disappeared into the house. She took another tissue and blew her nose. Interesting that her mother hadn't asked about her red eyes and blotchy face, or even the box of tissues that she carried. But that was Brooke. She was probably consumed with what kind of impression she would make on Sarah's family.

"Here you are." Steven came out of the front door. "I wondered where you were."

"Did you meet my folks?"

"Nope. Just saw them in the distance. They're all in the back now getting to know each other. Last I saw, Chris was trying to pry Carlos away from the smoker to come take part in the rehearsal."

Kaitlyn laughed. "That's Carlos, and Chris knew that when he asked him to be best man."

"I can't think of a better choice, though."

"No, not for Chris. He and Carlos have been quite a team since Chris first took over the Dip 'n' Dine. Did Carlos tell you what he's giving Chris as a wedding present?"

"No, what?"

"He's making Chris's chicken mole verde the Monday special."

Steven threw back his head and laughed. "You're kidding. He's actually letting Chris put something new on the menu?"

"Yep, he's going to surprise him. When Chris comes back to work after his honeymoon, there it will be on the whiteboard: Monday—Chicken Mole Verde."

"Outstanding." Steven grinned. "But what about the green chile stew? He's not taking that off the menu? There'd be rioting in the streets."

"No, he's going to make it an every day dish. People ask for it every day, anyway."

"That's just great. I'm going to make it a point to be there. I want to see Chris's face."

"You know the great whiteboard unveiling is going to take place at 5:00 a.m., right?"

"I'm going to make it a point to ask Chris all about it. Later." He held out his hand and Kaitlyn took it. "Shall we go watch the rehearsal?"

Before they left the portico in front of the house, Steven took his thumb and brushed it under Kaitlyn's eye. "You've been crying. Do you always cry at weddings?"

"Not all weddings, but I'll probably blubber through this one. What got me started, though, was Chris telling me that we're going to transfer Livvy's guardianship back to me when he gets back. It took me completely by surprise." Kaitlyn found her eyes welling up again, and she swiped at her nose with the tissue balled up in her hand.

"I'm glad." Steven brushed away another tear. "It's time."

"He said something about you making him promise?"

"Did he? He shouldn't have done that. Because I didn't make him promise. I didn't have that right. But I did ask him to consider what a terrific mother you actually are, and to think about it."

Kaitlyn nodded. "I guess he did."

Steven let go of her hand and slipped his arm around her shoulders. "So what's the sister of the groom's part in all these festivities?"

"Strictly behind the scenes. I'm bringing my bag of tricks and turning up at some unearthly hour tomorrow to do hair and makeup for Sarah, Nancy Jo, Elizabeth, and Sarah's sister, Kim. Oh, and I'm doing Livvy's hair too."

"What about your own mom?"

"Oh, no. Mom has had the same stylist for twenty years. She goes in every four weeks to have her hair cut and highlighted, and other than that, no one touches it but her. Same for her makeup. Truthfully, I'm glad I'm not doing her—too much pressure, not enough time. What about you?"

"Strictly front and center." He pretended to preen. "I'm escorting Gran to her seat. She said there's no way she's pushing a walker down the aisle at her granddaughter's wedding, so she's taking her cane and leaning on me."

Kaitlyn smiled. "I'll bet you're a good one to lean on."

Steven flexed a bicep. "Haven't dropped anyone yet."

The wedding rehearsal had already begun when they rounded the house. Chris and Sarah stood laughing in front of Brother Parker, flanked by Olivia and Sarah's sister, Kim, on one side and Carlos on the other. By the time they reached the big tiled patio where tables were set for the dinner to follow, it was over.

—∞—

"Well, that didn't take long." Steven held his hand out to Brother Parker. "Nice to see you."

"When you have five people in the wedding party and everybody gives you their attention, it doesn't take long. We just need to figure out who stands where and we're done." Brother Parker shook Steven's hand and smiled. "I've been meaning to tell you how nice it's been to see you in church lately. I think it pleases your grandmother too."

"Well, we've always said it's real easy to please Gran. Just do everything she wants you to."

"If that's what it takes, then good for her."

"Mom, here are some people I'd like you to meet." Kaitlyn brought Brooke over. "This is our pastor, Brother Parker."

"We met briefly before the rehearsal. How do you do, Reverend Parker?" Brooke held out a slim hand.

"I'm glad I finally got to meet you, Mrs. Reed. I have really enjoyed getting to know Chris and Kaitlyn. You must be proud of both of them." Brother Parker took her hand in both of his.

"Indeed I am." She withdrew her hand with a small smile.

"And this is Steven, Mom. I've told you about him."

"Oh, yes. Steven. You're the one who renovated Kaitlyn's salon. She took me over for a peek this afternoon, and I am so impressed. I'm not the only one either. Sheila, the designer you worked with, said she was expecting to be working with a handyman and wound up dealing with a master craftsman. She'd love to work with you again, if you'd ever consider coming to Scottsdale for a project."

"Mother, Steven's going into law enforcement. He begins his training in two weeks. I told you that."

"Did you? I suppose I must have forgotten." She smiled and put her hand on Steven's arm. "I think it's a waste of talent, anyway. We have hundreds, if not thousands, of police officers, and so few people who can turn a sow's ear into a silk purse the way you did with that old bar. I saw it the first time we ever came to Last Chance, and it looked like it would collapse if anyone even leaned on it."

"Mother!" Kaitlyn looked aghast.

Steven really did not know where to begin to answer Brooke, so he took a deep breath and plunged in. "Thank you. I like a good project, and fixing up my dad's old bar for Kaitlyn's new business was something I really enjoyed doing, but I can't see making that my life's work. As Kaitlyn said, I'm going into law enforcement, and I have to say, I am truly honored and humbled by the opportunity to join those hundreds, if not thousands, who are already out there putting their lives on the line."

"I see." Brooke's smile was fixed and brittle. "Well, all the best to you then."

"Brooke?" Nancy Jo came up to the little group and put her hand on Brooke's shoulder. Brooke stepped slightly out of her reach. "They're ready to start serving dinner now. Would you or David like to make the announcement? Or maybe Chris?"

"I'll tell David." She started to leave but turned back to Brother Parker and bestowed a gracious smile on him. "Reverend Parker, I do hope you will honor us with grace before we eat."

She moved away, and Kaitlyn banged her head softly against

Steven's shoulder. "I am so sorry. But in her defense, I have to say she thought she was giving you a compliment."

Steven shook his head and grimaced. "I didn't react very well. I'm going to have to figure out how to get back on her good side. What do you think my chances are?"

Kaitlyn made a face. "Oh, knowing you, I'd say pretty good."

"Hey, everyone." David stood in the middle of the patio and raised his voice. "They tell me we're ready to eat. I guess it would be kind of pointless to thank everyone for coming since you all were here already, and we're the ones who turned up. But I can't tell you how pleased Chris's mother and I are that we all can gather tonight for this happy occasion. Now, Padre, they tell me you're going to say grace."

Brother Parker asked God's blessing on the food and on the young couple. As soon as he said amen, Chris bellowed across the yard, "Carlos! Step away from the smoker. You're the best man. Come over here and sit down. Pete can do anything you can do with that smoker, and you know it."

Carlos came, though he didn't look too happy about it, and took his place at the bridal party table with his wife. Everyone else found their places at the appropriate tables, and the buzz of conversation began as platters of food were placed in front of them.

—~—

When the dessert had been served and eaten, and while Lainie and Ray and Sarah's brother, Justin, and his wife, Bethany, lingered over coffee, Steven thoroughly embarrassed Kaitlyn by grabbing her hand and standing up.

"You are wonderful people," he said. "But you are old and married and probably haven't even noticed that there's a full moon coming up over that mountain, so Kaitlyn and I will take our leave. Enjoy your coffee."

The folks at the parents' table looked up and smiled, and Steven waved. So did the bridal party, and Steven waved at them too.

"You missed the kids' table." Kaitlyn felt her face redden to the roots of her hair. "Don't you want to let them know we're leaving too?"

"Are you kidding? They'd just want to come with us, and I want to be alone with you."

The murmur of conversation faded as they walked around the house. Away from the lights and heat lamps of the patio, the stars, just beginning to come out, were brighter, and the air was cooler. Kaitlyn rubbed her arms.

"Cold?" Steven put his arm around her and briskly rubbed her arm.

"A little."

"Just a sec." Steven opened the front door and grabbed a jacket off the coat rack. Draping it around her shoulders, he pulled her close. "Better?"

"Yes, it is. Thanks."

"Here, let's sit over here."

He led her to the wooden park bench on the front porch and put his arm around her again when they sat down. For a while, they watched the moonrise in silence, but finally Steven spoke.

"What are you thinking?"

"Nothing very profound, I'm afraid. I was thinking about my salon opening next weekend."

"Well, that's romantic." Steven pretended to be miffed.

Kaitlyn smiled at him. "It is when I'm thinking about what you did for me to make it happen."

"All right then, since you put it like that." He sounded mollified. "Everything ready for the grand opening?"

"Are you kidding me? Rita's pretty much taken over. There have been radio spots for the last two weeks and flyers all over Last Chance *and* San Ramon. We're going to have a drawing for some free services. She really wanted a balloon rainbow over the salon, but I was able to talk her out of that. I'm telling you, if you want anything done, Rita is your go-to girl."

"Known that for years." Steven stretched his legs out in front of him and crossed his boots at the ankle.

Comfortable silence drifted down onto the porch again, and after a while, it was Kaitlyn who broke the silence.

"Do you think Chris and Sarah will be happy?"

"You can't know what the future holds, but I have never been surer of any two people than I am of Chris and Sarah." He looked at her. "Why do you ask?"

"It all happened so fast. They didn't start going out until last Thanksgiving, and in January, they got engaged. Who does that?"

Steven didn't answer for a long time. He pulled her closer and rested his cheek on her hair. "As I see it, two types of people do that. Really reckless people—and Sarah and Chris certainly aren't reckless. And people who have never totally crashed and burned. People who might still have reason to believe in happily ever after."

"Not like us."

"No, not like us."

They were quiet again, and the moon finally cleared the crest of the mountain and began its journey across the sky.

"Kaitlyn, I think the first time I told a girl I loved her, I was probably about eight, and when I think of the number of times I've said it since then, and the reasons why I've said it, I don't like myself very much. So when I think about saying those words to you—and I think about it a lot—they sort of stick in my throat."

She looked at him and slowly nodded. "I know. I know just what you mean."

He took her face in his hands. "These next few months are going to be so busy for both of us. You here in Last Chance, and me at the academy. Tell me I can think about you and Olivia coming home together and having dinner and doing homework and all the other things you do in the evenings. Tell me I can picture you working in your salon with the Desert Bluff walls. Tell me it's okay to imagine myself standing next to you and holding the hymnbook on Sunday mornings. Because whether or not you tell me I can, that's exactly what I'll be doing. And I'll be counting the days until I can come back to you and Livvy."

Still holding her face in his hands, he lowered his lips to meet hers. When he raised his face to look in her eyes again, she smiled.

"We will be here waiting."

Acknowledgments

My warmest and most heartfelt thanks to Marcy Weydemuller, who calmly and with warm encouragement keeps pace with my manuscript as deadlines approach and panic ensues; to Wendy Wetzel, editor extraordinaire and expert on seven-year-old girls; and to Naomi Sims, who first noted that Last Chance was sadly lacking a hairstylist and then set about helping me create one. I love you all. This book wouldn't exist without you.

Cathleen Armstrong lives in the San Francisco Bay Area with her husband, Ed, and their corgi. Though she has been in California for many years now, her roots remain deep in New Mexico where she grew up and where much of her family still lives. After she and Ed raised three children, she returned to college and earned a BA in English. Her debut novel *Welcome to Last Chance* won the 2009 American Christian Fiction Writers Genesis Award for Women's Fiction. Learn more at www.cathleenarmstrong.com.

Meet

Cathleen Armstrong

online at

www.cathleenarmstrong.com

AuthorCathleenArmstrong

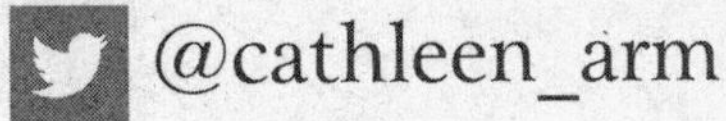

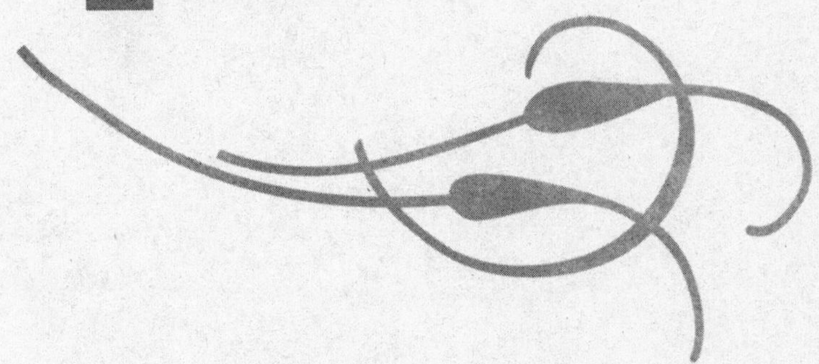

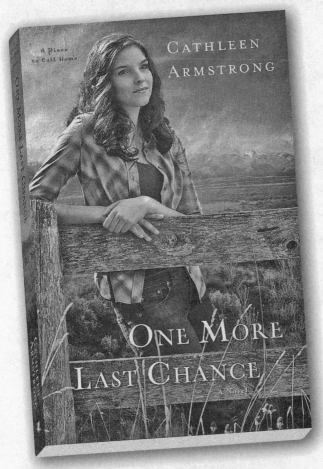